SEX WITH STRANGERS

MOLLIE MATHEWS

PRAISE FOR SEX WITH STRANGERS

"I absolutely enjoyed this story. I loved the storyline, I loved the characters, I loved the humor. I couldn't put it down. The descriptions were perfect.I loved everything about this book especially the humor. It was funny, sad at times, and I loved it."

~ Patricia Quinn

"At times playful and other times very steamy, Sex with Strangers was an interesting read. There are steamy between the sheets moments and elsewhere even if some are only in Ruby or Chanel's imagination! Chanel is definitely an x-rated life coach if only to get her best friend back in the dating game and more!"

~ JoAnne Weiss

"A really good, hip, fun book. It was a riot. Great fun!"

~ Robyn Donald

"I thoroughly enjoyed it. Just lovely."

~ **Daphne Claire**

ABOUT THIS BOOK

In love, the most dangerous enemy is saucy secrets

44-YEAR-OLD RUBY EVANS doesn't want to be a 'leftover girl.' But finding a 'forever' man is proving impossible.

Suddenly single after 20 years of marriage, her husband is the only man she has ever slept with. But the one bit of security she always thought she'd hold onto for the rest of her life is brutally ripped from her.

Humiliatingly and cruelly ex-ed when her husband trades her for a younger model, Chanel Zest, a long-time friend and motivational life coach, comes to her rescue. Together they embark on a quest to reclaim and rebuild Ruby's shattered life and begin the grueling process of dating again.

ONCE IN A PINK MOON, **Ruby has to play dirty...**

. . .

IF YOU LOVED **Brigette Jones's Diary and enjoy romantic comedy, you'll love *Sex With Strangers*.**

Full of quirky humor and the promise of a happily ever after.

Sex with Strangers is a clean romantic comedy with a few spicy bits.

1

GET A LIFE COACH

New York, December, 2005

P eople start over all the time. Why can't I?

My friend Chanel's a life coach here in New York. She's one of the best. She even has her own column in *The New Yorker.* Chanel has generously offered to help me. To be honest I really think I'm beyond help.

11 months ago my husband, Jon, left me for a younger woman and now they're having a baby. A baby! My life is a walking cliché. It's no wonder I'm still feeling lost, betrayed and empty. When Chanel turns up at my place unexpectedly, she tells me she thinks I have abandonment issues. No kidding! It's 3 pm on Sunday and I'm still in my pajamas, sprawled out on the sofa devouring romance novels.

"What on earth are you reading, Ruby?" she says, screwing up her nose. She picks up several paperbacks from the stack beside the sofa. "*The Virgin Bride*? As if! *Husband For Hire?* Why bother? Why on earth are you feeding your head with this stuff?"

"Princess Diana read Barbara Cartland novels and she married a prince," I say crossing my arms defensively.

"Yes, and how did that work out for her?" Chanel asks.

With my left foot I carefully slip Joan Lust's recent novella *Cuddle Up With A Prince* under the sofa. "Besides, they're not mine," I lie. "They're Millie's. I figured seeing as I'm not getting any romance I may as well read about people who are."

"These aren't your daughter's," Chanel says tossing the books back on the sofa. "J.K. Rowling is more her bag. You'd be better off reading books about wizards and magic than you would this stuff. People who *can*—date, and people who *can't* —write about it," she says dismissively. "Reading these— these fairy tales is not going to help."

I want to tell her that reading love stories helps hugely. That reading romance makes me feel less lonely. That reading romance lets me escape. That reading romance gives me hope. But I don't bother.

"The truth is you fear abandonment and this explains your reluctance to start dating again," Chanel continues. "Think Meghan Markle."

I stare at her blankly.

"What would her life be like if she clung onto her dead-beat ex?"

"Crap."

"Exactly. It's time you went looking for a new husband," Chanel says when I confess I haven't been out for months.

Well, that's not strictly true of course. Every weekday I go to my job in a towering office on Fifth Avenue where I work as a trainee public relations adviser for The Miss America Pageant. Believe me, there's a lot of work to do as we work to rebrand the organization. But I love that finally women are being appraised on more than big boobs and hairspray. And, after, the mass exodus of lewd members of the leadership team, finally, women are running the show.

I have other non-paid jobs too. Like walking my dog Snoutts in Central Park and running Millie, my fifteen-year-old daughter, around.

"I don't have time," I lie. "Besides I'm quite happy sitting here at home. Honestly," I protest, picking the anchovies off last night's pizza.

"Nonsense," she snaps as she brushes the dog hair from her expensive skirt. "Every woman needs a man. Especially you, Ruby."

I mumble through a mouthful of cold pizza, "But I'm enjoying my spare time—reading books, doing what I want, not having to race to get my make-up on before my husband got up and saw the real me. You don't care what I look like though do you, Snoutts?" I say, reaching down and patting the Dalmatian-cross I rescued from death-row.

Snoutts looks up at me adoringly.

I'm lying of course. The truth is I'm miserable. I miss my husband. I shouldn't after what he did, but I do. I miss being married. I miss having someone make decisions with me and dealing with things I don't want to, like taking the rubbish out and doing our accounts.

Actually, I miss sex the most. We had great sex, even after 18 years and 13 days. What if I never have sex again! That's my greatest fear. I don't know how I would even begin to meet a man, let alone have sex with a stranger.

"It's easy when you know-how," Chanel says. "Not only am I the queen of dating but in my professional role I've helped masses of women reclaim their sexual freedom."

I wish I had her self-esteem I think as I look at her. Chanel isn't the world's greatest beauty. She's got a prominent Jewish nose that would give Barbara Streisand a run for her money. But she has charisma like Jeff Bezos has money. She only has to walk into a room and men practically trip over themselves.

I've always admired the carefree way she flicks her vibrant orange hair, smiles demurely, and regales men with a mix of witty banter and sexual innuendo. I don't think self-consciousness even exists in her vocabulary. She wears clothes that leave little to the imagination, though she's not exactly Twiggy.

"I'm voluptuous, darling. Voluptuous. Men love women with curves," she says proudly.

I know her real secret, though, it's her confidence. I'd do anything just to have a smidgen of it. It's hard to feel confident when your husband's done a runner.

Chanel's also an expert when it comes to breaking up. From what I can remember she's never dated any man for longer than three weeks, and women pay her hundreds of dollars just for an hour of her time, eagerly drinking the wisdom she dispenses and coming back for seconds.

She's promised to give me her top get-over-a-break-up-quick tips. I tell her plenty of people have been giving me dating advice. It's just left me confused.

"A guy at work told me 'the best way to get over a woman is to get under another,'" I tell her.

Chanel rolls her eyes and groans. "Men have a different way of working through their grief, darling."

I tend to agree. For starters, everything I've gleaned from scanning men's magazines suggests they don't have an issue having sex with strangers.

"I can't imagine stripping off and being naked with anyone other than my husband," I confide. "Maybe the reason men are so untroubled is because there's a worldwide shortage of eligible men."

"Don't let statistics scare you," she says, when I tell her that in New York, women outnumber men three-to-one.

"That's not what scares me," I say. "For over 18 years my husband was the only man to see me naked. We always had sex with the light off. What if I meet someone who's into. . . well, you know, kinky stuff like doing it with the light on, or in car parks in broad daylight? I've read about things like that."

Fear clamps my stomach. "God, I couldn't bear it. They'd only have to see my stretch marks and my rolled-up tummy and they'll do a runner, too. My belly still hadn't bounced back," I say, pressing my palms firmly on my stomach. "In fact, the only thing it does is bounce."

Chanel's finger rests on her lips as though she is savoring diplomacy. "Breaking up is hard to do, Ruby. Everyone knows that but crying over spilled milk isn't going to bring him back," she says, her voice thick with intensity.

"I think 18 years of marriage is a bit more than a puddle of milk, Chanel."

"It's a figure of speech, Ruby. Of course, I *am* sensitive to the fact that you've been together a long time, but to be honest, you are rather dragging out the healing process."

She crosses to the shelf over the fireplace and picks up several framed pictures of Jonathon and me on our wedding day.

"Hanging on to happy-couple photos is definitely not the way to go. Never let yesterday consume today, Ruby." Chanel strides to the mahogany sideboard at the end of the room and throws the photos in the bottom drawer.

As she closes the drawer I fight back tears. Perhaps Chanel is right, hanging onto memories only pulls me back into a past that is no longer my future.

"If you can help me get over the humiliating fact that my

husband abandoned me for another woman and got his PA to send me a text confirming my marriage was over, you're a miracle worker. I just can't let go. I just can't move on. I just—"

"You just want your old life back," Chanel says, finishing my sentence. "Never gonna happen."

The truth knifes through me, jolting me to a stop.

"The text thing was pretty low. I know, darling. I feel it. But don't worry. Have faith. Life is about to get a whole lot better. I *am* a miracle worker," she says confidently. I hear that from my clients all the time. Trust me, darling. Before long you'll be thanking that vixen for taking him off your plate."

"Somehow I doubt that." I gaze nostalgically at the mahogany sideboard, then turn to her and force a smile. "Still I'm willing to be convinced."

"I'm going to share a few of my miracle cures with you. Are you ready for number one of my hot tips? "

I nod enthusiastically. Chanel's passion for her work and life is infectious. I've never, ever seen her down despite the fact that life has dealt her some pretty tough cards. I knew her when she was Zelda Abromovich. She changed her name to Chanel Zest when she was twenty. Chanel after her muse Coco Chanel, she told me, and Zest to better reflect her personality.

It all sounded plausible at the time but I knew the real reason was that she wanted to emancipate herself from her past. I wouldn't mind being able to liberate myself from my entire family—but we'll get to that later.

Chanel's come a long way since those troubled days. I figure if she can reinvent her life after all she's been through then she can help me too.

"Start keeping a journal. It's a wonderful way to start your day," she continues enthusiastically. "Early each morning pour out your feelings onto the page. Empty the horrible stuff out of your head onto paper, then write some positive intentions about how you want to feel. This will free you up and allow you to enjoy the rest of the day. I promise you."

"Hmm, sounds wonderful," I say, nibbling my nails. "I'd love to stop going over and over and over all the things that I must have done wrong to make Jon leave, and wondering about all the ways I could've have tried to make him stay. Things like if only I'd dressed more sexily, given him blow jobs—"

Chanel thrusts her hands in the air. "Stop! Blow jobs don't determine a happy marriage."

"According to Barbara Cartland they do," I say glumly. "She says that's why Charles left Diana."

"*Camilla* is why Charles left his marriage," Chanel says firmly. "Cheating spouses are why marriages end."

"Perhaps if I hadn't been crabby when I had my period or been more understanding when his favorite team got thrown out of the World Cup. Or if, let's be really honest, Chanel, if I'd be younger."

"You've got to stop with the terrible self-talk, Ruby. Do you have any idea what power your words and thoughts have over you? What are you feeling in your body right now?"

"In my body?" I look down at my chest and then my feet. All I can see is Mickey Mouse running up and down my flannel pajamas. "I've got no idea. It's not saying anything to me. Should it be?"

"Your body is your temple, Ruby. It speaks to you all the time. You just haven't been tuned into it before now. Notice what your body barometer does when you start going on and on and beating yourself up like that. It makes you feel depressed, doesn't it, darling? No wonder when you start affirming that kind of rubbish. *If only. If only.* I only you would start saying some kind, loving thoughts about yourself. Try it and see what happens."

Screwing up her nose Chanel picks up the remaining pizza and gives it to Snoutts who looks at it with disinterest. "Getting rid of that processed food would help too. It's not even really suitable for the dogs," she says turning back to face me. "Now, tell me right now five things that are great about you."

"Um. . .er . . ." I trawl through my memory bank and draw a blank. "Gosh, you'll probably think I'm a real sad-sack but I can't even think of one. You don't think I'm a lost cause, do you?"

"Of course I don't, darling. No judgment, Ruby. It's quite, quite normal. You wouldn't believe how often people struggle to think of anything nice to say about themselves. You do know there's a global self-esteem virus? Why else would so many people be popping Prozac?"

I avoid Chanel's gaze and wonder if I should be canceling my prescription of antidepressants.

"Well, there's your first bit of homework," Chanel says. "Keep two journals. One for recording all the sad-sack stuff —things like how you're feeling, times when you feel blue, angry, etc. Then get yourself a fun, funky journal. We'll call it the passion journal. Start collecting positive things people say about you, and record things that inspire you or make you feel good."

Chanel reaches into her bag and pulls out a small spiral-bound notebook. "Here's your first bit of feedback."

She rips out a page, and hands it to me, along with her favorite citrus-orange Shaeffer fountain pen. "Write down what I am about to say and then transfer it to your passion journal. *You are a kind, generous, loyal, intelligent and resilient woman."*

The pen crawls across the page. I feel like such a fraud. Tears bleed across my eyes as I write each word. But then I start to feel better. I hadn't realized how much I needed to hear someone say something nice about me.

I stand up and give her a hug. "I don't think anybody has said anything quite so nice to me in a very long time."

"I'm sure they have, darling. But words are like photos—unless we record positive memories we forget them. It's amazing how memorable criticism is though. Which leads me to my next top tip for getting over a break-up fast. Learn how to meditate. Meditation is the biggest thing since gluten-free bread."

"I don't know, Chanel. I really don't think I could handle shaving my head and I can't see myself wearing a yellow robe any time soon either."

"Don't be silly, Ruby. You don't have to go all weird and new age to meditate. Just saying some simple things over and over is enough."

"Like what?" I ask her.

"Like baaaa, lamb, sheep. . ."

"Sounds pretty weird to me, Chanel."

"I'm joking, silly. But the truth isn't too far away. Any word can be a mantra. Mastering the art of meditation is simply disciplining yourself to repeat the same word over and over again. By concentrating on only one thing you can gradually silence the thousands of random thoughts that are spinning around and around in your head."

Saying one thing over and over sounds easy enough. I decide to try meditation tomorrow. I'm keen to start feeling better and Chanel must know what she's doing because she's the life coach and has qualifications coming out her ears.

"The next tip is fabulous, darling. I know you're going to love it. Eat loads of chocolate ice-cream," she suddenly looks serious. "The ice-cream has to be *Mövenpick*."

I'm starting to wonder about Chanel. Her advice doesn't sound very normal. But then Chanel is quite possibly the zaniest person I know. I do like ice-cream, and *Mövenpick* is exquisite.

"The next tip is in the same box as getting rid of photos," Chanel says.

I brace myself.

"Delete lovey-dovey emails, bin the heart-wrenching texts and burn old love letters."

I bite my lip pensively. I'm a romantic at heart and asking me to throw away my love letters is like asking Linus or Baby Bop to throw away their comfort blanket.

I'm not sure if I'm ready for this.

"Hanging onto old emails is seriously bad relationship feng shui," Chanel insists. "Change the energy flow in your home, darling. Change your life."

"It sure would be great if all I had to do to get over Jonathon was press delete, and whammo he would be gone," I say.

"Believe me it is," Chanel says. ". . . that and dating and time. Of which, might I say, I think you've had quite enough. Grieve any longer than 11 months and you'll head down the slippery slopes of depression. Believe me, that's the last thing you want. It's a steep climb once you've plummeted. Besides, you don't want Jonathon to think he's won, do you?"

I shake my head.

"Good. I can tell you, both as your friend and life coach, that there is no way I'm going to let that cheat come out of this break-up better than you."

I suddenly feel self-conscious sitting around in my pajamas. Perhaps *I am* sliding toward the icy slopes of depression.

"I guess I can store my letters at my parents and retrieve the emails back from the trashcan if I don't feel better," I whisper tentatively.

Chanel's brows furrow into a scary frown. "What's the point of holding onto them?" Chanel says impatiently. "They're only words. Words from the scum that left you for another woman."

Ouch, that hurts. But it's true. I resolve to push delete as soon as I get to work.

"The next tip is a no-brainer but you'd be surprised how frequently people don't realize how unhelpful some of their friends can be. To really move forward it's important to surround yourself with friends who make you laugh. Friends who will introduce you to other single men."

"Other than you, Chanel, I can't think of anyone. Most of my friends were Jonathon's friends and those who have stuck with me don't laugh anymore. They're working ninety-hour weeks and are so stressed out that all they do is come home and blob out in front of the telly. Gosh, now that I think of it that's why so many of my girlfriends are like me—shagless and single. As for my married friends— well, it turns out they weren't really my friends at all."

"It's incredible how invitations to dinner parties dry up when you're single and dateless, darling," Chanel says.

"I know. And when I did go to a few I got the distinct impression some of the women thought I was threatening. As if! To be honest," I say, "I just end up feeling miserable. They're married and *I'm not.*"

"Which brings me to the next rule. Stay away from married friends." Chanel wags a manicured finger at me.

"And stay well away from anyone who looks even the teeniest bit like they might get married."

"Okay," I mumble.

"Definitely don't go to any weddings. You'll only get stuck on the singles table, and believe me," she says solemnly, "that's dating suicide."

"Really? I thought that would be a great way to meet someone."

Chanel lowers her chin and looks at me over the bridge of her nose, "Are you kidding me? Only the desperate go to weddings on their own. Far better to buy a date rather than go it alone. Desired people are desirable," she says. "Which leads nicely into tip seven: *Be glad that you were loved and that you had that person in your life.* Some people live their whole lives never being loved."

I sniffle as tears loom again. "I was glad. Really glad. I was happy loving my husband. I thought he'd be in my life forever."

"Don't be silly, Ruby. That's irrational," she says, handing me a tissue. "Nothing lasts forever. But," she says, her voice softening, "tip eight is relevant here: give it time. Grief does have its own sense of timing."

This doesn't sound like Chanel. "Are you sure?" I ask uncertainly, wiping my eyes.

"Just don't grieve too long. No one likes a sad-sack."

That sounds more like Chanel.

"On that note, and concluding today's lesson, is tip nine: find some fun! Book a holiday. Have a makeover. Spoil yourself rotten. Have something to look forward to or do whatever gives you a buzz. Which leads me to the next point," she says, reaching into her bag. "I've got just the cure. Do you remember my cousin Julie?"

"The pretty one who left her husband and ran off with a surf instructor from Malibu?"

"She did? Oh yes. . .that was ages ago. A year at least. She's been single since then and having a fantastic time. But we're keen to take our loving offshore and have some European fun. We're already booked," she says, passing me a travel brochure, "and the best part is, there's room for you!"

I take the brochure tentatively and thumb through it before returning to the cover page and reading, *Contiki for 18-35s. European Inspiration Tour: 19 days from London to Amsterdam, Berlin, Prague, Munich, Venice, Rome, Florence, Lucerne, Paris and more.* "I've always wanted to go to Europe. But Contiki? Don't you think we're getting a little old for this?"

"Don't be silly, Ruby. We're the perfect age. We're 35 -"

"We're over forty, Chanel."

"Don't say the "f" word, Ruby, it's not polite. Besides, we don't look a day over thirty. With our wisdom, experience and mature outlook on life, we know who we are and what we want. We're an asset to the young."

"We are?"

"Yes, we are! Men love confidence, and confidence comes with experience. Which Julie and I have. . . and you will soon. We've got it all mapped out, and Contiki is just the company to help us realize our dreams."

"What dreams, Chanel?" I ask nervously.

"We want sex," she replies matter of factly, "and lots of it."

"We do?"

"Absolutely. I read an article in *The New York Times* the other day that said one of the biggest regrets people had was not having enough sex. That and not marrying the right person. And you know about that already. I for one don't want to die with regrets. Do you, Ruby?"

"I guess not."

"You guess not? How many lives are you planning to have, darling?"

"Don't be silly, Chanel. Everyone knows you only get one."

"Not everybody believes that," she corrects me. "But for simplicity's sake let's assume it's true. Do you really want to use yours up crying over a disloyal prick of a husband or are you going to join our race?"

"What race?"

"Our race to conquer Europe. Julie and I have set each other a dare. We've got to bonk a guy in every city we go to. The winner gets to have fabulous sex with a bevy of European lovers.

"And the loser?"

"The loser gets to have sex—only with less strangers."

"I don't know, Chanel. This sounds a bit desperate and dangerous. I mean, gosh, we're middle-aged, and you already have a head start when it comes to picking up strange men. To be honest, it's not really my thing."

"Come on, it'll be good for you. A fresh start. A chance to sample some of the stuff you've been missing. Maybe have a fling with a younger man. Haven't you heard that old Chinese proverb about being as old as the last guy you screwed?"

"I can't say I have, Chanel. I think we must read different books."

"Yes, darling, we do," Chanel says, glaring at Joan Lust's novel stuffed under the couch. "Think of it as sexual healing, Ruby. The point is to have fun flings, not full-on relationships. Besides, having one night stands has been scientifically proven to boost your chances of finding love again. Not only do they broaden your sexual repertoire, but they also boost your self-esteem. And let's face it, darling, yours is pretty deflated. So what's to lose?"

"Scientifically proven?"

"Absolutely! 100 per cent guaranteed. Knowing you may never see your conquest again allows you to practice the one thing that will stand you in good sexual stead forever."

"Which is?"

"Saying what you want in bed."

For a moment I'm sure my breathing has stopped.

"I know what you're thinking. You're mortified right?"

"Have I gone a pale shade of white?" I hope my laugh sounds less self-conscious and more, *'this is going to be so much fun.'*

"Grinding your teeth together kind of gave you away," she says putting her arm affectionately around me. "Relax! Believe me—I know. Asking for what you want is the key to a happier life. One-night stands are the perfect way to practice. Oh, and news flash—sex outside of marriage is not a cardinal sin. This is the new millennium, the era of female empowerment, freedom, and choice. Don't waste your life making the wrong ones my sweet. Life's too short and too precious for that."

I do like the idea of getting away, and coming from a family of seven sisters has instilled a competitive streak in me. But racing to take European men to bed isn't exactly the same as grabbing the last potato at dinner. And everyone knows that European men are a lot less uninhibited. They're bound to want to do it with the light on.

I clench my hands over the cushions on the couch. "It's a bit of a stretch, Chanel. I mean, it's all right for the two of you —you're experienced. I wouldn't know where to start. Gosh,

I think I'd fall over if any man other than Jonathon looked at me in an amorous way."

I twist my gold wedding band. The divorce isn't finalized yet and wearing his ring still gives me comfort. It was like a neon sign telling the world someone had picked me. I was wanted.

"Don't worry, we'll get you up to speed. I'm a life coach after all. Helping people with relationship issues is my specialty."

Suddenly I'm more nervous than when Millie tricked me into going on the world's biggest, oldest, and most rickety rollercoaster. I'm half excited and half out of my mind with fear. Mostly it's fear I feel as I say, "It all sounds great. When do we start?"

Feel the fear and go dating anyway, right? Although in Chanel's hands at least I won't die.

Will I?

2

———

MID LIFE MELT DOWN

"Maybe I do need to see a counselor after all," I say handing Chanel a tumbler filled with refreshing gin and tonic the following week at home.

It's been a hard week at work and an even harder week personally. "I think I'm having a mid-life meltdown. I know I've never had one before so it's also possible it is something else. . .but Chanel, tell me what you think. You'll know. I mean you must have seen it all before."

"Darling, I'll need more detail to make an accurate diagnosis." Chanel places the tumbler down on the glass coffee table and looks around the room. "Now where did I put my stethoscope?" Laughing, she reaches behind the cushions on the couch. "I could've sworn I left them right here when I examined my last victim. . .er, I mean client"

"I'm being serious." I walk over the stereo unit tucked away in the floor-to-ceiling bookshelves and turn the volume down. "I don't feel quite myself," I continue, turning to face her. "In fact, I feel positively glum. I just feel so confused about everything."

"Everything? Like what everything?" Her lips still smile but her eyes study me seriously.

"Like who I am and what I'm doing and where my life is going."

"Oh, that kind of everything," Chanel nods sympathetically.

"I've been trying to stay positive like you said. I've been doing the running meditation - religiously in fact. Snoutts quite enjoys it. I end up calling his name so often trying to coax him away from all the female dogs, Snoutts has become my mantra. Why they have to sniff each other's bums? I'll never know. Anyway," I say, pushing my thoughts to the issue I hope Chanel can help me solve.

"I got rid of all my old wedding photos. I binned the lot of them. Well, not quite. They're in storage. But it's close enough and you were right it was incredibly freeing. It's just. . .well, despite all your fabulous tips I still feel down."

"What are your symptoms? Hot flushes? Night sweats? Mood swings? Panic attacks?"

"No nothing like that."

"Oh, that's good. We can rule out premature menopause then."

"Oh God, I've still got that to look forward to and I'm already depressed. Depressed and in a bit of a rut. I had my whole life mapped out. I was going to age peacefully into retirement knowing that I had my man by my side. If he'd told me he wanted more, something different - well I might have tried to accommodate him. If he'd wanted a mistress I might have turned a blind eye. Like the french do. But divorce! God no."

"You've spent your whole marriage accommodating him. You deserve a sufferance medal if you ask me."

"I know you never liked him. But I did. I loved him. Now

I feel such a failure. All of my sisters, all six of them, and my parents are still happily married. Not a blemish. Then along comes me. The Black Sheep." My voice began to shake. "A blight on the family album ever since I was born."

Tears well in my eyes. "I can't seem to do anything right, as my parents so frequently remind me. And I feel stupid, so incredibly stupid. Why didn't I see it coming? Surely there were been signs. Lipstick on the collar, weekends away—"

"Jonathan's such so tight when it comes to spending money I'm sure the whole affair happened in the photocopier room in his office."

I knew she was trying to use humor to lift my soggy spirits but I couldn't even manage a smile. "I never even saw it coming. Never." My lips begin to tremble then the flood gates open. For the first time in months, I ball my eyes out.

"I wondered when you'd finally crack," she says putting her arms affectionately around me. "Have a good old cry. Better in than out. You've been a pillar of stoicism. Keeping all your feelings inside. Trapping them beneath all your layers of propriety. I understood of course. You had Millie to think of. But it's no good keeping your emotions bottled up. That's a surefire way to aid and abet that demon depression. Think about it—de-press-ion. . .you depressed all those feelings below the surface. No wonder they're breaking free now. And bloody good job. They need a good airing. Then they can jolly well bugger off."

"Do you think I'm going mad?" I sob. "I'm so afraid. Afraid I'm losing my mind. I can't sleep. I eat all the time in some sort of desperate attempt to soothe myself. Now, look at me. I look like Mrs. Blob - Miss blob,' I correct myself despondently.

"You're not going mad. Quite the opposite really. The biggest mistake people make is thinking they can go around being all jolly, jolly all the time. Quite ridiculous. You've just been through a bereavement for goodness sake. And unlike other people I could name, you took your marriage vows very seriously. Literally by the book. That's you. Always has been. When the priest said til death do you part, how were you to know that God's will would be undone by United States Law and one determined long-legged blonde? Of course, you're not naïve. You did know divorce was possible, after all over fifty percent of all marriages end up in the divorce courts, it's just you never thought it would happen to you. Why would you? Not with your family history. Unlike me. My parents separated when I was one. They never bothered to get married. I guess that must have made things easier when they split," she says bitterly.

"But hey we're not here to talk about my messed up childhood, darling" She smiles brightly, reaches into her bag, and hands me a packet of tissues. "We're here to talk about you and your mid-life blues."

"I feel terrible, obsessing about my worries. I mean, if you'd rather change topic."

"Don't be daft. Stop putting other people first. I'd much rather talk about your problems than open the lid on mine" she laughs self-consciously, "besides I'm the life coach. It's my job to listen to you. And my pleasure," she adds. "So, tell me about this mid-life meltdown of yours."

"It's just, well. . . " I bite my lip. "I feel so frumpy," I blurt. "Look at me." I lift a few locks of mousy hair. The fine strands fall limply through my fingers.

Chanel nods. "Mmm. I see what you mean, darling. This definitely isn't your best look—sort of bag lady meets Charlize Theron in *Monster*."

"Chanel!" I cry. "Do you have to be quite so cruel?"

"Well, you did ask," she replies nonchalantly. "Besides

I'm one of your biggest fans and I wouldn't have said it if I thought you were beyond hope."

"Gee thanks."

"I know that under all that limp mousy hair there's a gorgeous woman waiting to be rediscovered. Kind of like that sculptor guy. What's his name? You know the one who said he could see an angel in the block of cold marble — his job, he felt, was to set her free."

"Michelangelo di Lodovico Buonarroti Simoni."

"Ahhh. Yes, him. That guy. You always were good with names. Ohh can you imagine what that man's hands would feel like on your skin?"

"Calloused I imagine."

"Oh, Ruby you are melancholic. Michelangelo was an artist, not a laborer. I thought this sort of stuff was your passion. You always loved art at school and look at this place. It's absolutely crammed with beautiful paintings. What you need is a creative man, someone like Michelangelo. Just imagine the attention he would bestow upon you. Think about him caressing your skin, exploring your body in every minut detail, feeling his way tentatively over every muscle, every bone—"

"Every lump of cellulite," I interrupt.

Chanel ignores me and continues with her fantasy. "Imagine him peppering your body with kisses before bringing you to a shuddering climax."

I shift uncomfortably on the couch. "He's gay Chanel, and all this talk makes me feel like some creepy voyeur. But I am curious about where this is heading. How exactly are you and Michelangelo going to do to help me break free?"

"For starters, darling, this has got to go," she reaches over and lifting some strands of my hair. "Chop it. All of it."

"But it's taken me years to get it this long," I place a protective hand over my head and slide it through the ends.

"Years to end up with long, thin mousy hair? I don't know why you bothered. It only makes you look old."

Chanel wasn't the most predictable of characters but one thing I could rely on Chanel for was her honestly. And she wasn't failing me now. It is tough to hear, but I need someone strong to motivate me into action.

I start to feel excited and nervous about what she might suggest I do. Chanel has always been a bit of a glamour queen, in an out there, outrageous kind of way. Perhaps not in the style that I might want to emulate, I think as I look at her flaming orange hair.

She often wears it piled high onto her head and twisted into a top knot. Her fringe is cut short so that it almost reaches her hairline. A blonde peroxide skunk-like stripe runs through the middle of it. I get up and walk over to the mirror which hangs over the mantlepiece and study my reflection in the mirror. Drab. Drab. Drab.

"Hmm, I guess you have a point," I say, turning to her, "but no persimmon orange."

"God, no darling. Orange on you would be terrible. I wouldn't dream of it." She picks up one of Millie's fashion magazines which are sprawled over the coffee table. She licks her forefinger and thumbs quickly through the glossy pages. "What about his?" she asks, lifting the magazine and pointing to English actress Sienna Millar.

"Jude Law porked his kids' nanny and she did a Bobbitt," Chanel says. "She didn't cut off his penis, which in my book she should have, but she did cut off her hair. And now look at her. The press loves her and her career's never been healthier."

"To be honest I preferred her hair longer. Is there anything a bit less severe-looking?" I wasn't quite ready for hair that barely touched the top of my ears.

Chanel points to a photo of the singer Faith Hill sporting a new layered bob.

"Ohh, I quite like that," I say, beginning to get enthusiastic. "Did her man jilt her too?"

"Nope her hair was so badly frizzled she was left with no option." Chanel studies my hair intensely, "yours is pretty frizzled too, Ruby."

"It's stress."

"It's hardly surprising. You've had the two major stressors—make that three, in the space of one year. Separation, cheating, change of financial circumstances—oh, and career. So that's four. I'm amazed your hair hasn't dropped out completely."

I look at her with horror. "You don't think it's going to, do you?"

I could see it now. Bald, fat, and single for the rest of my days.

"Not if we act fast and give it the chop. How about a combo, darling? Let's blend a little bit of Meg Ryan's tousled just-got-out-of bed-hair, Faith Hill's sleek and sexy, and Sienna's Millar's blonde bombshell."

"Me blonde? I can't imagine it? I'll look like mutton dressed as lamb."

"Not a chance. Not with me as your creative director."

I threw her a dubious look. Stripped stockings, orange cardigan, mauve skirt—okay so they were all designer labels - but subtle Chanel wasn't. She looks more like an impressionist painting. A riot of color clashing in an orgasmic symphony.

"I know what you're thinking. But just because I dress like this doesn't mean I'm going to create a clone. This is my signature look. My brand. My statement. My *je n'est sais q'uoi*. My DNA, darling." She threw her hands around her as she spoke.

"Alright. Alright. I get it. It's your secret sauce." Secretly I envy the way she lives her life with color. She knows how to wear clothes that suit her personality. I can't think of many people who can throw together such an eclectic array of clothing. She's like a person throwing together a salad with whatever strange ingredients are on hand and pulling it off.

"Yes, darling. One hundred and fifty percent me. I wouldn't replicate me for all the tea in china. Not even for you Ruby-do," she says giving me a hug. "Now get dressed and get ready to have ten years knocked off your dial."

"Where are we going?"

"Kenneth Amore, style queen and hairdresser to the stars."

3

———

GETTING BACK IN THE SADDLE

Get back on the horse, my friends tell me, but not one of them tells me how. Besides, when did being divorced by the man you thought you'd spend the rest of your life with equate with being bucked off a stallion?

"Well, for starters it hurts like hell," Chanel tells me the night she drags me out to a singles bar. "Here, take a swig of this for courage." She hands me a highball glass full of ice and a dazzling amber-colored liquid.

Obediently I take a take a long sip. "Cripes, what's in this? My head is spinning already and I've only had a little bit.

"You always were a cheap date," Chanel giggles. "It's a Long Island Iced Tea, darling. The fun thing is there is definitely no tea in it whatsoever. Just loads of vodka, rum, tequila, triple sec and—" she turns toward the barman, "Joe, darling, what else goes in this?"

The barman flashes Chanel an alluring smile. "Half an ounce of gin, Kitty Kat." His eyes linger on her voluptuous breasts before he saunters off to the other end of the bar.

"Kitty Kat? How well do you know this barman, Chanel?"

"Intimately, darling. Intimately. Isn't he divine?"

I cast an eye over him. He's not exactly my type, but then I don't know what my type is anymore. As I check him out I begin to see what she might find attractive in him.

With his blond hair stylishly tousled, blue eyes like Robert Redford's, flawless, copper-colored skin, chiseled jaw, and the best smile in Manhattan, Joe is handsome in a *Cleo-centerfold* kind of way. His physique more than matches his looks.

Dressed in a skin-tight white tee-shirt he has pecs to die for and a flat taut stomach that I'd give me eye teeth for. As he moves around the busy horseshoe-shaped bar I can't help but steal a look at his tight, muscular, butt cheeks. Why is it men are always blessed with the kind of bodies they desire in a woman—except, of course, for the lack of breasts.

Mortification turns my face crimson when, my eyes still riveted to the seat of his pants, he turns back toward me and winks. I thirstily gulp my drink.

"I'm glad you like the cocktail, but what do you think about the eye candy? He's more than a pretty picture—he's a blimmin' good lay too." Chanel slides her fingers up and down the straw. "Whew, it's hot in here," she says picking out a cube of ice and tracing it across her breast.

"Chanel Zest, you are wicked!"

"Wicked is the new good - haven't you heard? It's time you got a bit more wicked too, Ruby."

"I don't know, Chanel. I'm not judging you or anything, but this flirting with the ice thing and slipping and sliding with the straw. It's not really me."

"How do you know? Once you try it you might just find it's more like you than you think."

"Maybe," I say dubiously.

"Like I keep saying, getting over a break-up is like riding a horse — first you have to be willing to get on the horse, secondly you have to learn a few tricks. It's easy when you know how, especially when you have an expert rider like me to teach you. Thirdly, no one says you have to stay with one horse. It pays to ride a few before you partner up with your next stud."

"Uugghh, that's gross. Besides, I'm a one-man-woman. You know that."

"You were, Ruby. You were a one-man woman but now you're a no-man woman. I don't mean to be harsh, but you've got to face facts. He's not coming back."

"But I still love him."

"Loved him. Past tense. Any man who runs off with a two-bit showgirl like Jon did, and then sends you a text telling you your marriage is over, isn't worth loving. It's time to move on."

"I know you're right. It's just that it's so hard. Everywhere I look there are reminders of him. The waiter looks like a tad like him and now they're even playing our song."

What are the odds of a mid-town Manhattan bar playing *Love Me Tender?* Next to zero. But fate has decided today had is the day for Elvis to croon out the words which played when we were married.

"Hey, Joe, Darling, " Chanel calls out, "do you mind picking another tune. My friend's allergic to this one."

Chanel reaches into her bag and pulls out her signature pen, as Joe selects Elvis's *Hound Dog*. "Perfect choice, darling," she says to him as she slides a couple of paper serviettes toward me.

"The problem is you've romanticizing him. I see it all the time. Clients are always focusing on the things they loved about their partners and conveniently forgetting the things they didn't like. It's classic Pollyanna thinking."

Chanel slips another drink to me and passes me her pen. "Do you know in all this time I've never heard you badmouth him. It's not healthy to put people up on pedestals, Ruby. More than that, it's not realistic. I want you to write down a list of all the things that you didn't like about him. Remember no one's perfect - even Jon Sugar Jnr."

"I feel mean doing this. I know he left me, but obviously I wasn't what he wanted anymore. I can't really blame him for that, can I?"

"Forget about blame Ruby, and quit with the martyr self talk too. Just write down the things you didn't like — things that if you'd had the chance you'd have liked to change. Imagine you're designing your dream man and that by writing down the things you didn't like you're getting clearer about what you want in your new husband."

"Ohh, that would be cool. I'd love it if I could just write a list of the things that I wanted in a man, send it to Amazon, and he'd get couriered to my door."

"What if I told you it is. I'll let you into a wee secret. Reality begins in your mind. Not the way we're been conditioned to believe. Your thoughts create your intentions and your intentions guide your actions and everything else flows from there. The secret my darling is the law of attraction. Start telling the universe what you're looking for in a man. Let it know what you want to attract. Come on write it down! What are you waiting for girlfriend?"

"Well, okay—here it goes. If I'm honest Jon could be incredibly domineering and bossy. Ohh, and stubborn. I've never met a more stubborn man. He was incredibly lazy too, expecting me to pick up after him all the time. I blame his mother. She over mothered him. He was way too serious as well, especially about work. He'd come home really wound up, go up to the bedroom, flick on the TV and not come out for hours."

Chanel gestures to the paper. "Write down, *uncommunicative during times of stress* and then turn it around so that you're affirming what you want, like *great communication skills even when things are difficult.*"

"Definitely!" I scrawl the words down in big bold letters across the napkin.

"Now turn the other things you said around — the last thing you want to do is attract all the things that annoyed you."

I write down, *collaborative, easy-going, flexible, and helpful.* I'd never stopped to consider what I was looking for in a man before and until I starting writing I really couldn't pinpoint what it was about Jonathan that always had me a little on edge. It felt really freeing — both naming the things that weren't right in our relationship, things that I had bottled up for years like rust that never really sleeps, but also getting clearer about what I wanted.

"Anything else?"

"This sounds silly. Promise me you won't laugh, but he had incredibly bad underwear. He always wore those horrible white Y-fronts. I never complained - I mean they were practical, and easy to soak and keep white, but not exactly sexy if you know what I mean. Yet he'd rant and rave if I ever wore beige underwear. That's the other thing. He had a terrible temper."

"You can always tell a man by their underwear, Ruby. It's been scientifically proven."

I look at her skeptically and write down, *must have great underwear — Calvin Klein or similar. Even if there's no science behind correlating men's underwear with positive personality traits I'm going to make that one of my non-negotiables.*

"Not a bad list, Ruby. Anything more you want to add before we file it away and get onto my next coaching intervention?"

"Wow, you're really working me hard," I laugh. "But if I could change another thing it would be the fact that he always had the TV on. I mean *always*. Boxing, baseball, sports. . .all we ever watched was the sports channel. Because I wanted to do things as a couple I sat there with him. Eventually, I learned a bit about the games but I can't say I ever enjoyed them. It would be nice to meet someone who shared the same interests as me. Someone I could talk about music and art with and maybe even go to shows with. Someone with a great sense of humor who could crack me up wouldn't go amiss either."

"Coming right up. You wait and see, Darling. Just by saying you want these things you've begun to make your dreams a reality. Happiness will come when you least expect it."

"Sounds like the Long Island Iced Teas talking."

"It takes more than two drinks to knock the sense out of me. It's like the horse scenario. You can say you want to ride a horse, even visualize it, but unless you get on the damned thing you're going no where."

4

"So here's riding lesson number one, Ruby. Whenever you enter a bar or any other place where there are loads of potential suitors, survey the room as soon as you arrive. Make sure you look in every nook and cranny. You never know where Mr. Right will be lurking."

Just the thought of going into bars knowing that I was on the hunt made me cringe, never mind being so obvious about it. "Why don't I just wear a sign around my neck, *desperate and dateless?*"

"Now there's an idea, but to be honest I really don't think it'll work. Subtlety is key. Men like to feel like they've had to work hard to catch their woman. They like a challenge."

"Gee there's a lot to learn Chanel."

"Dating is like fishing. You need to take it seriously if you want to reel in a prize fish. This is where Step Two counts. Once you've scanned the room, position yourself so you are as close as possible to the number one hottie and can be seen by as many other hot guys as possible. This is essential. Whatever you do don't turn your back to the room. Even if no one immediately catches your eye a hottie might walk in at any moment. The last thing you want to do is not be seen. That's dating suicide."

In a blinding flash it occurs to me that that was what Chanel did every single time we went out. She never went for the most comfortable seat, away from the hustle and bustle so we could hear ourselves talk. No, she always positioned herself in the thick of the action. I leant forward and listened with fervent interest to the next tip.

"Step 3 is the make or break of flirting. You have to maintain eye contact with any hotties - but scan their wedding fingers for any sign of a prior commitment. Only losers waste their time on married men."

"The blonde bimbo who stole my husband ended up the winner."

"Yes - well - that was different. She — er - she obviously set out to snatch him. Anyway I'm not convinced she won anything worth keeping. Most times married men never end up leaving their wives. Besides, you're just not the kind of girl to get involved with a married man. But you are the kind of girl who tends to always see the best in people. That's why I mentioned it. You can't afford to be so trusting. It's a big, bad world out there. To survive you'll have to keep your wits about you. Not everyone is as honest as you."

"Okay, so I've maintained eye contact," I say, keen to avoid dredging up the past."What happens next. Is this the part where the good looking guy I've been giving the eye to glides over, lifts me onto his flying swan and carries me toward my dazzling new future?"

Chanel sighs with exasperation. "You've been reading those romance novels again haven't you, darling?"

"A little escapism never hurt anyone.It gives me hope."

"Fine, but save the escapism for the comfort of your own home. Right now we need to get real. Most of the time guys are just as afraid of rejection as women are. More so, in fact. Women often make the fatal mistake of assuming that the man will take the lead. But most men need a little encouragement, which is the basis of step 4, *Say something personal*. But don't make it too easy for him. Tease him a little. Work the room rather than make a beeline for him. That way he can watch you work your magic and see how other men respond to you. Men are competitive, especially against each other. If he senses another man is attracted to you you'll drive him crazy with desire."

"Won't he think I'm a floozy? If I saw a guy working the room after he'd just given me the look I'd think he was shallow."

"So you say, but you haven't had any experience of that yet, have you? I'm telling you that jealousy is the way to a man's heart. It's the old primal hunter-gatherer thing. Why do you think men spend masses of money searching for game-fish like marlin?"

"I have absolutely no idea. I think it's barbaric."

"Barbaric or not they want the challenge of going after something that's rare and that other people can't catch. So you've got to be a little elusive. . .but not too elusive."

I cast my eye around the bar. A twinge of envy encircles my heart as I notice a couple gazing into each other's eyes. Momentarily lost in my nostalgic thoughts I don't notice the lingering gaze of a florid-faced man, with a receding hairline, sitting slightly to the left of them. I look quickly away in horror when our eyes meet briefly and he raises his glass in my direction.

"I see you have an admirer," Chanel giggles.

"Very funny!" I quickly turn my chair around to avoid attracting any more unwanted attention. "It's a minefield out there. The ones you want to talk to are busy chatting up someone else and the rest just seem desperate. I think I'll give up now. It's taken me awhile but I've got kind of used to living on my own."

"I thought you told me you didn't want to die never having experienced great sex, darling. I thought you said you wanted to meet someone funny, relaxed, and fun. I thought you said you were *in the game*. Do you want this or not? Nothing worth having comes easily. Unless of course you are deliberating sabotaging your chances of success."

"I seriously doubt I'm going to meet that extra special someone in a bar. My true soul mate will find me. That's how destiny works. I shouldn't have to go and hunt him down."

"Really, darling? So remind me again, how did you and Jon end up together?"

"My mother. . . okay, so I did have a little hand."

"A little!" Chanel splutters, choking on her drink.

"She practically set you up from birth. And didn't you join the cheerleading team at college just so you could be at every game of football Jonathan ever played?"

"I tried to join the team," I correct her, "but I was still too much of a tomboy back then and they wouldn't have me."

"Whatever." Chanel interrupts. "I just remember that both of you were incredibly proactive. Which supports my point perfectly. Destiny doesn't happen to people who sit at home waiting for Mr. Right to knock on their door, Ruby. Sure, it's a bit of a game, but maybe if you changed your attitude then it wouldn't seem like such hard work. Try seeing it as a fun sort of game and focus on the end goal. Besides, you have to work at anything worth having. If it was easy more women would be dating, darling."

"Okay. Okay. Point taken. I'm not trying to be a sad sack. I just feel a little awkward that's all.," I say. "So what happens after I've said something personal?"

"Then the fun really begins. All you need is a little more practice," she says, her eye following a hot looking guy who has just entered the bar. "Watch this," she says walking toward him.

He glances up as she approaches, probably because he feels her eyes boring into him. She flashes him her winning smile and runs her fingers through her hair tucking it behind her ears in a playful flourish. He turns his body toward her expectantly as though he expects her to sit beside him.

But instead of doing the predictable thing she veers slightly to the right and starts chatting with a couple of complete strangers sitting at a table nearby. I watch gob-smacked as she laughs and jokes with them, occasionally looking coyly in the direction of Mr. Hottie. The nerve of the woman, I muse as admiration for her effortless charm grows.

As she predicts he doesn't take his eyes off her. Even when he pretends to look at the football on the television screens plastered around the bar his radar seems tuned to her every movement.

I only look down for a second to get my credit card out of my bag so I can order another round of drinks, but that was all it took for her flirty fishing to hook the bait. When I look up again Chanel has reeled in Mr. Hottie and is back at my side.

"This is Robert. Robert, this is my friend, Ruby. Ruby was telling me that she thought she recognized you, so I thought I'd bring you over so she could be sure. She's a little short-sighted."

I'm stunned, but play along. After all she had told me we'd be doing some experiential learning, whatever that was, and the last thing I wanted was to look like I hadn't caught on.

"Oh, I'm sorry, I think I was mistaken. You look so much

like a friend of mine," I stammer. I kick Chanel discretely and shoot her a warning look.

"No problem. It happens to me all the time."

I scramble for words but the well is dry. Even though only seconds pass, the silence is unbearable and seems to last for hours. He slings his drink down his neck and then looks at his watch. "You ladies have a great night."

Chanel nudges me and mouths 'go and get him' as he walks away.

"Jeeze, Ruby, I bring you a live one and what do you do? Clam up and freeze!"

"What was I supposed to do, Chanel?" I protest. "I've never met the guy before in my life and you were making out like he's some long-lost friend. You're lucky I played along or we would have looked like a right couple of dicks."

"But we didn't did we, darling. In fact it was a great teaching moment. Sometimes not doing something right can be the best way to learn. Flirting Tip 5 is *keep the conversation going like you're talking to a friend*. Most women get too hung up on worrying about whether the guy will like them. The focus should be on just getting to know people and showing an interest in who they are."

"I'm crap at that. Maybe all those years of being drowned out by my older sisters has zapped my skills in this area, or maybe because Jonathan always dominated the conversation. Whatever the reason was I've never felt very good at initiating conversations with strangers. I always feel so tongue-tied."

"But you make a living talking to people all day long, Ruby."

"Not really. Probably ninety percent of my work involves writing. Plus taking to people for work is different. Easier somehow. I can separate who I am from what I do. This is. . . well, it's way more personal."

"Well the fab news is once again practice makes perfect. So your coaching homework for the next week is to practice the art of small talk, darling. I want you to initiate conversations with at least twenty complete strangers."

The horrified look on my face does not escape her.

"Relax. Most people love talking about themselves, so begin there. Just before you could have said something like, '*So, Robert tell me a little about yourself.*' Or, '*so Robert what's a nice man like you doing in place like this?*' Cliches are perfectly acceptable. Or just commented on his clothing, '*great tie.*' That sort of thing, darling."

"I don't have the gift of the gab like you do. I work to a script. All the things I do at work are planned, then planned some more, then planned again, and then passed on for review, critique, rewrites, edits and more critiques. Nothing, but nothing, comes out of my lips without being staged first. It might look like spontaneous dialogue but it's far from it. Nothing in PR is ever left to chance."

"So there's your answer, darling. Go out, plan, practice - write a script if you have to. But get out there and have conversations with strangers."

CHANEL's hot flirting tips might seem obvious to most girls but it is all new to me. I have never had to do any of this in my life and it scares the heck out of me. I don't know how I would cope without the benefit of Chanel's wisdom. . . and her nagging. She reckons her tips will probably end up shaving years and years off the time it would normally take me to hook up with someone new.

"As you know Ruby, I'm blessed with the ability to pick

up men like drivers in Manhattan pick up parking tickets. I know the dating strategies that work and those that don't. So I figured why not share them with people who could really benefit? I think it's my life purpose. Really I do."

"Have you ever thought of writing a book? That way women like me could refer to it when we're in dire need."

"It's funny you say that, Ruby. So many of my friends and clients have said the same thing. I'm working on a draft at the moment. I thought I could get you to try out a few of the ideas I haven't got around to using."

"Ahh, now I get why you've given me all this special attention. You want me to be a social guinea pig."

"Don't sound so horrified. It's not as if I'm going to inject you with drugs or weird hormonal stimulants, although that could be a new technique worth exploring. Kind of like social Botox. Ohhh, I can see it now. Have you got a pen? I need to write that down before I forget."

I hand her my pen and watch as she quickly scribbles down her idea.

"Social Botox! That's the title. I love it. It could be a real money spinner. Absolutely! Imagine if all you had to do was inject yourself with positive hormones that instantly made you more socially confident and irresistible to men."

"Like perfume?" I ask.

"Yes, only way more powerful, darling. Speaking of irresistible perfume, I've whipped up a little aromatherapy blend to help boost your confidence."

"Aromatherapy? I think it's going to take a bit more than a few flowers to boost my confidence."

"Trust me, Ruby. Remember I'm the life coach. I do know a thing or two about what works and what doesn't. Lots of people pooh-pooh aromatherapy as though it's some hippie type concept. But the truth is scientists have been raving for years about the power of smell and how it can activate dormant chemicals in the brain. Here, take a whiff of this and tell me what you think, darling."

Chanel thrust her neck toward me. I lean closer and inhale.

"Smells like rosemary and something else I can't quite put my finger on."

"You're spot on with the rosemary, and I added a few other confidence bolstering essential oils. Rosewood, Spikenard, Chamomile, Helichrysum, Italicum, Cedarleaf, Fir Needle, Balsam and something else I forget."

"What no bats' eyes and wizards' whiskers?"

Although Chanel shakes her head it wouldn't surprise me if she has dropped in a few other odd ingredients. Ever since I've known her she's been fascinated with white magic and mystical things like tarot cards, psychics and angels.

"I haven't heard of half of the things in this stuff. You sure that stuff's safe?" I ask.

"No, it's not safe. It's gloriously dangerous!"

A peel of laughter sweeps over me like a golden ray of sun.

"Once it hits your system you'll be unstoppable, darling. Smell plays an important role in the dating cycle. I've left out until now because we had to get the foundation right. Which we're doing step by step by rebuilding your confidence and self-esteem. Things like the hair cut, your diet and affirmations have all helped. Of course we're not there yet but every day things are on the up, aren't they darling?"

I like the way she says 'we.' It reminds me that I'm not on my own.

"Next we need to wear a scent that is attractive to suitors so that like bees they are drawn to your honey pot, darling."

"There's no way I'm ready for any man to come sniffing around my honey pot."

"Not yet. But you will be once you're armed with my hot tips for flirting and all the stuff we're doing to rebuild your shattered self-image, darling. My prediction is that you'll end up surprising yourself. You'll see."

The word prediction raises my hopes. Chanel looks happy too.

"You're enjoying yourself aren't you? "

"What's not to enjoy? Helping people redesign their lives is a very creative and rewarding process. I'm like the Van Gogh of people's lives. Plus I get to help my best friend rediscover her true fabulous, sensuous, authentic self."

"I like the sound of that — but you might want to pick another namesake. Van Gogh killed himself."

"Good point. You're the art expert. Who do you suggest?"

"Pierre Bonnard would be a better match. He's colorful like you."

"Wonderful darling. Pierre it is. I just adore the French. Did I tell you about the gorgeous French sommelier I shagged last week? Divine. Absolutely divine. The funniest thing was his name. Can you believe his last name was Tazain. Like Tarzan! Get it?" She threw her head back and laughed.

"Those French know a thing or two when it comes to seduction. . .and wine." Chanel gazes dreamily at the ceiling before smiling at me and handing me a small brown bottle. "Take this potion. . . I mean blend, and massage it into your skin day and night. Then sit back and let it work its magic."

I take the amber bottle and hold it to the light. "I won't come out in a rash, will I?"

"No, it's perfectly safe, darling."

Still not convinced I hold it to my ear. I can't hear any ticking and there's no croaking toads.

Chanel rolls her eyes. "I told you it was safe. She takes the bottle back and shakes it vigorously before twisting the cap off. "The way it works," she says dabbing some of the contents on her finger and patting it behind her ears, "is that differing aromatic rings are contained with essential oils. When we smell these the odor is transferred into a nerve message. The message is sent to different parts of the brain where the process of stimulating different hormones is undertaken. What this wee magic concoction will do is trigger the hormones that tell your brain, 'I'm sexy, confident and wonderful, and I relate easily to all the new, wonderful men that are about to step into my life.'"

"Gosh, so much in such a small bottle. Who would've thought?"

"Here you try some," she holds out the upturned bottle and dropped some of the oil onto my palm."

"Just call me Genie. Only don't rub my tummy. I think I've had one too many Brandy Alexander's," she says laughing. "So Ruby, now you have all the tips you need to succeed in the world of dating. Are you ready to take the plunge and put it all into practice?"

"Ready as I'll ever be," I say surprising myself. Perhaps the confidence blend has already begun to work its magic.

5

S mothered in my confidence blend, I head to a downtown bar after work so I can practice Chanel's *Hot Flirting Tips*. I pray I won't make a fool of myself, take a deep breath and walk into Rockside—commonly known in Manhattan as the meat market—only they don't sell sausages there.

I subtly give the room a lingering, longing glance just as Chanel has coached me to do. So far so good. Chanel has arranged for her cousin Julie, the Shania Twain look-alike, to meet me for a drink.

Shania is waiting at a table against the far wall sipping a long, exotic-looking aqua drink. The only spare chair is positioned opposite her. Sitting there would mean that my back would be facing the rest of the patrons. That, Chanel, had warned me, would be flirting suicide.

Normally I hate drawing attention to myself, but tonight I am a woman on a mission. I have to flirt fast or Chanel will have my guts for garish garters. So I pick up the chair, turn it to face the bar and plonk it next to Julie's. Julie is obviously a pro because she is already sitting with the best view of the house.

"What are you doing?" Julie asks.

"Sitting next to you so I can hear you," I lie. Chanel had warned me about the perils of going flirting with other single women.

'Things can turn nasty," Chanel had said. 'The claws come out if it even looks like you might both be on the prowl and it just complicates things. Act like you're not flirting but make sure you don't forget to flirt."

My head is still spinning from that bit of advice and to be honest, I'm not sure how I'm going to master it. According to my friends, I'm an open book. Still so far, so good. Julie hasn't cottoned on at all.

Ping! I spy him. My very own Mr. Big. From the length of his legs which just out from under the table, I judge him to be at least 6ft-2-inches. I can't pick his nationality. With skin that olive he had to be from somewhere exotic like Spain or Italy, or maybe even somewhere further afield like New Zealand. A couple of my friends had moved there and shacked up with the most gorgeous Maori men.

Best of all, Mr. Big knows how to dress and hold down a professional job judging from his attire. He is wearing a crisp white shirt, lemon tie, dark wool trousers, and matching jacket which hangs carefully over the back of his chair.

Mr. Big is sitting with several other men and judging from the way he stands up and shake their hands I figure it must be a business meeting.

But what really knocks me out are his eyes. They are lagoon blue, the color that you'd expect to see on a blonde guy, not one with black glossy hair the color of licorice.

Even from a distance, I can see how they sparkle and dance when he speaks, like the sunlight bouncing off the water. His smile is dazzling, and a little mischievous. I try to think where I've seen a smile like that before. Then it clicks.

He has a Robbie Williams smile. Naughty, playful, promising.

I am so lost in my fantasies I don't see him staring at me at first. He is hot. Seriously hot. And he is looking right at me. . . he keeps looking and then looks some more. . . and I look right back. Yes, I do!

I feel the color rise to my cheeks. *Maintain eye contact. Maintain eye contact,* I will myself. It is excruciating. I want to look away. I feel naked. Exposed. Vulnerable. Panic-stricken. Stupid.

Why is my confidence blend failing?

Mr. Big grins and keeps his eyes on me. Damn now we are in a serious eye-wrestling competition. Chanel's tips completely elude me. I've caught the fish, now what the hell am I supposed to do with him?

Panic rises in my stomach. Blood rushes to my chest, my neck, my face. Great now I look like a cross between a hot-house tomato and a red deer caught in headlights.

"Are you okay?" Julie asks. "You look kind of weird."

Weird. Damn. Sexy in some strange stage-fright, blushing-bride kind of way would have been better. Weird isn't good. Not good at all.

"I'm trying out a new thing. That's all," I say. "Don't laugh but I'm trying to flirt."

Ignoring my plea completely Julie lets out a hearty chortle. "Yes, Chanel did mention you had flirting homework to do. Brownie points for moving the chair by the way", Julie says. "So who's the object of your affection?"

"It's that guy over there. The one talking to the other suits. Don't look."

Julie cranes her head and swivels it back and forth like a periscope, searching for the target. She couldn't have been more obvious if she tried. Mortified, I slink into my chair and cover my eyes with my hands. This is not going well. Not well at all.

"Where is he?" she says, too loudly. "I can't see him."

I roughly sketch a seating plan of the bar, mark where we are, and draw a line to indicate Mr. Big's table. Happily, my ploy distracts her. But alas, not for long.

"Him? He's not your type," she says, coiling her hair around her finger and smiling at him.

Why was it that everyone but me were experts on my type.

He glances toward me again and we hold each other's gaze momentarily. My body tingles in places it shouldn't. Especially if he's not my type. But Chanel was right this is fun. . . and addictive.

Julie nudges me under the table. "Keep practicing. He's obviously intimidated because I'm here. Guys don't like approaching groups of women, especially women in pairs. I'll nip to the loo, powder my nose or something. I guarantee that when I'm gone he'll saunter over."

With Julie momentarily out of the room, Mr. Big and I continue to look at each other. I feel ridiculous but excited. I haven't felt this giddy in years. Not since going to Disneyland.

Mr. Big gets up from the table and heads my way. I think all my hens have come home to lay eggs. Julie was right. Practice makes perfect. He is going to come over and whisk me off for my first night of passion.

I begin planning our first date and imagining what our children will look like. With my new blonde hair and his lagoon blue eyes, our children will be models.

As he walks toward me I study my drink and pretend not to notice him. Play it cool, I mutter under my breath, keep him keen.

In hindsight that's probably when I blew it. The moment I droppped eye contact everything went downhill. He walked straight past me and headed for the men's toilets. He must have kept walking because I never saw him again that night. Come to think of it, I didn't see Julie for ages either.

"Surely men can't be that insecure," I protest when I meet Chanel the following night to give her my progress report.

"I told you, they need reassurance."

"I gave him the eye. What more did he need?"

"You did good there, Ruby. That's real progress. But how was he to know that you don't give the eye to everyone? You need to be more active. That's the whole point of Step Four. What happened to Step Four by the way? Did you say something, anything, personal?"

Oh, Step Four. Say something personal! I knew there was something I forgot, I say inwardly.

"I never got the chance. Believe me, I tried. We even did what you said and tried to create an opportunity where I was on my own. Julie sent herself off to the toilets and everything. But all he did was sit there and smile and stare at me - and I mean seriously stare. The way that man looked at me it was practically like having sex—only with our eyes."

"So he was hot but shy. So then what happened? Did you work the room?"

"Julie came back and we got talking. The next thing I knew I looked up and he was gone."

"See there you go again—focusing on someone else. You completely forgot about your own goals. While it's nice to be concerned for others you need to stay focused on yourself."

"Never mind," her tone softens, as though she registers that I am feeling like a total failure, "In a city the width of

Manhattan you're bound to bump into him again. Forget the size of the population. Just think square mileage. The main thing is that you stepped out of your comfort zone and gave it a go. Next time you'll know what you need to do to actually reel in your catch. Like any new sport, it's a matter of practice, practice, practice."

It had taken all the courage I could conjure just to get that far, I think as I head home. Surely there must be an easier, less humiliating way to upskill. Then like a zig-zag of lightning it strikes me. I could practice from the safety of my very own apartment.

How? I hear you wonder.

Using my computer..

I've always imagined a fantasy life as a novelist or a scriptwriter and Chanel's book idea gets me thinking. Why don't I blog my way to romance? It's the ultimate medium to seize control over my destiny and start having sex with strangers. I could create the characters and scenes exactly as I wanted. And I would have the lead role. How cool would that be?

Very cool.

Forget about rejection.

Forget about shyness.

Forget about stretch marks and lipstick on my teeth.

Forget about years of being the good girl everyone expects.

I'm going to throw caution to the wind. I'm going to discover the real, sexy, other-worldly me.

6

─────────

I t sounded so easy. Until I faced my computer. I stare blankly at the screen. What am I going to type? I have no idea whatsoever.

The English tutor in the on-line creative writing course I enrolled in when Jonathan and I split, tells us, 'Just write. Get out of your head and write whatever comes.'

Tentatively I start. I have no idea where it is going to go. I just know that I wanted to make my failed attempt last night at Rockside have a hipper, happier ending.

Like a scene in a corny movie, I looked across the room and there he was. He was hot. Seriously hot. As I stood at the bar waiting for a drink he came up to me and whispered in my ear, " I want you."

"I want you too," I purred. "But where?"

He took me gently by the hand and led me to the male toilets.

. .

I look glumly at the screen. Oh God, this is crap. Literally. I can't even write a decent sex scene. No wonder I'm still single and shagless. And where did I ever get the idea that male toilets were sexy? Perhaps those tales of people having sex on airplanes pierced my conciousness. I wouldn't mind hooking up with Ralph Fiennes. Would you?

But Mr. Big is not a superstar is he? And We're not flying to the Caribbean.

I delete my entry. But I'm not prepared to admit failure just yet. The key, I had gauged from reading other tantalizing blogs in the past, was to write as though you were having a conversation with your online audience.

This sounded alright in principle but as I was never going to tell anyone that I had a blog I was pretty certain no-one would ever read what I wrote.

But this was okay because the fact that nobody will read it is a benefit. I will not have to worry about looking ridiculous or having to censor my words. It will be just for me.

I can write without fear of retribution or censorship, and that, I must admit, feels quite freeing.

Inspiration strikes again. My fingers dance over the keys. I am buoyed by a renewed sense of optimism.

Naughty. Playful. Promising.
I finally took the plunge. Smothered in my Hot and Sexy aromatherapy blend I went to a hot new singles bar and practiced the Hot Flirting Tips I'd picked up in the latest copy of Elle. The articles promised I'd be able to haul in even the most elusive catch—and believe me they worked fabulously.
As soon as I walked into Rockside I spotted the most gorgeous guy I've seen for a very long time. I just knew we were going to have sex—wild, hot, passionate sex.
Within minutes of locking eyes, he sauntered over to where I was sitting and offered to buy me a drink. The rest is history.

By the end of the night, we were making out in his Penthouse apartment.
Talk about leaving me breathless. The guy was built like a stallion and knew how to give a woman pleasure. I must have orgasmed over nine times.
Sleep? What sleep? Why would I? Would you? Of course not! But I'm knackered now. . . you would've been too. I must have tried out every position there was in the book. I can hardly walk and I seem to have a permanent smile spread right across my face.
I know you know that feeling, girls. I'm addicted. Addicted to sex with strangers.
I have to go now to score my next conquest. I'm no Dracula. I don't drink their blood. But I am thirsty. Thirsty for more hot man-hattan loving. Stay tuned.
Wishing you lots of hot summer loving—Sandy.

I SIT BACK and re-read my entry. I like the name I've just invented for myself, but the rest of it was still crap. I sound like a cross between a sexual predator and a nymphomaniac. An inexperienced, naïve nymphomaniac.

Still, all things considered, my inexperience in the area of sexual conquests for one, I decide it isn't too bad a job. My finger hovers over 'publish.'

"Fear the fear and publish anyway," I affirm out loud. "Just do it." I push my inner perfectionist forcibly to one side and click 'post' before I change my mind.

Oh, my god! My blog is live! A rush of adrenaline spikes through my veins. I giggle at the sheer absurdity of what I've done.

Mr. Big and I are officially live in the universe.

Even though I can hide behind my pen name, to give my content authenticity, it is clear that I am either going to have to get more experienced sexually or borrow some ideas and techniques from someone else.

I glance over at the stack of Mills and Boon novels lining my bookshelves. Of course! If anyone knew how to write sex scenes it was the men and women who churn out those saucy stories. I walk over and run my palm over the racy red spines. Marcia Siren's *Sex Goddess* yells, *'pick me!'*

I slide it out and study the cover. A scantily clad woman with fiery-red hair is surrounded by several bare-chested men —all clamoring for her attention. I can handle that sort popularity I tell myself as I mentally project myself onto the cover.

The blurb on the back cover hints at the sexual escapades of a recently divorced middle-aged woman who longs to escape her humdrum life. After concocting a magic elixir she becomes irresistible to men.

I remember the day I bought *Sex Goddess* as clearly as if it was Monday.

It was two months to the day after Jonathan had finally had the rest of his stuff removed from the house.

I'd gone for a walk, not wanting to be there to witness the finality of it all. I stumbled into a bookshop full of wonderful romance novels and casually flicked through the books on the shelves to pass the time.

When I came across this one it jumped out at me. I found myself instantly uplifted. I knew no elixir was going to cure my woes. But as I eagerly devoured the pages I was transported from my life of relative emptiness to a world where a divorced woman got her groove back and reigned supreme.

As for the sex scenes! Well, they really got me going and

I think it was then that I started to have my first inkling that perhaps there was more to sex than the missionary position.

I remember that I have dog-eared the pages of some of the hottest scenes. I pad downstairs and make myself a cup of tea, then head back. I sit down and study the passages.

A surge of excitement laps my body. I could really let my hair loose, go global with my sexual antics, and nobody would ever know it was me!

How delicious.

7

GAME ON!

"Sit down, Chanel. I've got some exciting news. I've finally broken the drought and it's all thanks to you. You really are a fabulous life coach."

"What? Fill me in." She sits down on my couch, switches off her cellphone and gives me her wide-eyed attention.

"Well, you know that guy I met in the bar the other night?"

"Don't you mean, the guy you didn't meet, darling?"

"Do you want to hear this or not?"

"I'm all ears!"

"I went back the other night and he was there, and just when I was about to give up and leave he came up to me and asked if he could take me to dinner."

"Wow!"

"We were walking to his car when he scooped me into his arms and peppered my neck with kisses. For a moment time stood still while my organism shivered with anticipation."

Chanel frowns. "Your organism, Ruby?"

"Do you want me to tell you what happened or not?"

"Of course I do. . . but your organism? It sounds so

mechanical. Is that really how you feel about your body, darling?"

"Chanel!" I scowl. "Will you let me finish? I haven't even got to the exciting part."

"I'm just happy to hear that you actually got asked out on a date. The fact that you scored is. . . well, it's a miraculous testimony to how my coaching has transformed your life."

"Our mouths connected, disconnected, connected again. It was me who groaned in ecstasy as I crushed my mouth to his in a hot spurt of desire."

"You dark horse, Ruby!"

I smother a giggle and read on. "I hadn't let myself feel this way before. Even when I first clapped my eyes on him and he'd stirred that sleeping urge to life I'd been careful not to feel desire. Until now."

"Too right! A girl's got needs!"

"Chanel, will you let me finish? You're putting me off. I feel weird telling you this anyway."

"Sorry. I'm just so proud of you, darling!" She leaps up and gives me a hug.

"I wanted him, all of him. His hard, male body, the ripe taste of him and the feel of his hard, stiff. . ."

"Ohhh, I've got tingles! What happened next?"

"Be patient, all will be revealed." I took a languid sip from my decaffeinated coffee and stir in a teaspoon of *Sucral.* Reducing stress and losing weight are big priorities right now.

Chanel is on the edge of her seat. I slow my stirring, enjoying the effect my night of passion is having on her.

"The sultry dancing of tongues, the teasing nibble on my earlobe, the thrill of feeling a heartbeat in unison with mine. I let out a scream of pleasure when he lifted me up and placed me on the car. He kissed me again. I kissed him back. I set off tremors in him that pounded like pulse beats. Quiet sounds of longing vibrated in my throat. . .”

"Go on. Go on, darling," Chanels gasps.

"That's all."

"What do you mean, *that's all you're telling*? You can't leave me there! What the hell happened next?"

"I need to know what you think so far," I say. The truth was I was feeling all steamy just telling her about it and I need to take a breath. Plus, I am trying not to giggle.

"I'll tell you when you finish the story. Now go on!"

"Need flooded my body, hot and welcome. Riding on it, I pulled up his shirt, arching my aching body against his hands. I trembled as they slid over my flesh. He felt as horny and impatient as a teenager as he lifted me in his hands and tried to open the car door. 'We need to go somewhere private,' he gasped as we continued to strip off our clothes. I loved his kisses. I wanted them all over every part of me."

"I wouldn't say no either, darling," Chanel says as she closes her eyes. "He sounds hot."

"He was," I purr. "He needed a little bit of guidance though, so I said, 'Here, baby, right here,' and moaned, arching my neck as my fingers wrestled with his jeans. He kissed my ears, my neck, and then lowered his mouth to my breast. I quivered beneath him, a simmering pot on the verge of boiling. . . Chanel, I can't go on, I'm sorry I have to stop."

"You have to go on, Ruby! As your life coach, I demand to know what happens next." Her cheeks flush and her pupils are so enlarged I fear they will burst.

"Are you drooling, Chanel?" I point to the saliva forming at the side of her mouth.

"Of course I'm not! That's. . . well, that's. . . oh, for goodness sake, Ruby, put me out of suspense. Did you get screwed or not, darling?"

"I'd love to tell you," I giggle, "but that's as far as I'm up to in my book."

"Your *book*?"

"By Joan Lust. You must have heard of her. She's America's most popular romance writer. *I* memorized a scene from one of her books, *Slave to Desire,* and that's what you just heard. Though I made it sound as though it was actually me in the car with the super-hot hero, Brad!"

"Now I'm convinced you've lost the plot!"

"You told me to *act as if.*"

"I did?"

"Yes, Chanel, you did. You gave me that book by Jack Canfield, the dude who wrote those *Chicken Soup For the Soul* books, and told me to start acting as *if* what I wanted had already happened and I was now living my ideal life. Like a walking affirmation."

"Oh, yeah, *The Success Principles*. Wow, Ruby, you were pretty convincing! I must read that sometime myself. Good work! So tell me, how did you feel, darling?"

"It was weird at first, telling you about my romp in the back of the car with Brad, but now I want to get into the action for real. I even started feeling sexy just thinking I was Adele. She's the heroine in *Slave to Desire.* She's kind of like me anyway. Except she's run away from her man. He used to beat her and was a real control freak. My husband was a control freak, but he didn't beat me, so I guess I was lucky there. Mostly I feel hopeful. If it can happen for Adele after all that she's been through, it can happen for me!"

"Excellent! As that New Zealand supermodel Rachel Hunter—you know, the one that married Rod Stewart— once said, '*It won't happen overnight but it will happen.*' Though the sex scenes need a bit more work if you don't mind my saying!" Chanel says.

"It's hard to have sex and think about how you're going to write about it. I bet those romance writers do hours and hours of lips-on research," I say.

"Lucky cows!"

"My friend Gerald says everyone should be a romance writer at least once in their life."

"You know what, Ruby? Romance writing might be great therapy for you. Kind of an extension of the act-as-if principle."

I nod enthusiastically. "The other good thing about writing romance is writers like Joan Lust make millions and millions of dollars writing stories about women just like me conquering their fears and their men. She's seriously hot! I want to be just like her."

"In what way, exactly, darling?"

"Every way possible. It's so freeing. Just being able to use words like *penis, breast, and sex* without being censored."

Chanel laughs."Welcome to my world, honey!"

"I feel like I've turned a corner. I've got you and Joan Lust helping me be free to be me."

"That's your homework, Ruby. I want you to find out what it takes to be a romance writer. See if there is a club or something you can join. Just remember when you make your first million I want ten percent!"

This is the best homework Chanel has given me so far. I wish I could tell her about the blog and my fantasy life. Only I can't.

Not yet.

She'll probably tell me I need to see a shrink. Besides, I'm not really being that dishonest. I'm just trying to do things at a pace that's comfortable. If Chanel had her way I'd have bonked half of Manhattan by now. Maybe after a few more blog entries and after I lose a few more pounds I'll feel more confident.

Even though not a word of what I write is true it really is beginning to make a difference to how I feel, and every day I can feel my confidence growing.

Who knows, maybe one day I actually will end up shagging someone. The exciting thing is that all this imagining what *might* happen is helping unlock my creativity. It's great for self-expression too. I feel like a new woman.

Or could it be that I'm discovering the real me?

Before I got married I used to be really creative. I loved to paint and draw and spent hours and hours writing stories. But both my parents and my husband didn't approve.

So I gave it all up. But now I am free to do what I like and I love it. When it comes to my sex life, even though when I sit down to write I never know quite what's going to happen, with whom or when, at least I am in control.

And I can always press delete!

THAT EVENING when I return home I have another go at writing my own sex scene. I'm sure, with practice, I could match Joan Lust's talent.

The timing's perfect. Millie is downstairs deeply absorbed in a video, so odds are I'll get a clean run at writing a decent sex scene.

Where to begin?

I'm temporarily lost for words. Then a flash of insight pops into my brain. Everyone knows I haven't broken the drought for real. Shacking up with Joan Lust's hero doesn't count.

Why not invent a real-life situation? That way I can

stretch my creative writing skills and gain some 'real' experience at the same time.

I log into my blog and create a new post. I title it, *Let go and live*. Satisfied it's suitably symbolic, I begin to type.

Within minutes of bumping into Luke, a guy I'd dated years ago, I knew we were going to have sex. Luckily he lived close by, so in less than five minutes we were in bed at his apartment.

"I have needs," I purred, flinging an arm across Luke's body and snuggling closer.

"I forgot you were a spooner," he said, drawing me closer and placing his arm around me. I turned and kissed him. He stroked my hair and smiled as he gazed into my eyes. "I like your hair blonde."

"And I like the way you help this blonde have some serious fun." I purred, lightly scratching his smooth, muscled chest with my red painted nails. I moved my fingers gently down his chest. "How are your cowboys?" I said cheekily, lifting the elastic band of his underwear.

He followed my gaze and checked his underpants. "Rearing to go," he said grinning, picking out the cowboys and Indians machine-printed across his caramel boxers.

"Ride that cowboy!" I laughed, careful to give him an eye full of cleavage as I sat up. I slid a leg over his body and straddled him. I lowered my mouth onto his lips. They were soft and moist. He kissed me back passionately. His hands reached up and cupped my breasts. He French-kissed me and our tongues encircled each other. I felt like a child spinning on a merry-go-round, unwilling or unable to stop the ride. Luke began to nibble my ear lobe, then moved down my body lightly peppering my neck with kisses. When he began licking my nipple I moaned with pleasure.

I felt his shaft harden beneath me. With eager fingers, he pulled my lace underwear to one side and traced my sex with a moistened finger. I arched my back and moaned with pleasure. He slid down under me until his mouth was over my. . .

I TAKE a break from writing and rack my brain. I know doing edits as you write is a no-no. My tutor says we should always write forward and leave edits to later. He's right.

I'm no longer in the zone. No longer in Luke's apartment. No longer being seduced and made love to by a young stallion.

I'm here. Alone, upstairs, in my brownstone.

But I had to stop. How can I go on if I don't know what to call my bits and bobs in a way that doesn't sound like I'm a gynecologist?

I'll have to check out Joan's books again and see what words she uses! Vagina isn't exactly sexy, is it? And clitoris doesn't quite do it either. Womanhood is odd. Honey pot? Eve's den?

No, those stray too far.

Actually, now that I think about it. I'm not sure Joan's heroines ever get to have oral sex. Do you know that in some places in the U.S. oral sex was banned?

It probably still is.

I wonder if Jonathan can trace his ancestors back to one of those more puritanical states. He never once came down on me but was always poking and prodding his penis in my direction.

It's late and even though I'm too tired to write anymore I

do feel I am making progress. Hopefully, I'll hear back from the short story contest I entered last week.

It would be good to get some independent feedback and even better to win. Just think what a boost that would be for my writing career!

8

The next morning as I sip my coffee I flick through the pages of *The New York Times* until I come to the best sellers list.

I've decided that if I am going to be serious about my writing the best place to start is obviously to take my lead from people at the top of their game. I scan the brief reviews for fiction paperbacks and put a mark beside a few that catch my attention.

First up is *Misty's Kiss* by Laura Love. The blurb was enticing. 'After Sarah O'Shea gives up her job as a P.A. to assume her duties as a faerie princess, she must prove her fertility through sex with her step-princes.'

It's a tough job, but someone's got to do it!

Next on the list was *The Inheritance*, by Pauline Glengarry. I really love her writing. The promo reads, *'Politics and treachery in the court of Henry VIII, narrated by three women, two of them his sometimes wives.'*

I'd love to write historical fiction but I don't think I have the patience and attention for detail you'd need to pull it off.

But perhaps I could borrow from the author and weave some politics and treachery into my story.

Perhaps I could try a modern-day-Clinton type tryst. Or would Trump be more popular? No, I decide, I don't want to have sex with too many strangers. And I want to be respectful.

Of course, a best sellers list wouldn't be complete with something by Joan Lust. The last book I circle is *Last Impressions*. Amazingly this was written in 1994 and here it is in 2020 top of the best sellers. Now that's staying power!

I like the idea of writing mainstream romances. It would be far more respectable than the slutty stuff I am writing on my blog.

As I've already mentioned Joan Lust earns millions and millions writing about love, lust, and passion. Even thousands of dollars would feel good to me right now. Euros would be even better.

I long to gain my own financial independence. Every time Jon's alimony and child support payments are siphoned into my account I feel like a kept woman. I hate it. I suspect he derives some perverse pleasure from my still being under his control.

I wrap my robe tightly around me and walk downstairs to the front door. My adrenaline spikes as I spy the large white envelope.

Last month I'd entered a short story competition. Even though writing romance is vastly different from writing press releases I thought I'd done pretty well. Now I will see.

My hand shakes as I force the seal. I read the covering letter pinned to my type-written story.

Excitement turns quickly to disappointment.

'*Dear Stella,* (I've got so many pen names now that it's hard to keep track)

Thank you for entering our short story contest. Five thousand, four hundred and two entries were received. Although your entry did not gain a final placing, I hope you will feel that you have benefited from entering the contest.'

Disappointment turns to despair as I read through the judges' comments.

'Unpleasant characters. A shallow heroine and crass hero.'

Ouch.

'The story seemed more about sex than emotion.'

Boo.

I blame Chanel. I keep telling her *I can't* have sex with strangers. *I can't do it with someone I don't care about.*

'Lumpy and forced.'

Oh crap.

My hopes and dreams of becoming the next Joan Lust crash to the floor like a detonated skyscraper.

Writing is way, way harder than I thought. Just like finding someone to love. I pick up my phone and call Chanel to confirm I can meet her for afterwork drinks.

"I've ordered for you already," she says, as I walk into Harry's Bar, just around the corner from the office. "This should cheer you up. It's a Mai-Tai."

It was definitely the most cheerful drink I'd seen outside of a beach resort. A bright pink paper umbrella pierced a plump, glossy, cherry and dangled elegantly on the edge of the cocktail glass.

"I'll never be a writer." I pass Chanel my rejection letter. "Nothing's going right. They hate me and I still haven't even been on a date with anyone and. . ." I pick my happy drink up and lift it to my lips.

The cherry speared to the umbrella falls from the glass and lands in my lap. I stare at the large raspberry stain tattooed on my white dress. "Oh perfect. Now I can't even hold my alcohol."

"Look on the bright side, Ruby. At least you received some helpful feedback," Chanel says.

"Sure if you think the comments were helpful. '*A shallow heroine and a crass hero make this story annoying to read.*'"

"You're focusing too much on the negative, darling," Chanel says.

"It's hard to find anything positive. I worked really hard with that story and despite all my efforts no one really fell in love with my characters. But I loved them. I really did."

I grab a red serviette from the counter, dip the end in a glass of water and dab my white dress. "Great. The serviette's not colorfast," I say as a coil of red bleeds over my dress.

"Problem solved. Now you have a pink dress, or you will if you keep dabbing your skirt with it. As for your writing, all you need to do is create characters readers can fall into love with." Chanel looks around the bar. "Take him for example."

I follow her gaze. She's so predictable. Tall, dark and handsome, she never strays from the same type of guy.

"Simple you may say. But I don't think you can make somebody fall in love. It just happens. . ."

"Shit just happens, Ruby. Love you have to work at. It takes time but with a little bit of focused attention you can help cupid along, darling."

"Since when did you become an expert? I don't think I've ever heard you talk about *love*. Sex yes but love, no. Have I missed something?"

"Yes, Ruby, you have," Chanel says coolly. "You've totally missed the point that we are not talking about me. We are talking about your crass hero and your shallow heroine. The fact that your readers can't identify with them tells me that they are obviously not well suited. You need to think more like a matchmaker. Try aligning their horoscopes."

"What?"

"You need to build believable characters. Make them real. Give them birthdates and then see how their signs gel. Take you for example. You're a Libra. There is no way you should ever hook up with a Capricorn."

"But Jon was a Capricorn," I say.

"Exactly. The relationship was pre-destined to fail. If you'd been born in India a marriage like yours wouldn't have been allowed."

"I did have an arranged marriage, Chanel."

"I hardly call your mother's meddling and your infatuation an arranged marriage. Other cultures take love far more seriously. People often ridicule horoscopes but it's ancient wisdom which has been around way before any of us were conceived, darling."

"Don't you think we have a bit more control over our lives than that?"

I thought I'd dealt with the whole *Jonathon-meets-pretty-girl,-ditches-wife* cliche, but now Chanel's comments about predetermined compatibility leave more questions than answers.

Why hadn't I thought about that before? Possibly because Jonathon and I had married young and I hadn't even stopped to consider the possibility that there might be someone better for me.

Were Jon and I always predestined for disaster? Could I have saved myself this sorry ending by never getting involved with him to begin with? Was everlasting love really as simple as finding someone with a compatible star sign and then the magic would begin?

Who was my heroine compatible with, I wondered? Forget about my heroine. She can wait. *Who was I compatible with and why hadn't I found out before?*

9

I'M IN LOVE!

I head up to my room armed with a box of chocolates and log in to Liz Greene's astrology site. I am determined to find out if cyberspace and the cosmic field hold the key to helping me find a love mate.

Once again Millie was out with her friends and I had the house to myself. Time was running out. Before long she'd be off to college and moving in with friends. If I didn't get my skates on I'd be living here all alone locked away like Rapunzel in her tower.

Only my hair is so super short now, even if a prince did come along, he'd never be able to climb and whisk me away to my happily-ever-after.

In the realm of romantic fiction, there was still hope of a rescue in the form of paranormal heroes like wizards and warlocks. Or maybe a half-bird, half-man creature who could fly to my aid. As long as he has all the bits in the right place.

Right now I'll take nearly anything I could get. As long as we were compatible, of course. I decide to take a peek at my daily forecast to see if Liz is on the money.

'Your sensitivity to and awareness of the subtler aspects

of the world around you is greatly increased. Sometimes this influence accompanies a period of dreaminess, in which you spend much time fantasizing.'

Yip! Bang on. Liz really is the real deal. I don't know why I hadn't thought to look at compatibility tables before. I am now officially totally open to anything that will prop me up and give hope. Whatever it takes, right?

I've decided to re-write my heroine and make her a bit more autobiographical. My writing teacher says that most first-time novelist's books are autobiographical because it's easier to master. From then on, he says, it's easier to write for real—or non-real.

Secretly I feel pleased with myself because I am well on the way to writing proper fiction. Everything on my blog is totally made up. But I can't tell my tutor that. Nobody must ever know, for reasons you and I both understand. We are sworn to secrecy, aren't we?

So in the interests of efficiency, my heroine has metamorphosed from a fiery Scorpion into a diplomatic Libran woman.

On Liz's site, I click on the icon labeled '*love, flirtation, and sex*' to find out who my heroine is compatible with sexually.

"Who she goes with, I go with," I vow as I read Liz's overview.

'You are *addicted to physical beauty and grace in sexuality.*'

That explains the attraction to Jonathan and why it has been so hard to let go. No wonder I'm having withdrawals. I had to go cold turkey. One text and our marriage was over. Who wouldn't have suffered?

I stuff a chocolate in my mouth and continue to read. Yes

I know I'm supposed to be dieting. But allow me this one little addiction, won't you?

'You are a very steady and reliable partner in a love relationship. When you make a commitment, you intend to stick by it.'

Yip, bang on the money, again. Jonathan was not a Libran like me.

'You will generally take a lover only after the two of you have become fast friends.'

This is what I have been trying to tell Chanel all along. I can't be rushed. I must show Liz's website to Chanel.

Okay, I've done the self-awareness bit, now let's get down to the business of finding my lover-friend.

I can't seem to find out how to do this on Liz's site. You already have to have a partner and then put in his birth date. Then she'll tell you if you're compatible or not.

I don't have a partner. And my heroine doesn't want to close down her options.

I spend fifteen minutes searching on the web before stumbling across another site that tells me straight away that my best love-sex-friendship match is with an Aquarian.

This leads to even more research as I try to find out what exactly this means.

You're probably thinking this is a huge waste of time and energy or you may be nodding your head in agreement. All I know is that all this research and thinking for the first time about what would make me really happy is a whole new, brave, courageous world for me.

All my life I've been so caught up with everyone else's views about what is best for me. *I've been to paradise but I've never been to me.* Do you know that song?

Anyway, I digress. I feel like a kid in a candy store able

for the first time to pick and mix whatever I like in a man. It's liberating.

I zip back to the profiles and read more about Aquarians. My excitement builds as I read through the list of characteristics these possess.

Humanitarian, friendly, independent, quirky, willing, progressive, an original thinker, inventive, creative, and loyal.

Wow! I'm in love! After years of living with a serious, determined, cautious and cold man, Mr. Aquarian sounds just like the fun, good-time man that I need.

I immediately sit down and rewrite my short story, importing all the positive aquarian traits into my hero, Zack.

I am now officially in love. Before he was a little dishonest, a bit shallow, morally corrupt and a man-whore. What was I thinking! Yes, you're right—I was thinking about Jonathan.

Now, complete with bio and horoscope Zack is a fun, exciting, caring, aquarian male with an unconventional streak that I just love. Think Paul Newman, John Travolta, James Dean, The Mad Hatter (!)—they are all famous Aquarians. I'm not sure I can see myself with The Mad Hatter but James Dean, definitely.

I surf back to Liz's site to see if she approves of the new match. Yip, she's happy. We are predestined to have a wonderful relationship. This is a sassy, exciting pairing of two similar souls that is sure to be a hit.

It doesn't matter that I know zero sexy, single Aquarian males. What matters is that I now have hope and if I can't achieve it in my own life, at least I can bring love to life on the page.

I enthusiastically typed up a new character profile for my hero. As I proofread it I fell more in love by the minute.

Before you think I've gone absolutely mad, falling in love

with your characters is very common. Look at all the women who fell in love with Heathcliff, Mr. Darcy, McDreamy and Mr. Big (of Sex in The City fame).

They're not real people but we love them anyway.

In a burst of spontaneity, I text Chanel and ask her to keep an eye out for any Aquarian men for me—in the interests of research of course!

She texts back immediately!

'I know one! I was going to see if u wanted to go a blind date today but u said u were off men. He is *sooo* lovable and has just written a script for a movie.'

My heart stops. My first reaction was panic. A blind date? That is way scarier than anything I have done yet.

For one thing, I would have to be me. Really truly deeply me. Not Stella, my creative writing pseudonym, or some other invented character—but me.

This is scary.

The universe has sent me my perfect match. Our horoscopes are aligned for goodness sake. And Chanel, who knows me better than I know myself, thinks we could be a good together.

She's given him the seal of approval—'he is sooo loveable.' Note the three *ooo's*.

He even has the same interests as me. So what is the problem? You got it. Self-doubt. What say he doesn't like me? I hunt around the room for my confidence blend. Where is it when I need it?

Deep breath. *Fake it till you make it*, I remind myself. I text Chanel back trying to sound upbeat and super confident.

'I am definitely interested.'

I rub my jaw and resume breathing. Feel the fear and do it anyway.

Just for one day.

The blind date was a total disaster. The guy Chanel set me up with not an Aquarius. And he wasn't a scriptwriter. Everything was a lie.

None of that would have mattered if we'd had one grain of anything in common. But we didn't, and we sat over dinner looking like two stunned mullets. Only, and I don't mean to be cruel, he looked more like a muppet.

Graham was fifty-five and wore a toupee. I'm sure he'd put it on back-to-front. Either that or radiation in the atmosphere had caused it to shrivel and lurch dangerously to one side of his head.

"I can't believe you did that to me," I curse when I meet Chanel for breakfast the next morning.

"I thought you'd appreciate the practice," she says seriously. "You did say you hadn't been on a date so I thought it was time to break the drought."

"Not like that. It was humiliating. We looked like one of those old married couples that go to dinner and look bored out of their brains, staring at anyone but each other in total silence."

"Graham said he had a lovely time. In fact, he's keen to see you again."

I roll my eyes. "You are kidding."

Chanel breaks into peels of laughter. "Of course I'm joking. Graham's the ex of one of my clients. He needed to build up his courage muscles — he's a bit shy around women. I thought of you immediately. Win-win if you ask me. You did go easy on him didn't you?"

"I recognized he felt as badly as I did and I tried my best to make the evening pleasant. He doesn't really want to see me again, does he?"

"Relax. He was only in town for an Actuary conference." She glanced at her watch. "I expect by now he's on a plane back to Minnesota."

"Whew, What a relief. You know I've never been any good at saying no. If he asked me out I'd go out with him just to avoid hurting his feelings."

"Yes — we need to work on that,. But right now we need to get you dating. I can't believe you still haven't shagged anyone."

"I'm warming up to it."

"Well not soon enough. Antarctica could melt before you warm up. It's time to move you on to the next step, Ruby. It's time to go dancing!"

"You're joking! I've never danced in my life. To hook a man you have to be super cool, not mince around looking like someone having an epileptic fit."

"The point of going dancing is to learn how to dance," Chanel says seriously. "Besides, it's a well-known fact that loads of single men go to dancing classes to pull the babes. It's way easier to score a woman by twirling her then it is buying her a cocktail. And you get to wear pretty girlie dresses without looking like a twat."

"I don't know, Chanel. I'd feel kinda awkward."

"Come along on Wednesday and check out the class and see how you feel. It's a walk in the park really and you can chalk it up as another FTE — first-time experience. You may even find you love it more than you thought."

Somehow I doubted it, I think as I reluctantly agree.

"Who knows you may meet someone you can model your romance-writing skills on," she says, enthusiastically.

11

———

DANCING MY SOCKS OFF

My stomach tightens as I hesitate at the doorway to the dance studio. "I'm not so sure about this." I turn and look longingly at the cab as it pulls away.

"Relax," Chanel says, taking my reluctant arm and dragging me up the threadbare steps. "This is dance heaven and we are its dancing fairie, darling."

"Speak for yourself. You could have told me you were dressing up."

Chanel looked gorgeous. She was wearing a hot-pink flared tulle skirt that splashed around her calves as she moved.

Her shoes, although much more practical than she normally wore were still outrageously high. Hot-chili satin ribbons extended from the shoes crisscrossing around her legs like a ballerina.A slightly ruched chiffon blouse with a plunging neckline only barely concealed her breasts.

I, on the other hand, had assumed that Ceroc would be quite aerobic and therefore thought something more practical would be the order of the day.

Flat black shoes, jeans and a beige tee-shirt with the

words *'make peace not war'* splashed across the front of my chest. I'd purchased it from one of the stalls lining the anti-war rallies held earlier this year. Somehow tonight the words seemed especially apt. I definitely didn't want to step on anyone's toes, nor leave anyone bruised and bloodied.

I squeeze against the wall to make way for a couple bouncing up the stairs. The girl brushes past, giggling. She wore a flared skirt that barely covers her plump, dimpled thighs. A lycra boob-tube struggled with the weight of her heaving chest as she bounces up the stairs. A pair of strappy sandals wrap tightly around her ankles, and folds of skin billow over the leather straps.

While I am obviously underdressed, the sight of a normal, overweight, supremely confident woman made me relax. Perhaps it won't be so bad at all, I think as I reach the landing.

My confidence was horribly short-lived. My worst fears were confirmed. The room was full of lean, leggy women with waists the same size as my wrists.

Okay, I'm exaggerating. But the place looks more like an audition for America's Next Top Model than the dance class I was hoping for.

"Are you sure we're in the right place?" I ask Chanel.

"Absolutely!" she says. Her arms are outstretched as she saunters toward a gorgeous blonde taking money at the door.

I follow like a wary lamb.

"Darling," she cries, kissing the blonde on both cheeks. Very European I think, as they mutually adore each other in the way that very sociable people who know absolutely everybody do.

I scan the room looking for my chubby soul mate. I catch sight of her briefly as she disappears into a side room. A door with a sign *tango for beginners* snaps shuts behind her. Damn.

"Paula darling, this is Ruby."

"Welcome!" Paula cries, wrapping her lithe arms around me and kissing each cheek. "Look at you. You're so sweet. Very Audrey Hepburn in your pumps."

I can barely hear above the noise.

"She's a virgin!" Chanel says loudly, just as the music softens to a stop.

I stand bewildered, my cheeks reddening. Everybody is looking at me.

"Your first time. . ." Paula continues loudly, "can be a little uncomfortable but once you've been through a few partners it gets easier. . . like riding a. . ."

As they both stand grinning like Cheshire cats I wish the ground would open up and whisk me down a tunnel to the safety of my warm and cosy bed.

Thankfully the room darkens and I'm out of the spotlight. A strobe glints seductively over the floor. Figures appear like stray cats from the corners of the room. Men with outstretched hands pull women they've obviously singled out before venturing from the blackened edges.

"Come on then. Let's get you started. This is the warm-up dance," Paula shouts , as Donna Summer's *Hot Love* belts out from the speakers.

Paula points a supremely long, shimmering pink nail into the darkness, curling it repeatedly as she beckons to a tall, muscular stallion clad in black.

Oh my god, it's Patrick Swayze, I think as he saunters over. A pulsating beam of light illuminates his face momentarily. No, it's not Patrick (duhh) but this guy is hot! Hot! Hot! Too hot for me. He's more like Antonio Banderas. I break out into a nervous sweat. If ever I wished I didn't have two left feet it's now.

"Mauro daring, this is Ruby," Paula rests a hand possessively around his waist.

He places his hand longingly on her butt, squeezing her cheeks playfully. Not that there is much to squeeze— because an arse like the rear end of a bus this woman does not have. Her bum's so flat I could iron Millie's hockey gear on it.

Chanel, who has disappeared to the ladies room to apply yet another layer of tangerine lipstick, suddenly appears. I swear that woman has a man radar!

"Mauro," she cries, gliding across the floor and sandwiching herself between him and Paula. "How's my favorite Latin love machine."

His white teeth are blinding as he smiles. "I am wonderful."

"You certainly are," Chanel drools, ignoring Paula's attempts to cut in.

"Mauro is going to show your friend some moves — unless you have other plans for him," Paula says. She is smiling but her words are sharp, carefully chosen, and not without threat. I momentarily forget about my two left feet.

Mauro takes my palm. Looking coyly at both ladies he lifts my hand to his lips and kisses it. They both visibly stiffen, their smiles momentarily frozen to their faces. He slowly traces my hand with his moistened tongue. It tickles and I giggle. Paula frowns, her eyes narrowing as she is momentarily caught off guard.

"If I didn't know you better I'd think you were trying to make us jealous, Mauro," says Chanel. She walks behind him and pinches his bum before licking the back of his neck. I hear her whisper to him, "You're a naughty boy and you will be punished."

"Just teach the girl some moves Mauro," Paula hisses as she walks off. "Leave the Latin love routine at home."

My brain is spinning. It's war out there. I recall Chanel's earlier warning, *'Even your closest friend can be your arch-rival.'*

Somehow I doubt Paula is Chanel's close friend anyway. Still, it's disconcerting. The pickings are thin. Everyone knows it. Women statistically outnumber men all over the world.

As I scan the room, the imbalance is noticeably visible. Like musical cushions, only on a bigger scale, and it's not cushions that are missing. It's men. Even though the thought of looking like a fool on the dance floor scares me, the idea of being a left-over girl, glued to one of the benches that line the perimeter of the room, troubles me more.

Mauro leads me onto the dance floor. "I can't dance," I warn him in advance.

Before I can protest he draws me tightly toward his oiled chest. He is wearing a black shirt, buttoned only at the navel. Wiry black hair and body oil sizzle against my skin.

"Relax," he says, massaging my tense shoulders. "Do not be afraid of dance. Let your body be moved."

I nod. But my bod has a mind of its own. For some reason, it has decided to lock up on me completely. I'm stiff as a coffin.

"In the arms of the right man, a man of, shall we say Latin origins. . . a man strangely not too dissimilar to myself," he smolders, "you would be putty. Soft, malleable, able to bend and mold your breasts into mine. We would dance as one. Instead, you are cold. Unresponsive to my touch. But this, I think, I can change. I will lead and you. . . you will follow. You will respond in very little time to that. No?"

His supreme confidence verges on arrogance. We'll see I

think silently, as he lunges toward me. With one deft maneuver, he flips me sideways until I am suspended in his arms and my head is almost touching the floor. As I reach to put my hand out to cushion my fall he flips me up again until I'm standing.

"How was that for you? Good I think," he says.

"Mind-blowing," I reply shakily as I try to relocate my head back into my neck. I swear I must look like ET. The force with which he threw me to the floor and back again must have elongated me ten-fold. I'm sure my jaw has dropped several inches too. I run my fingers tentatively across my chin. Phew. Everything seems to be okay.

"See. It is as I told you. But still, I feel you are too. . . how do you say. . . too. . . erect. You are stiff like a boner on a holy man. This I think is not so comfortable for you, no?"

I suddenly wish I wasn't such a visual person. "No," I say quickly as I look for the nearest escape route. The images he's described stick in my mind.

"Perhaps we will try something a little more to your liking. I have a special talent of finding that special place for the woman. . . the g-spot, no?"

"Errr. . . n. . ." Before I've even got the word *no* out of my mouth, he's lifting me off the ground. Suddenly I am surfing over his head. All I can think is thank god I have jeans on as one hand clasps over the back of my neck and the other under my arse.

As he spins on his feet, taking my wooden totally petrified body with him, I feel increasingly dizzy.

"Please put me down," I beg. "I'm afraid of heights." But he doesn't hear me, The noise is so loud and unhappily for me, he seems to know every word. They're playing Bon Jovie's *You Give Love a Bad Name.* I should have gone to Ballroom for Beginners.

"Eeeeeeeewwwww" I squeal as Mauro plunges his hand between my legs, flips me upright and lowers me to the ground.

I'm speechless.

"Ahhh, I see I took your breath away. So you are not so stiff now."

He lowers his face to meet mine. The fact that I am doubled over in pain, fails to register.

"Is this a new move? I do not know this one. But I like to try all the positions."

I feel suddenly totally inept. I'm terrified. Terrified of what moves he'd like to try with me. Terrified of looking like a fool. Terrified of walking off the dance floor, my tail—or should I say, the memory of his hand, between my legs and everybody looking at me.

I force my mouth into a tight smile. My mouth feels tight and dry. My legs like deadweights. But I'm determined to go on. If this oddball can manage to master the dance moves, surely I can too.

Besides, when I wasn't feeling terrified there is something exhilarating about being whirled, twirled, and pirouetted.

Or is the fact that for the first time since separating from Jonathan a man has finally touched me—*down there*. I swear something stirred. Now that's got to be progress. Only I'd prefer it didn't stir while I was mid-air.

"Mind if I cut in?" Paula says sharply.

I wondered where she'd got to. For a moment it occurs to me I could say, 'yes I do mind'. But I've never really been good at standing up for what I want. As she falls into Mauro's open arms. I'm a little miffed. I was just beginning to relax.

I stand awkwardly in a sea of dancers for a moment before another man in black approaches.

"Mauro thinks he is good but I am better," the stranger

says in a toneless voice. He offers me his hand but does not look at me. His eyes are firmly fixed on Mauro.

Feeling it would be impolite not to accept, I figure 'why not?' I'm keen to have another crack at it.

He pulls me toward him, my body follows. My mind tries to anticipate his next move. I fail miserably as suddenly once again I find myself horizontal only centimeters from the floor. My body tenses. I'm going to hit the linoleum this time. I'm sure of it.

But no the man in black has timed his move to perfection and pulls me up just in time. Here's me thinking dance was supposed to be elegant. Not another competitive sport.

I think I've pulled a muscle. My new flat shoes rub the emerging blister on my heel. But there's no time to lick my wounds. He has me in his grip. He firmly clasps my left hand then wrenches me forward as though I am a little bit of string on a spinning top.

He flicks his wrist and lets me go, sending me spinning into the couple beside me.

"You are supposed to grab my other hand," he growls.

"I'm sorry. . . this is my first time."

"I saw you with Mauro," he says in an accusing tone.

"Yes, but he was teaching me."

"Now you have learned another. Please don't make that mistake again," he says grabbing me by the wrist again. I feel increasingly uncomfortable. I don't even know his name. He never smiles. He's snappy. I thought dancing was supposed to be fun.

I try to make conversation. After all the whole point of being here is to meet men. Perhaps I have been too quick to judge I think as I introduce myself.

"I'm Ruby," I say.

An awkward silence follows.

"How long have you been dancing?"

His face is expressionless. "Six years," he says in a deadpan voice.

More silence as he concentrates on his moves. His eyes look past me at Mauro and the bevy of beautiful girls he is dancing with. They all move supremely. I can't help but think I must be the only first-timer here.

"I'm sorry. You must think I'm a terrible dancer."

His smiles tightly but says nothing to reassure me. Why he persists in staying I can't fathom.

"If you'd rather dance with someone else I understand," I say.

"I never leave mid-song. It is bad luck," he says.

I get the feeling he feels obligated to continue. That I'm kind of like a kid sister he's been forced to lug around. He seems the dutiful, military type.

The music mercifully slows to a stop. A polite thank you vaporizes into the air as he glides into the distance. I can't help but think he has chosen the furthest point away from me. I am left standing alone looking like Nancy-no-friends. I want to go home.

I spy a Mexican girl with glossy black hair and a wide smile. Her full lips are beautifully completed by a row of dazzling white teeth. I watch as the mute stranger holds out his hand. He takes her in his arms and they glide across the room, perfectly anticipating each other's moves.

Her hips sway seductively to the Latino music. They make it look so easy. I attempt to copy the sway of her hips.

Chanel bounces over to me, a tall Nordic-looking man in tow. "Are you okay? Do you have a pebble in your shoe?" she asks breathlessly.

"Chanel, this is useless." I sway my hips more vigorously to accent my point. "I can't get the hang of Ceroc."

"Now you look like a blender," she laughs. "Why do you always think you have to master things the first time you try? You are allowed to look foolish you know. It's not the end of the world. As Donald Trump says, 'Talent is like money. It has to be developed. It has to be nurtured. It has to be used properly. It takes time, work and patience.'"

"Well I don't see Donald here and I've never seen him on *Dancing With the Stars*. So I'll take it he wasn't talking about Ceroc and if he was he was probably referring to people who had talent to begin with."

"You'll feel better once the proper lesson begins," she says brightly. Her eyes follow the couple dancing. The music has stopped and the bright overhead florescent lights flicker on.

The dream couple continues to dance seemly oblivious to the mix of admiring and envious stares.

"Sexy aren't they?" Chanel pulls the orange scrunchy hair tie from her hair, As her flame-colored locks tumble free she tips her head upside down and shakes her hair vigorously.

"This is Jean-Jacques," she says as she slips her hair back and then piles it on top of her head. She twists it into a smooth knot again. Jean-Jacque a tall- blonde, olive-skinned Nordic god looks at her admiringly. A twinge of jealousy surprises me. I wish someone would look at me that way.

Jean-Jacques takes my hand and kisses it softly. "Enchantee," he says. Not Nordic. French.

Before you start thinking the room is full of hotties let me correct you. *Big time*. The three guys I have met so far are the only good looking men here. I later learn that they are all quite high up in the dance world. As part of the dance community thing they regularly help out to keep the girls coming back. That, and to give the new guys something to aim for.

It makes sense. For one, guys are competitive. And two, most guys would run a mile if they thought they were going to be teased and called effeminate.

These guys are macho, sexy, and lusted after. Something I am sure all guys aspire to. If I was a better dancer I seriously feel like I could really learn to surrender into their arms. But I'm not. Not by a long shot.

I scan the room as men and women begin to form into lines. Hope turns to despondency. There must be about 100 people and at least 70 percent of the class are women.

I can't help feeling like I must look desperate. My odds of meeting anyone here are zippo. Besides the fact that at least sixty nine other women are competing for the same men, the only guys worth going for are the three guys I've already danced with.

Good looking they may be, but charming, loving and into me, they are not.

"Come on, Ruby," Chanel cries enthusiastically. She grabs me by one hand as Jean-Jacques pulls her onto the dance floor. "The lesson's about to begin."

"It's alright for you. You have a partner," I whisper into her ear.

"Everyone gets a turn. You'll see."

The man in black and the Mexican princess take center stage. "Pick a partner," they shout into their microphones.

Pick a partner. The dreaded words.

As Chanel and Jean-Jacques stand opposite each other I shuffle on my feet and look around the room expectantly. Surely someone will take pity and pick me.

There is a rush of activity as men race to secure a partner. All the younger women are snapped up first. Then the ones in pretty flouncing dresses.

I stand stiffly a tight smile frozen on my face as I try to

cover my embarrassment. A late comer enters the hall. Tall, dark haired and blessed with a disarming smile he walks toward me. Relief!

A wave of excitement lifts me up and holds me in the air. I hold my breath wondering if he is going to ask some other girl to dance. It's nerve wracking. He continues toward me his smile broadening. Perhaps this Ceroc thing is going to be alright after all, I muse as he approaches.

I smile at him nervously.

"Ohh, I'm sorry" he says looking startled." I thought you were my wife. "From the distance you look so…" he tries to explain. "I have a new prescription." He points to his eyes, smiles awkwardly. "Apologies," he says as he leaves.

I so wish I could leave too.

"Don't worry," says Chanel brightly as the man in black and the Mexican princess show us the first move. "We'll change partners soon."

For the next thirty minutes we are led through a variety of dance routines. On their own the moves appear easy. Put together, they're a riddle. A stretch for any middle-aged memory.

Our teachers make it seem effortless. The men concentrate intensely, acutely aware that in the dance world they are the movers and shakers who must show their partners the way.

This must be the last bastion of old fashioned male superiority. The one place where they lead and women follow. It's a phrase I am reminded of many, many times during the night.

"I think you like to be the boss," says my first partner, a tall gangly Indian man with exceedingly sweaty palms. I hesitate briefly as he reaches to take my hand again for the next move.

"Dancing is new for me," I try to explain.

He puts a long, ET-like finger to his mouth. "Sssh. I am the boss. Please allow me to do my job."

The music begins and I stand mortified as his body begins to shudder and his legs fly out from beneath him.

At first I think he is having an epileptic fit. Then I realize he is dancing. How exactly I'm supposed to follow his lead I have no idea. His plaid trousers are too short, revealing mismatching socks and Adidas sneakers. He moves erratically like a fly doused in insect killer.

Mercifully the music winds down and stops him dead.

"Thank you," I say politely.

"I'd ask you out," he says, smiling nervously, "only I don't think you will say 'yes'."

The music drowns out my reply. A very clear, *'thanks, but no thanks.'*

I'm suddenly very grateful that rotation occurs every five minutes, as I move onto my next partner. He is a squat rotund man. His shirt is almost two sizes too small for him. I assume by the crumpled state of it, he must have had to wrestle to get it on.

He concentrates intensely as the dream couple guide us through our next move. He wears horn-rimmed heavily frame dark glasses. The left corner is held together with tape. As he moves, the lenses fog up with the combined effort of his very animated dance technique and the force of his concentration.

I swear I see steam coming from his head. His body odor is pungent like a mix of wet socks left inside a plastic bag for days, overheated synthetic shoes, and animal urine.

"Do you have pets?" I ask as he lowers me to the floor. My nose is right near his feet. It's a miracle I don't throw up.

"Just a dog? Why?" he asks, tipping me back onto my feet.

"Oh, nothing," I say, as he twirls me beneath his sweat soaked arms. Thankfully, it's time to move on again.

I have to sit out several dance moves due to the lack of male partners. Other women opt to dance solo. It just looks sad.

I wait and wait until finally another partner shows me his moves. But by now I don't care. After my initial good run I'm over Ceroc.

My decision is confirmed when I meet my next dance partner. His bald, shiny head and dwarf-like height remind me of the actor, Danny DeVito.

His face only just reaches my breasts. Thank god I didn't wear a low cut dress. He looks disappointed. It doesn't stop him from standing unnecessarily close though. He presses against me repetitively and I realize with horror he has an erection.

"Call me," he says after our turn ends. He slips a torn piece of paper into the back pocket of my jeans as I move toward my next partner. I feel strangely violated.

I look around the room for Chanel. She has managed to monopolize Jean Jacques. So much for rotating partners.

"Ready to make music," my next partner says, reaching for my hand. He is also short and also smells. With a skillful flick of the wrist he sends me spinning and then catches me in his arms. What he lacks in height he makes up for in confidence.

"Was that good for you?" he asks taking both my hands in his. His palms are rough like a tradesman's and heavily calloused. The texture reminds me of fish scales, or is it the fishy smell that floats through the air as he draws near?

His hands chaff mine as he grips my hands. As we dance the smell progressively worsens. It's impossible to avoid. Every time I take a breath, pooh! This incredible stench.

What is it with this place, I wonder? Why do the guys stink.? The fishy smell is especially off putting.

"I'm Sperious," he says as he grips my hands and draws me to his left side. "Sperious Oppidopolus—fishmonger extraordinaire." He says as he pulls me vigorously toward his right side.

That explains the smell.

"Have you come straight from work?" I ask hoping he will get the hint.

He nods and grips my hand and then forces it back sending me into a spin. "I'm good with my hands. . . " he grins. "…and I can do you a great deal on fish. You've probably seen my ads."

I hold my breath and brace myself as he prepares to pull me under his legs. The stench of fish bits and pieces is excruciatingly strong. "I can't say I have," I mumble as I come up for air.

"If you want a lover, or a piece of groper," he continues, oblivious to my discomfort, "I'm a great catch!" He throws his head back and roars with laughter. "Get it!"

"Ummmm…" I mumble.

"Grope-er. Groper! Catch. Great catch!" He clutches his stomach and laughs uncontrollably. "I'm a regular laugh a minute me!" He raises his clammy calloused hands until they hover over my breasts. "Don't you get it? Grope…"

I freeze, temporarily caught by surprise, as he curves his stumpy fingers and cups a breast in each hand and squeezes.

Regaining my senses I step back and shriek in horror. A chorus goes up around the room "Hooter tooter. Hooter tooter."

Needless to say I'm mortified. The groper is only encouraged and his hands follow, still clamped to my breasts.

"If you want a father for your child, a walk across the

beach, or just damn good shag, I'm your man!" He leans forward and whispers in my ear. "If you don't mind me saying you seem a little tense. A good shag could be just what you need."

I try to free myself from his clutches. Thankfully Chanel comes to my aid. She clips him playfully over the head. "Back off Romeo."

"You know this guy?" I ask.

"I should've warned you. He doesn't mean harm. . .he's a bit . . .well. . .simple," she says as we walk away.

"You're not kidding!" I throw her a you-could-have-warned-me look. "You know what? This really isn't my scene. I think I'll call it a night. You coming?"

"So you don't want to dance with Kilt Man?" she says nodding in the direction of the guy destined to be my next dance partner.

Kilt Man is a middle aged guy, wearing a kilt (no surprise there!), a Bon Jovi tee-shirt and Doc Martin boots. What's left of his receding hair line is gathered into a pony tail — or, to describe it more accurately a long thin strand of hair that kinks like a rat's tail.

"Thanks, but no thanks. Right now, Snoutts is looking like my best option. That and a good Joan Lust novel."

12

CAN THE INTERNET FIND SOMEONE FOR ME?

Chanel runs a moistened finger around her highball, as we meet over a lunch-time drink. "It helps if you get clear about what you're looking for first, darling."

"Otherwise you'll waste your time looking in the wrong area. For the purposes of this competition, you want to score, but that doesn't mean you still can't have standards."

"But I had what I wanted," I replied, trying to ignore the seductive glances she was throwing a Ben Affleck look-a-like at the other end of the bar.

For all the years I've known her I could never understand how she managed to stare at a man's crotch that long. Crotches aren't the most fascinating things in the world.

"Don't start with that old thing again, darling. You're beginning to sound like a stuck record," she warned, maintaining her seductive, lingering gaze on Ben's crotch.

"And you can add *quit talking about your ex* to my list of tips." She swiveled her bottom on the barstool and gave me her full attention. "If you forget that one, darling, all the rest fall over. Now here's what I tell all my clients who are looking for gap-fillers. . ."

"But I'm not your client, Chanel. I'm your friend."

"Do you want my advice or not?"

I didn't have the heart to tell her I think I'd rather read a romance novel than go out looking for sex buddies.

"It depends how much it's going to hurt," I joke feebly.

"This one's easy. You can check out a whole variety of men on the Internet and no one will ever know. After all that time kooked up with one man you'll be amazed at what is there is on offer."

"Really? There must be a catch."

"Nope. It's simple. Log onto www.findsomeone.com and type in your criteria, and watch more men than you can shake a stick at strut their stuff on your screen."

"And no one will ever know?"

"Look at your face, darling! Anyone would think I'd just invited you to have a threesome. Relax."

"I don't know. . . it sounds a bit desperate."

"Do you have a better idea?"

"Well, no."

"Then get cracking and call me tomorrow. Remember, Ruby, you only have one life and you're not getting any younger. Everything you do today either takes you towards or further away from your dreams. Which way are you heading, darling?"

"Up, Chanel. Up!" I give her a thumbs up to assure her her counsel has motivated me to do succeed.

I leave Chanel to do her thing with the Ben Affleck clone and head back to work. Can the Internet really find someone for me? Why would anyone pick a 39-year-old woman when they can have a twenty-year-old with fewer miles on the clock? Can I lie about my age? Would that be a sin?

Chanel's parting words break through the clatter of my

negative thinking. "Stay positive in everything you do, Ruby. Be your biggest fan at all times."

I repeat *I'm a wonderful person. I'm a wonderful person,* over and over until the bad thoughts give up and go away.

I close the door to my office and sit down in front of my PC and navigate to the dating site. Chanel says that finding a new guy is like finding a job or a new house. You've got to check out quite a few before you find the one that's right for you.

I look over my shoulder to make sure no one is peering through the glass doors as I log on. I scroll through the profiles of available men between thirty-nine and fifty. She's right. There are literally hundreds and hundreds of men. Lonely, available, balding men.

Maybe I should change the search criteria to men between twenty and twenty-five. If younger men are good enough for Demi Moore perhaps they're good enough for me. Then I remember, Demi was abandoned for a young model too.

I opt to persevere with men my own age for a while longer. As I read through their introductions I feel increasingly nervous. I can't help wonder if they aren't seriously screwed up too.

I'm one of nature's smartarses - I can run fast and laugh at the same time. . .

"You can keep running. Bye!" I say, clicking off his profile. God, I'll never find a normal man again. Not one I want to bonk anyway. I know I'm only looking to practice but the prospect of finding a relationship online is feeling like a big waste of time.

I'll be single and shagless for the rest of my life if I don't make more of an effort, I convince myself. I persevere and read some more profiles.

Still exploring the different paths called life. Searching for a new star in the sky. Maybe extra sunshine over my. . .

Click!

I tune in to my body barometer. The nauseous feeling in my stomach tells me I'm just not ready yet. Besides, I feel kind of like a voyeur clicking through people's profiles.

But Chanel has given me strict instructions that I am not to log off until I've looked at least twenty profiles.

"Most people give up too early. Hang in there. Trust me. The Internet can find someone for you. It's worked for millions of people all around the world," she said.

Reaching into my bag I pull out a bottle of Rockstar. The energy drink promises its for those with active lifestyles. I take a big swig and hope the extra caffeine shot will give me the boost I need to win the Internet dating race.

As I read through more profiles I can't help feeling sad.

Sad and anxious.

I've been single for nearly a year now. What say nobody ever picks me? Secretly that's my biggest fear. That and worrying about how my daughter Millie will react if I did meet someone.

Old memories begin to stir, reminding me of all the times that nobody ever picked me to play on their sports teams. Just as I'm beginning to feel really sorry for myself the next profile startles me.

SpongeRodFreak39 from New Jersey. Just a guy looking for love. She is out there. I wont give up.

What sort of a guy calls himself SpongeRodFreak and hopes to seriously attract a woman? If his rod is what I think it is and if it's spongy I doubt he'll ever find a shag—let alone true love.

I'm started to seriously doubt the Internet could ever find

someone for me when the profile for *NiceGuy114, 42 from Central Manhattan,* appears on the screen.

He looks seriously cute. But as I read through his profile hope turns quickly to disappointment.

I have found a wonderful woman through this site. So sorry, I am taken well and truly.

Damn! Just when I thought I had found someone, no pun intended, he's taken. I can't help but feel that if I hadn't lingered over lunch with Chanel things might have been different.

When it comes to the Internet it seems like even two minutes delay can make a huge difference to your luck. If I'm going to succeed I'm going to have to get a whole lot faster. I might even have to get really brave and try out speed dating.

I'm feeling encouraged, just knowing that someone like *NiceGuy* is actually out there. Buoyed by my near success I scroll through another thirty profiles. It's lucky I'm having a quiet day at work! I have to pinch myself when I come across Harry's profile.

I see his drop-dead-gorgeous photo first and think perhaps this Internet dating thing might not be so bad after all.

Harry439, 43 from Hoboken.

I am a compassionate caring person who enjoys life. I have had a major loss in my life but do not let that get in the way of my desire to. . ."

Ohh, I'd love to know what he desired. But I have to sign up to the dating site to do that, and I'm not quite ready to yet.

But this guy Harry has a seriously cute photo and I think it could be worth registering just so I can email him. Actually he looks so good that he could be an Armani model. Even models must need help finding someone sometimes.

I'm surprised at how quickly he has pulled my heartstrings. I wonder what major loss he's had. I wonder if he got dumped as I did?

Selfishly I think that would be great—then there would be at least one person in the world who really understands how it feels to grieve.

I feel reassured that I am already fantasizing about having sex with Mr. Armani. I was beginning to worry that I might be frigid.

As excited as I am about Harry, I can't help wonder if there might be someone even better out there for me. I should have quit while the going was good because the profile of the guy after him is seriously weird.

Luscious, 41 from Soho.

I love to crossdress, strut my thang around the house, and just do things. . . I think strange isn't the case. . . I just. . .

I'm feeling a little freaked out now. In my protected life as a married woman, I haven't really come across too many out-there, alternative kind of people.

My husband was your typical all-American guy; he played football at school, loved his sports and cars, and never, ever got into anything remotely kinky. When it came to sex it was always lights off, him on top and no distracting noise. That's how he liked it. And definitely no dresses!

But this Internet thing is opening my eyes to a whole new world and I'm not sure I like it. I've come across guys who want to be women; guys who want to do it with other guys; guys and their wives who want to do it with other women and their husbands. Even, dare I say, and this really shocks me, guys who want you to do it with animals.

I force my thought back to hope. My friend Jeremy is a family lawyer who got divorced recently. He's been dating online for months and he told me that he's met some fabulous women. He even flew to New Zealand to be with some woman he met on the Internet.

I log off the *FindSomeone.com* site and log into the web address he gave me, *Adultslookingforfriends.com*.

As I wait for the site to come up Matt Loews suddenly bursts into my office.

"Surfing porn sites, Ruby?" he sneers.

Mortification doesn't cut my reaction as I scan the pages.

It sounded such a nice site, and Jeremy is such a nice guy. But it just shows that you can't judge a book by its cover or a person by their job. This site, I discover to my horror, specializes in helping people find someone to have sex with and 'swing'.

Thank god Matt's phone rings and he leaves.

I didn't know what 'swing' was before, but I sure as hell do now. On this site you can find someone for one-to-one sex —I guess that's normal sex (?)—threesomes and group sex, bondage, exotic chats, phone or email fantasizing, cross-dressing, exhibition and voyeurism, sadism and masochism, and something called miscellaneous fetishes. I dread to think what those involve. Perhaps having sex with your shoes on, or something else?

It's just dawning on me how protected I've been for all these years. It never even occurred to me that so much variety existed out there. To be honest I'm not sure I'm the sort of girl most men seem to be looking for.

Now I'm even more nervous and the odds of meeting anyone who's into 'loving sex' seems beyond reach. Heck, there's not even a category for 'loving sex' on any of the sites I've looked at.

The fetish site has over thirty million subscribers in the US alone. Doesn't anyone do love anymore? Maybe Chanel's right. Maybe I need to lighten up a little and be prepared to experiment.

I'm still not convinced about online dating though. Other than with Harry, of course. He looks very honest and trustworthy. But can you trust the Internet?

I've heard so many scary stories. Only yesterday I read about a woman who met a guy on online and when he picked her up for their date he forced his way into her apartment and robbed her. She's lucky money is all he stole. Maybe it was SpongeRodFreak. I mean, who has a name like that? It just isn't normal!

13

A DATE WITH CHRISTMAS

I finally take the plunge and email Mr. Armani. It's way, easier than I thought and after several emails, Harry and I arrange to meet.

Everything about him seems so perfect and on paper. I consult my wishlist and he meets most of my criteria. He is handsome, his emails are witty and cheerful and his punctuation and general command of the English language tells me that Harry is both an intelligent, widely read man and a man well-informed about international events.

I yearn to be with someone who could stimulate me and widen my knowledge of things beyond the American continent.

I should've known it was too good to be true. I'd been so careful and had followed Internet dating suggestions by the letter. I hadn't rushed to the first face-to-face meeting for starters. We'd emailed for a period of time.

I read and re-read each message to reassure myself that the object of my attraction is not too weird or bordering on psychotic, and then arranged to meet in a very public place.

You can't get more public than Macy's Herald Square

store, between 34th and 35th on Broadway. With ten floors of shopping and the pre-Christmas sales, the place is mayhem.

The fact that Harry suggested Macy's is just another bonus. Hallelujah, a man who loves to shop as much as me.

He told me that he would be wearing a red trouser suit and that he would be instantly recognizable. I did think a red trouser suit is rather odd. Jon always wore charcoal grey pinstriped suits to work. But then Harry does look like an Italian model and everyone knows what style-setters the Italians are.

Harry is seriously hot, I figure. Red-hot. Besides the new me is totally into color, and anything that brightens up my dull life right now is fine by me.

"Other than your red suit how will I recognize you?" I typed.

"Don't worry. Come to the seventh floor. You won't miss me. I'm one of a kind and I can promise you it will be a date you'll never forget. I'll be the guy, holding a bunch of presents, searching for a beautiful girl called Stella to give them to."

Stella is my new Internet dating name. That is another Internet dating safeguard protocol. Avoid giving out personal information until you have met and established that this is a guy you seriously want to see again. Otherwise, you could end up with a bitter and twisted stalker on your hands.

I've heard that lots of guys take rejection very personally, while others get infatuated to the point of obsession. Having someone obsess over me could be nice for a change, I think. It would certainly beat the waning affection that corrupted the latter years of my marriage.

"Tell me, Stella, are you feeling playful?" Mr. Armani asked in one of our many emails.

I don't think anyone who knew me would think of me as playful. Cautious maybe, but playful definitely not.

"Sure, playful is my middle name," I lie.

"Great. Just outside the main doors, there's a West Indian dude selling fake Playboy merchandise. Pick up a set of bunny ears and pop them on so I can spot you in the crowds. Ohh, and don't worry about going home and changing. I love women dressed in business suits. It turns me on."

My heart lurched. Playboy bunny ears? He's turned on by a woman wearing a suit? What is this guy on?

Still, the ears did sound like a sure-fired way of standing out in the Christmas crowd. Unusual, yes, but novel and just a little bit out of my comfort zone to chalk it up as another one of Chanel's FTE's.

I hate to admit it but a little bit of me felt quite excited, and just a little bit turned on. Having fun is high on my list of priorities and breaking the drought especially with someone like Mr. Armani isn't bad either.

I catch a cab to Macys' straight after work. It is way too cold to battle the streets and the subway is crowded.

I wanted to arrive looking sexy and casual—not pale and covered in sleet with clothes trampled in the commuter crush.

I choose to wear my favorite Cavalli tuxedo-inspired pantsuit. The black pants suit and jacket had shimmery, crepe-de-chine satin accents that lent it an elegant yet empowered effect.

It is not exactly the most colorful thing I had in my wardrobe but suited me way better than bland beige. Plus, it is the perfect piece because of its versatility.

I've only worn it a couple of times and had bought it in anticipation of getting my promotion. I absolutely adore it. Italian designers understand the curves of the feminine form and know how to use them to accentuate the body without being too risqué.

You can be professional and sexy at the same time. I can wear it dressed up for a gala night-time event or dressed down a bit for the daytime when I have to meet with important clients or act more confidently and powerfully than I really feel.

So it's ideal for tonight because I'm nervous as hell. What say Mr. Armani doesn't like me? I'm anxious to create a great first impression. That's the other reason I'm wearing this suit. It's flattering and shows off my fuller-figure curves.

The pants are boot-cut and give a slimming effect to thicker ankles and calves. Perfect! The pants are low waisted and comfortable. The blazer goes in at the waist and out at the hips to give an hourglass effect. It screams,'sexy'.

I hope.

Macy's isn't called the world's biggest department store for nothing, especially during sale week. The walls are heaving with a frenzied crowd of bargain shoppers.

For a brief moment I panic. Finding Harry will be impossible. Then I remind myself how easy it will be to spot him in his red suit. I excuse my way through the crowds and take the escalator to the seventh floor.

I stand on my tiptoes and crane my neck in a futile attempt to see over the crowds. Still no luck. Being short is definitely a disadvantage. But then I remember the Bunny ears I've just purchased.

I draw them slowly from the bag and glance around. Whew, everyone is too busy with their noses in the bargain bins and rummaging through sales racks to worry about what I'm wearing.

I reassure myself that people have more important things to look at then to be distracted by a woman dressed in a corporate power suit with Playboy bunny ears perched on her brain.

Sexy woman are confident, I mutter as I placed the band over my head. I*'m a confident, sexy woman*, I affirm. Tentatively I looked around the store. My face heat and flushes crimson. I feel ridiculous.

I hope Harry will find me, and soon. This is definitely way out of my comfort zone. But, I start to get a few admiring glances from men, and I begin to feel more playful.

How would Stella handle this, I wonder? Stella would be super confident, cool and sassy. She'd strut her stuff, and think she is the hottest thing since gluten-free bread.

I decide to be Stella. Right now. Right here. Right in my bunny ears. Besides, I'm tired of being good, safe, cautious Ruby. Somewhere deep inside me is a naughty, rebellious playful vixen. I just know it.

I reach into my bag and pull out the new deliciously sexy red lipstick I have just brought. I totter over to a mirror and apply a thick, over-generous layer. The effect is instant. I suddenly feel like a mix of Mae West, Marilyn Munro, and Caroline Bissett-Kennedy. Chanel would be proud of me, I think to myself.

Suddenly a warm breath in my right ear makes me spin around.

"Merry Christmas."

"Merry Christmas," I say tentatively. I didn't know Father Christmas did the rounds of Macy's. And I certainly had never seen him go up to single women and breathe into their ears.

"How about a kiss for Santa?"

"I'm sorry? Do I know you?" I say in my most officious voice.

"Know me? No, not really. . . not yet. . . but I'm hoping

after tonight we'll know each other a whole lot better." His long white beard twitched as he spoke and his watery green eyes never moved from resting on my cleavage the whole time.

It can't be?

"You're not. . . " I stammer. No way, surely someone is playing a cruel joke.

"You look hot," he looks me up and down, left and right. He is short, seriously short. Roughly my height, 5 ft 5. But I have my stiletto heels on and towered over him.

"Hot and sexy. Just like I imagined you, Stella."

He knows my name?

"I love that suit. . . mmmmm. . . shows off your curves to perfection. I'm glad you didn't ruin the view by wearing a shirt underneath it." His eyes linger on the swell of my breasts. "I'm nearly finished my shift. Let's go somewhere comfortable and play with those bunny ears of yours."

I stand there gobsmacked as he walks off to get changed. I mean, how was I to know that Harry, the Armani super-model, would have a job masquerading as Father Christmas. It's a far cry from what his Internet profile told me he did for a living.

Maybe he's embellished his resume, and lied about his height and his eye color but I hope like crazy that under all that Father Christmas garb there might lurk a handsome, charming, sexy man after all.

My instincts tell me to cut my losses and get the hell out of there, but manners and curiosity get the better of me and I wait patiently for him to return.

My heart sinks as a short man, with runny green eyes, dressed in tatty jeans, sneakers and a Metallica tee-shirt bounces toward me.

Crap.

Harry is definitely not what I have imagined. Not at all. I'd been fantasizing for days about meeting my very own McSteamny. But there is nothing McSteamny about Harry at all.

For one he is short, and his hair is tomato red, with wispy tendrils that curl at the neck and recede at the forehead.

A tuft of ginger hair crawls across his lips and a small patch of fluff nestles on his chin. Mustard freckles the size of dollar coins scatter across his face.

Adding further disappointment is that the protruding Father Christmas stomach I'd thought must surely be stuffing appears to be his own. I fling my hands to my mouth and suppress a cry of horror. Only my Catholic upbringing stops me from doing a runner.

Do unto others as you would have them do unto you.

Damn those commandments.

"Hey, baby. Ready to play?" Santa says encircling my waist with an eczema covered hand.

"I'm sorry, but I think there has been a mix-up," I say freeing myself from his tentacles. "The Harry I was expecting is tall, dark with brown eyes and olive skin, and the most adorable smile. . . and well. . . to be honest, you just don't match your profile. Not at all."

"I may not be Brad Pitt, but I've got the stamina of twenty DiCaprio's. Check out my fingers, look at the length. Look at the width. That should tell you something. . .if you get my drift." He winks and pats my bum.

A wave of nausea sweeps over me. I get his drift all right and it makes me want to puke. This is not the man I have imagined spending my first night of passion with since splitting from Jonathan. I didn't care how well endowed he was. After 18 years of sex with the same man, I hoped for someone sexier. Harry, if his name really is Harry, looks like a cross between a toad and Rumplestiltskin.

"Your profile. . ." I say.

"Great bit of marketing, don't you think? Creating some positive spin they call it. I tell you it's a real winner. I've been inundated with women. Man, I've never had it so hot. But you're the first one who went for the Playboy bunny thing. That's always been a fantasy of mine. I did get a girl to come along as Little Bo-Peep the other day."

The wretched bunny ears. I'd completely forgotten. I pull them from my head and scan the store to make sure no one is looking. Then I see him.

Jonathan.

He is *s*tanding with a smirk on his face, his arm around The Cheerleader. God, this is turning into a nightmare.

"The ears suit you," Jonathan says as he walks toward me. "So are you going to introduce us to your new squeeze?" His lips curl into a smirk as he looks Harry up and down. Mostly down.

"Not exactly the sort of guy I pictured you with, but hey whatever spins your wheels, Ruby."

"Ruby?" Harry says. "I thought you said you said your name is Stella?"

"Hey looks like we have more in common than we thought. We're all a pack of liars, " I shout as I throw the ears on the ground and ran.

When I got home I find Millie lay stretched out on the couch, a bowl of popcorn, smothered in hot chilli ketchup balanced on her stomach. "How did your date go Mum? "

"Terrible. Just terrible. I thought I was meeting an Italian centerfold and instead of ended up with a cross between

Rumplestiltskin and a toad. I know it's unkind, but I can't help it. He lied about everything. He was so horrible."

"Horrible like a cross between Beauty and the Beast and the Frog Prince, horrible?"

I nod.

"Maybe you should have kissed him."

"Sadly, Millie, frogs only turn into princes' in fairytales. To make things even worse your father and The Cheerleader were there. I looked like a right idiot and he..well, your father looked as handsome as ever."

"It's not really fair to compare other men to Dad," she said. "It's just not that normal to be so good looking. Besides you're not getting any younger. You might have to settle for frogs."

My jaw plummets in astonishment. "You don't really mean that do you?"

"Yes, mom, I do," she replies looking briefly at me before turning to the Plasma screen and tuning into America's Next Top Model.

"Young people can be so cruel," I mumble as I pad upstairs to my room. I sit down at my computer and sign into my blog site.

Too old? Bollocks, I mutter. I'll empower myself. I'll create my date, I tell myself. If nothing else, at least I can have a bit of harmless fun and heal myself with writing.

He told me that he would be wearing a red trouser suit and would be instantly recognizable. I did think a red trouser suit was rather odd; but then he was Mr. Armani and everyone knows what style-setters the Italians are. This guy is seriously hot I figured, red-hot.
"Don't worry. Come to the seventh floor. You won't miss me.
I'm one of a kind and I can promise you it will be a date

you'll never forget. I'll be the guy, holding a bunch of presents, searching for a beautiful girl called Stella to give them to."

Stella is my Internet dating name. Sexy Stella! I love the idea of changing my identity, it makes me more mysterious to men and it's my little way of staying in control.

I can tell you from experience that men like to be controlled. They deny it of course, mainly because they fear being dominated. But deep down every man harbors a desire to be dominated. They want to be licked and whipped into submission.

"Tell me, Stella, are you feeling playful?" Harry asks me.

If only Harry knew, I smirked. For now, I'd let him assume he was in the driver's seat. Give a little then take a mile. It worked every time.

"I'm not sure, what did you have in mind?" I reply coyly.

"Just a little dress-up idea. Nothing weird. . . unless of course, you're up for it."

Harry was testing the water. Poor dear. He really didn't know me at all. Just the thought of blowing his mind made me hot with desire. I wanted him badly.

"Dress-ups? Ohh, that sounds like fun, I always liked dress-up games at school," I said, putting on my best cutie-pie voice.

"Great. Outside Macy's' you'll find a guy selling playboy merchandise. Pick up a set of bunny ears and pop them on so I can spot you in the crowds. Ohh, and don't worry about going home and changing. I love a woman dressed in corporate clothing. It's sexy."

Dressing up in playboy bunny ears wasn't the most imaginative thing he could have asked me to wear, so as I left for work that morning I brought along some of my own props and buried them under a pile of client files in my leather satchel.

I caught a cab to Macy's straight after work. I chose to wear my favorite Cavalli tuxedo-inspired pantsuit. It's the perfect piece because of its versatility. Italian designers understand the curves of the feminine form and know how to use them to accentuate the body without being too risqué. You can be professional and sexy at the same time.

I can get away with wearing it at work with a silk shirt and still be taken seriously by my male colleagues and then at night whip off the silk shirt and wear the jacket with nothing but a sexy lacy bra under it.

It's cut so long that it leaves nothing to the imagination. I chose to wear my favorite push-up bra for high impact. Imagine two voluptuous breasts practically bursting out of the bra like Italian puddings and you'll get the picture.

Macy's wasn't called the world's biggest department store for nothing, especially during sale week. It was heaving with a frenzied crowd of bargain shoppers.

For a brief moment I panicked—finding Harry would be near impossible. Then I reminded myself how easy it would be to find him in his red suit and pushed my way through the crowds and took the escalator to the seventh floor.

I stood on my tiptoes and craned my neck in a futile attempt to see over the crowds. Still no luck. Being short was definitely a disadvantage. But then I remembered the bunny ears I'd just purchased.

I drew them slowly from the bag and placed them carefully on my head. The last thing I wanted was hat hair. I'd spent house curling my locks so they had mountains of volume and looked as natural as Bridgett Bardot's.

The moment I put the ears on they stirred a naughty,

rebellious sexy vixen in me. I sauntered over to a mirror and reapplied my deliciously sexy red lipstick.

The effect was instant. Men were clamoring at my feet. I suddenly felt like a mix of Mae West, Marilyn Munro, and Caroline Bissett-Kennedy.

A warm breadth in my right ear made me spin around.

"Merry Christmas."

"Merry Christmas," I said tentatively. I didn't know Father Christmas did the rounds of Macy's and I certainly had never seen him go up to single women and breathe into their ears.

"How about a kiss for Santa?"

"I'm sorry? Do I know you?"

"Know me? No, not really. . . not yet. . . but I'm hoping after tonight we'll know each other a whole lot better." The bulge in his trousers gave him away. That and his earlier reference to wearing a red suit.

"I've been a naughty girl, Santa," I said, twisting my hair around my fingers and fluttering my eyelashes. I moved closer toward him and discreetly put my hands down his pants.

"Ohh Santa," I enthused, is that big package you've got down there for me?"

"Yes and no, Stella. You've been a naughty girl. I don't know if you deserve it."

"I'll be good, really good. Please, I'll do anything to make it up to you."

"What you need is a good spanking. Follow me. . ." He led me through the crowds towards Santa's Grotto. "Beat it will you," he said to the pimple-faced photographer. "I'm going to be. . . Er. . . let's just say I'm going to be tied up for the next 30 minutes." He flicked the sign which read, 'Santa's gone to lunch. Back in an hour ' and led me into his Grotto.

How did he know he was going to be tied up? I thought that was going to be my surprise.

"You look hot. Hot and sexy. Just like I imagined you, Stella. I love that suit. . . mmmmm. . .shows off your curves to perfection and I'm glad you didn't ruin the view by wearing a shirt."

"Silence," I ordered taking command of the situation and bringing out my bag of tricks. "Santa has been a bad boy. Very bad." I whipped him playfully and tied his hands behind his back.

Digging deep into my bag I brought out a can of whipped cream and seductively slid my knickers to my feet.

"Suck me!" I said, forcing his head toward my crotch. I didn't need to ask twice. He has a tongue like Gene Simmons from the band Kiss. Long, lean and rapid.

I literally exploded all over him. I pushed him to the floor and straddled him. I took off his belt buckle and whipped him lightly. He flinched a little so I whipped him harder and told him not to complain.

His manhood was already stiff but his erection grew with excitement. I pulled his red Father Christmas pants down to his knees.

I laughed when I saw his underwear. "Helicopters and fighter jets! My, my, Santa. I'd expected reindeer."

He arched his back. Jump on my throttle stick, Stella. Make me fly!" he pleaded.

"With pleasure, Santa, with pleasure." I laughed plunging my body down onto his manhood. The remaining 25 minutes flew as we shagged like rabbits.

"You're amazing. That was the most mind-blowing sex, I've ever had," he said, climbing back into his pants and buckling his belt. "When will I see you again?"

*"Next year, Santa," I said casually, blowing him a kiss.
"Thanks for filling my stocking."*

I push back from the desk and reread what I have written. I giggle to myself. That was fun! Heaps of fun—much better than real life. I suddenly have an urge to rewrite all my humiliating attempts at dating.

I click onto 'Create New Post' and run down the stairs to the kitchen and pour myself a drink and then sprint back and settle back down before the computer.

Before I even knew what I want to say the title appears. *The Mile-High Club.*

14

———

THE MILE HIGH CLUB

"Where the hell has this come from, and what's more where is it going?" I wonder out loud as I update my blog. My fingers glide over the keys and began punching an effortless flow of words.

I always wondered what it would be like to screw a fabulously sexy pilot in the toilet of a Boeing 747-400 series jet airliner. I've yet to test my theory but believe me I will. There's nothing like a man in uniform to get the flames of passion burning. Last night though I had to content myself with the bland attire of some nameless waiter at my favorite Manhattan bar. I'm not going to say where, because you'll all rush over there and want a piece of the action. But believe you me he is HOT! I'd been watching his tight little butt all night long, fantasizing about locking tongues with him in some dark shady corner of the bar. Then suddenly it dawned on me. I could do some pre-flight research.
It's tough work but someone's got to do it. He seemed kinda shy which surprised and excited me. He had the complexion

*of a newborn, but the rod of a man. I measured him. . . but I'll
get to that later.*

*One smoldering look from him and I was hot and horny. I just
knew we'd end up having sex. Judging from the bulge in his
pants something tells me he knew it too.*

*The bar was crowded and everyone was pressed against each
other. Other men were hot and horny too. I could tell. It's not
that hard when you can feel a baton against your back and
there's not a cop in sight.*

*But I wanted him. Young, gorgeous, inexperienced and a
dead-fire Johnny Depp look alike. I was practically gagging
for it.*

*My pupils were dilated and my heart was racing. I walked to
the ladies to freshen up, glancing coyly over my shoulder and
ran my tongue provocatively over my lips. It worked like a
treat.*

*I hadn't even reached the loo when he grabbed me around the
waist and pushed me toward a side door. Plunged into
darkness, at first I panicked. I mean, it wasn't exactly what
I'd planned. I'd wanted to be more in control and lure him
outside and down the side alley.*

*But that's what I love about young guys they just seize
the day.*

*He pushed up my skirt and pulled my knickers down around
my ankles. Not so naive after all, I thought as he whipped out
a condom and skillfully slipped it on while fondling my
breasts.*

*Lusty and lewd in the broom cupboard, there was hardly
room to move. But he made the best use of limited space,
lifting me and pressing me firmly against the wall, while he
thrust his hard cock inside my moist pussy.*

*The walls vibrated with each thrust and for a split moment, I
feared I'd fall through the paneling. But then he gently placed*

me on my feet, and slid down and buried his face in my snatch. Thank god I remembered to douche.
He had a tongue the length of Gene Simmons from Kiss and used it with similar skill, flicking it in and out, until I exploded all over him.
He drank the creamy liquid as though drinking his favorite cocktail, then lifted his still dripping face to me. I went down on him.
He had the stamina of a bull. No sooner had he shot his load than he was ready for more.
Exhausted but thoroughly satisfied, I pushed him off me. I pulled my knickers up and pushed my breasts back into my lacy d-cups, buttoned my shirt, popped on my shoes and then cool as a cucumber slid out the door and slipped through the crowds into the cool night air.
That's definitely a bar I'll be going back to :)

I RE-READ what I've written and then for some strange reason feel compelled to hear Marvin Gaye's sensually-geared song, *Sexual Healing.*

This must be some sort of weird sign, I muse as I obey my intuition and rummage through the CD rack downstairs.

"What's got into you?" my daughter asks.

If she only knew.

"I'm reinventing myself," I giggle happily.

15

"The trouble with you, mom is that you're too fussy," Millie says as we go out for brunch.

"I am not," I protest. "I just don't see why I should settle for second best."

"If you are not careful you'll end up alone," Millie said.

"But I'm not alone. I've got you."

"Aww gross," Millie cries as I cuddle her affectionately.

Chanel gave Millie a kiss on the cheek, totally unaware of the other café goers who had turned to stare at her as she made her dramatic entrance. "My ears are burning, darling. . . you must have been talking about me."

Sweeping quickly past the quiet café crowd, she threw her canary yellow coat and tangerine scarf onto a neighboring table with theatrical flair. "Here this is for you," she says, passing me a beautifully wrapped parcel. "I know your birthday was months ago but I've been searching for the perfect gift."

I take the parcel in my hands and study it, "Ohhh, yay, it's wrapped in gold my favorite color."

"Yes, every girl should have gold—and lots of it, darling," Chanel laughs as she looked around for the waitress.

I try to open the metallic gold paper as carefully as I can but excitement, or is it impatience, gets the better of me. I rip the contents free of the wrapping.

I study the red cardboard box, and read out the beautifully written words embossed in gold. "Poppy's Love Tarot: Instant Answers to Your Love Life."

"I thought of you as soon as I saw it," Chanel says. "The poppies mostly, and the fact that you still haven't got your love life sorted. I thought they might help speed things along a bit."

"Tarot cards can provide instant answers to my love life? Gosh, that would be fabulous," I say.

Millie throws her hands over her eyes and slumps in her chair. "Oh, mom, this is so embarrassing." Peering through her splayed fingers she turns her head slowly and scans the café to see if anyone is looking. "If you guys are going to sit here pulling those things out I'm going home."

"Come on it will be fun, darling," Chanel says, nudging me to open the box.

"No Chanel, it won't be fun, it will be embarrassing. Besides I don't see how a pack of cards is going to help mom meet another man," Millie says.

"O ye of little faith," Chanel laughs. "Stick around and watch. You might just learn something."

"Thanks, but no thanks. I'd rather go home and watch Johnny Depp be a pirate in the Caribbean. Honestly, sometimes you two act like you're my age. The only things is that kids believe in wizards, and fairies and goofy stuff—not tarot cards."

Millie scoffs the rest of her food, gulps her hot chocolate and gathers her things before getting to her feet, "Call me if your destiny gallops into the cafe on a white horse," she says kissing my cheek.

"Don't let her spoil our fun," Chanel says as she watches Millie leave, She takes the pack from out of my hands. "Let's see what the tarot has got in store for you."

She pulls a large deck of brightly colored cards from the box and pushing aside our coffee cups, spreads the pack on the table. "Pick a card, darling."

"Don't you think we should read the instructions?" I peer into the box and take out a small piece of paper lying on the bottom and unfold it carefully.

"Not, really. Here give that to me. I'll tell you what to do and then you do it. I'm the coach after all."

"Do you normally do this kind of thing with your clients, Chanel? I mean, it seems kind of weird and not. . .

"Not what?

"Well, not terribly scientific."

"It's holistic Ruby. Nothing to do with science. Good grief, if we all sat around waiting for people in white coats to have breakthroughs we'd still think the world was flat. When it comes down to what's real and what's not, what works and what doesn't, it takes people in the field. People like Drake, and Einstein, and well, let's face it, people like me. Folk like us who are at the coalface helping everyday people with everyday problems."

"I'm sorry, Chanel. I didn't mean to question your competence, it's just. . ."

"I know..it's just that all this is new to you, darling. But don't worry, you *are* in safe hands. What with the tarot and all the other things I have up in my toolbox to help you, we'll have you up and dating the man of your dreams in next to no time. You'll see. Now. . ." Her brow furrows.

"Why are you frowning? Have you seen something? Oh

god, I'm never going to meet anyone, ever again, am I? I knew it. I'm going to be a spinster for the rest of my life."

"Ssssshhh, stop catastrophizing. . .I can't concentrate, this pack is more complicated than I thought."

"That's good isn't it?"

"Yes and no. Yes, we want the process to be robust. But no, not if I can't for the life of me work out what I'm supposed to be doing. I hate reading instructions. . . " she says, looking despondently at the guide.

"Okay, I think I've got it. . . but first I need to get my energy centered. Can you go grab me a coffee, Ruby? Ohh, and a piece of that cherry cheesecake? It looks divine."

"Okay," I mumble.

"Right where shall we begin?" Chanel says when I return. "First you've got to ask the oracle a question," she says, lifting a fork full of cheesecake to her lips.

"Who's the oracle?"

"It's you, Ruby. You're the oracle?"

"What do you mean it's me? If I had the answers I wouldn't be sitting here with you, asking you how to get my life sorted"

"Not you-you—but YOU. The way these things work is that by focusing on something you want help with you are leading and tapping into your subconscious. Some people call it accessing your intuition or divine intelligence. Others call it accessing your super-galactic thought neurons."

"I prefer intuition," I say. "If I start talking about galaxies I'll start thinking about Martians and it won't be long before someone at work finds out and they'll have me committed."

"Concentrate, Ruby or you'll disturb the cosmic flow. Put your mind on choosing what you want the tarot to reveal."

Chanel picks up the box again and reads out loud, oblivious to the curious stares of people seated nearby. "The written messages on the cards can show you strong future possibilities and help give you some insight and guidance," she says loudly.

"Oh, cool! That sounds great," squeals the waitress as she carefully navigates the tarot cards and places fresh coffees on the table. Chanel gives her her best *'don't interrupt, can't you see I'm holding a coaching session'* look. The waitress scuttles away.

I pick up the subject cards and read through my options. *Finding new love; in a love triangle; will we get together; choice of two lovers; how is current love?*

"Well the fact that I don't actually have a lover eliminates most of these for a start," I say.

"What about that new guy who messaged you? Dave? I get the feeling you still haven't put him to one side yet. Let's try him out just to see if it works. What you have to do is layout all the cards in the *will we get together category,* Chanel studies the instructions intently, "shuffle them and then pick eight cards."

I pick all the 32 cards and shuffle them. I pick eight at random and then flip them all over.

"No not like that! You're supposed to turn them over as though you are turning pages in a book—not reveal them all at once."

"Oh no!" I look down at my cards with horror. "Have I've jinxed my future? That's all I need."

"Undo what you just did and then do it again. The right way this time. That should fix it."

Her confident tone reassures me. She is more experienced, so I do as I am told. I hold my breath as my future unfolds before me. Mesmerized I completely forget about all the people in the café and my coffee, which has gone cold.

"Oops. We forgot about these cards. . ." Chanel says,

"quick do these two—one's your identity and the other's your essence."

"Now you've really lost me," I say, looking at the two lost cards.

"You can't really go wrong. Destiny is destiny no matter how you deal with the cards. Everything is working out as is should."

My hope fades briefly but my spirits pick up when I turn over the first card. Against pale blue writing, the golden words, *potential lover* promises hope.

The *essence* card is less optimistic.

"D*ispute*. That doesn't sound too good, does it? And look the image on the card has an upside-down tear. I've done enough crying to fill the Nile. The last thing I feel like is more arguing and more tears."

"Just wait, will you? We don't know what it all means yet. You've got to read the other eight cards from left to right and then we can interpret all the signs."

"Okay. . .okay," I reply dubiously, casting my eye back to the dispute card. *A new love opportunity yet to present itself with someone else.*

"I bet you that's what the dispute is about. Dave is not someone new is he? He's old news. So it's him who'll be crying because he's got his heart set on you. Read the rest, this is looking good."

My heart races. The cards are working. They're really working. In my heart even before I'd done the reading I hoped and hoped that Dave and I wouldn't end up together. I'd been putting off replying to his email just in case.

Everyone has been filling my ears with stories about the worldwide lack of eligible men and the last thing I want to do is to throw a live one back in the sea.

Except, the inescapable fact is he isn't alive to me. He is a cold, wet fish.

I pick the next card up and study it before reading it out loud. "*A daughter; issues with motherhood.*"

"No surprises there, Ruby," Chanel says. "Millie's not exactly the most compliant child, and she's sharp, razor-sharp. But then you're lucky because if you come home with a tosser she'll be able to spot a dud a mile away. Millie's always been perceptive when it comes to people."

I bite my lip and continue, "*Faithfulness; loyalty and understanding.*"

"That's me!" laughs Chanel.

"Or it could be the fact that Jon was unfaithful but that my next lover won't be," I say. "He'll be faithful and understand how hurt I still fee by my husband's betrayal."

"Hey, you're a natural at this, Ruby. You sure you've never done this before?"

"Yes, Chanel. I'm sure. I'll leave the psychic, white-witch dabbling for you. How is your course going anyway?"

"It's fun! I get to mix potions and make spells and learn how to create mischief."

"Really"

"No. I'm joking. Learning to use your psychic powers is a very serious business. I've got exams next week."

"I hope they don't test you on this pack, you don't seem very familiar with it at all, Chanel."

"I'm just not properly tuned in that's all. Normally I wouldn't dream of doing a tarot consultation in a café. There's way to many free-ranging spirits floating around. Besides this is just a fun pack for your birthday and we're just doing girlfriend stuff. Now, what does the next card say?"

"*Jealousy from a friend—hold your own counsel!*" I faked a suitably accusing scowl.

"What are you looking at me like that for? I like blondes and you like dark guys. No competition!" she laughs.

"*Not that confident in love (don't rush things); not feeling worthy*," I read.

"Bang on the money, darling. But it's not something we can't fix," says Chanel.

I stare at the next card. *About to happen/happening now*! "Do you think Millie was right? Maybe my white knight's coming to this café," I say, showing Chanel the card.

"Imagine if your destiny is sitting somewhere in this place waiting for you to notice him," Chanel says. She stretches her neck and starts scanning the restaurant like a Meerkat looking for its mate.

"Whatever you do don't make a scene Chanel," I warn, as she swivels in her seat.

"Besides I've already checked the place out," I say, proudly. "Ever since we started our coaching I never go into any bar, café, restaurant, anywhere without lifting my gaze and checking to see if there is anyone even halfway handsome that I could possibly try and start a conversation with. Believe me, it's exhausting but I have been doing it."

"What about that gorgeous hunk over there? I haven't seen you look at him at all."

"Fourth finger on the left hand," I say.

"Ohhh…good spotting…taken already. . . okay, so maybe it's not happening right now, but it is about to happen so keep your eyes peeled. I can feel him, " Chanel says. "Two more cards to go. What's next?"

"*Caring and thoughtful*. Yes, please," I say. "The only thing Jon cared and thought about was himself and how much money he could make and how many people he could impress with it. I seriously think all I ever was to him was a trophy wife. A pretty thing to hang off his arm at cocktail parties."

"Self-loathing doesn't suit you. Besides you're being hard on yourself."

"Am I? I don't think I can ever remember a time when Jon actually ever put me first."

"You were more than a trophy wife," Chanel says. "He was just a selfish, egotistical fool. Honestly, I really don't know what you saw in him, and I sure as hell don't know why you're still wearing that wedding ring? It's been nearly a year now. Wearing that band of gold is like bars in a prison. It's holding you back."

"I know. . . it's just. . . I've tried. . . I really have. . . but my finger looks so naked. . . leaving it on makes me feel less like a loser. . . less like a leftover girl . ..." I twist the ring between my thumb and forefinger. Our wedding vows repeat in my mind. *To love and obey, in good times and in bad.*

"What really got me was the way you used to run around after him. He treated you like a doormat, and you took it," Chanel says, scraping the last crumbs off her plate, and piling them into her mouth.

"I did agree to obey, after all. It was in our contract. Besides I loved him. You'd be surprised what woman will do for the men they love. And he took care of me."

"Can't argue there. He gave you everything money could buy—luxurious houses, cars, holidays overseas, jewelry, but never the thing you most wanted. Time together."

"His work was demanding," I say.

"The one good thing he did for you was leaving you your house. Lucky for you he's a property developer with an eye for a bargain. Your place must be worth millions."

"Four million, seven hundred and twenty two thousand to

be exact. The latest property valuation just arrived." I say smiling.

"Not bad, not bad at all. So Jon Sugar Jnr. turned out to be your sugar daddy after all. If you want to keep hold of that rotten old ring, then you do it. But I'm telling you, as long as you keep wearing that thing, you're never going to meet another guy — at least not the kind of guy you want to meet. Cool guys don't go after married woman just like cool girls like you don't go after hunky dudes like Mr. Married over there," Chanel says glancing over at the handsome man sipping coffee. "I've got to go but first read out the last card and let's see what fate has in store for you. . .

I read out the last card. "*A woman of Celtic background, or with auburn/red/strawberry blonde/brassy hair.* Oh terrific Chanel, my next lover is going to be a woman!"

"Not unless there's something you're not telling me. Besides, nothing in life happens without intention. Right now, you're living in two worlds. You've still got one foot in the past—and hanging onto that ring and idealized fantasies about Jon aren't helping. The other foot is tentatively reaching out to step into the future you want to have. Only you're not quite there. You're thinking is all blurred. You need to focus. Before we next meet I want you to think about having a ring melting ceremony. You're creative — I'm sure you can think of some wonderful thing we could transform that wretched thing into. Something to symbolize the new, groovy, free, independent, sexy you.'

I rub my forefinger over the smooth golden band. "I'll think about it, Chanel. I really will."

"While you're at it, write down all the qualities you are looking for in a man. You can start by recording all the things that irritated you about Jon and then turn them into your wish list for your dream man. Number one on the list should be a man who prioritizes spending time with his family over making zillions of money from crooked real estate deals. And don't forget to write down, 'must be in touch with his emotions.' There's nothing worse than a man who can't talk about the stirrings in his heart."

"Is this my list or yours, Chanel?" I ask.

"I want what you want, Ruby." She stood up, and dredged the last centimeter of coffee from her cup.

"Why don't you summon the artist in you and draw Mr Wonderful. Make sure you give him chocolate-brown eyes. I've got a strong sense about that. I'm sure your Mr Wonderful has simply delicious eyes. Not all cold and icy blue like that drip you married. Ohh and he'll be well endowed too. No point wasting your time with a wiener."

Chanel's voice trails off as she disappeared out the door and hailed a cab. But the legacy remains. The whole café, and I mean the whole café, is staring at me.

"She's, my life coach. She's madder than a March hare. " I smile feebly, and pretend to be deeply ensconced in my tarot cards.

Still what doesn't kill you only makes you stronger, right? And the positive thing about having Chanel as my life coach is that each time she leaves me in a totally embarrassing situation the level of my embarrassment shrinks.

I am quickly going from being someone totally obsessed with securing everyones good approval, to getting more and more comfortable with not giving a damn. And I have Chanel to thank for that.

I go to the bathroom, and then come back and pack up my tarot cards and go to leave the café. I only make it half way to the door when the handsome man with the wedding ring stops me.

"Excuse me. I don't mean to embarrass you further, but —" he says.

I draw a shaky breadth as I look into his eyes. *His dark, dreamy chocolate eyes.* "Your skirt is caught in your underwear. . ."

For what seems like the longest time I stop breathing. The whole world stops. Nothing Chanel has ever subjected me to has prepared me for one of the most humiliating experiences of my life.

Blood rushes to my face as I quickly retrieve the end of my skirt from where it tucks into my knickers and run from the café. A chorus of laughter chases me.

So much for the new, groovy, sexy, *I don't give a damn me*.

16

I can't believe it. After six months of writing in blissful anonymity, suddenly *Sex With Strangers* has followers. Thousands of them. All unsolicited and all hungry.

Hungry for my tales of sexual conquest and seduction. They are peeping toms and voyeurs and people with nothing better on their minds.

I sound like a meanie. Actually I'm chuffed. It's been kind of lonely sitting here in my room, writing to myself. If I had met The Beatles I could have been the inspiration for their song lyrics, '*where have all the lonely people gone.*'

But I'm not lonely now. I have Mary from Connecticut, for example. Mary is a big fan. '*You rock. All power to you girl. Thanks for showing me how it's done.*'

Then there's Dan, from the UK, '*Great to meet a girl who's sexually liberated. Anytime you want a shag, email me.*'

The appetite of my followers is voracious and to appease them I have to write constantly. That's the thing with blogs— they're like hungry chicks. Unless you feed them regularly, after a bit of squawking, they'll fly off somewhere else.

Now that I've got some fans, I kind of want to keep them. I guess The Rolling Stones feel the same. Unless there's a crowd who wants to play? Except, and this is a big except, I'm not sure that playing to such a large audience is such a good idea. What say I've said something that inadvertently leads some sexual predator to my door?

One thing my blog has given me, besides a bit of very timely therapy, is the chance to meet people from all over the world.

My blog has become a virtual guestbook. Sort of like the rich leather bounds ones that you see at expensive and niche resorts. Visitors from all around the world scratch their comments in my online journal.

Millie is out again tonight. It seems as though these days she is never in. I don't blame her. Lately, I have been working horribly long hours. I'm sure my boss keeps me back just to irk me. There's absolutely no need for me to do those kinds of hours.

If he was a bit more organized or spent less time schmoozing clients over long liquid lunches I wouldn't have to work until 9 pm and 10 pm most nights.

Plus, he's a pervert. He always stands so close to me. I'm sure he hasn't a clue about personal space at all. There's something creepy about the way he looks at me, too. But that's another story.

THE HOUSE IS dark when I get home from work. Dark and silent. Even Snoutts isn't there to greet me. I walk to the refrigerator and retrieve the bowl of organic salad I've prepared the day before.

I may not be following everything on Chanel's list but at least I'm sticking to my food regime. As I stare down at the bowl of quinoa mixed with chopped parsley, onions, capsicum and tomato, it takes every bit of will power not to toss the whole lot down the waste disposal.

Chinese takeaways are just a phone call away. But I stick to my goals. Mostly, because I'm starving and mostly because I'm dying to see who has logged into my blog. Plus, I hate eating alone.

As I sit down at the computer I feel a bit like Meg Ryan in the movie *'You've Got Mail'.* I can't wait to see who has written to me.

I haven't updated my blog for ages because of all the late nights I've been doing at work. My fans are practically gagging for news.

Tonight Sarah from the UK has stopped by. *'Love what you're writing. Can't wait to see what else you get up to. Thanks for the tips on having multiple orgasms in the bath.'*

It's always nice when I receive success stories.

I can't help but chuckle. If only I really knew what I was talking about. Most of the tips I pick up from Chanel. If anyone should be writing this blog it's her. But she's too busy having orgasms to write anything.

Within weeks the comments have quadrupled and more people have subscribed. I have no idea how people found me in the first place but now that they have my blog has reached into the furthest corners of the earth. I even get comments from Peru, China, Romania, and New Zealand. If only I could tell them who I really am and then perhaps I could go and visit.

Here's little ol' me, Ruby Evans, a relative unknown from Manhattan with over 100,000 visitors a month. 100,000 a month!

To them though, I'm Sandy Lee. Sex nymph. Loved and hated, sadly, by over two million readers. How I became a cult I'll never know. What I do know is that it's awfully hard to stop being popular.

There's a huge responsibility. My fans want to know what's happening, how I do things, what I'm going to do next and with who. I feel like J.K. Rowling—only smuttier.

Nearly everyone wants to know me. Many of them depend upon me for confidence in their own sexual affairs. They hang off my every word. Some tell me that they want to be me.

Others say they are me. They are copying the things that I am doing (only I'm not, of course, so I do feel a little bit envious, but also proud.) Ironic isn't it? But I'll tell you something heartwarming. I feel like I am really doing something good in the world.

Something to empower women. *We are more than our boobs.*

They write in asking me what they should do. Even the guys do:

'Dear Sandy. I've been following your blog for months now. I was hoping you can help me. I can't orgasm without looking at porn. My girl's not happy. She says I love porn more than I love her.

Secretly, I'm worried I'm addicted. Can you help me get my love life back on track? Please help — Derek-in-the-dog-box, Virginia'

I take my new role very seriously. If only I could ask Chanel for her tips. But I can't keep risking it. No one can know about the blog.

Besides if I tell her she'll know I haven't had sex yet. She'll know that I lied. She'll know that every single intimate detail that I've shared with her at our catchups has been pure, uncensored fiction.

I glean from her what I can when we meet. She's always

got some new techniques. Last week it was hanging from the ceiling, legs in the air, while her man, a trapeze artist, straddled her.

"It was a real clitorial rush, darling," Chanel said.

If that was me, the blood would be rushing to my head and nowhere else. Somehow she always manages to look supremely divine.

I type my replies, not as a columnist would do, as in straight question and answer. But as a storyteller—à la *Sex With Strangers* style.

But right now, I'm just free-ranging and sharing my experiences. Does it really matter that they're fictional? I mean, I'm not hurting anyone.

'He had eyes like Johnny Depp. Dark, intense, dangerously appealing. His limbs were like Rudolf Nureyev, the most famous dancer of all time, strong, smooth, lithe and muscular. All the better for gripping me as he deftly lifted me in the air and suspended me from a hook in the ceiling.
"You've done this before," I gasped as my body rippled in a wave of pre-orgasmic trembles.
His room was tailor-made for mid-air sex. Long chains, some with wooden bars others with heavy plastic rings dangled from the ceiling.
He jumped like a gazelle into the air and gripping one of the rings, gently lowered his naked body onto mine.
I spread my legs to make room for his throbbing manhood. I was pleased to see he was the real deal. There was no padding in this man's tights.
He nudged me gently with his chiseled jaw, making my body involuntarily flip.
Flip!
That's an understatement.

As he entered me from behind I was flipping right out of this universe as my body exploded with multiple orgasms.
If you want the ultimate orgasm I' recommend men in tights who know how to turn your world upside down—oh, and I've also heard oxygen deprivation also helps!

I REREAD MY NEW ENTRY, and after doing a quick spell check post it.

Recently, one of my fans wrote me a cranky email saying bad punctuation distracts from good sex. I must remember to thank him. He was totally right.

I WAS PLEASED when Derek from Virginia wrote back several weeks later.

'Tights have never looked so good. I definitely don't need porn now. Because I look like a porn star myself.

I've also kitted out the bedroom and invested in a few accessories. I even managed to track down a Johnny Depp mask and a Pirates in the Caribbean costume.

My girlfriend's so into me and I'm so into her. Your advice has taken our lovemaking to a whole new level. So much so that we've gone live. You can check us out on Pornstar.com.

Not only has our sex lives improved but we've got a home-based income now too.'

I'm thrilled! My blog is proving to be a great bit of therapy for me but I'm also helping people in the process.

Already I feel more confident, better about myself, and useful. It is as though I've found my life purpose. I say 'though', because suddenly I started getting hate mail.

Not everyone thinks I'm making the world a better place.

I've been called a wanton hussy, a whore, a slapper and had my whole character called into disrepute.

Take Eugene from Utah, for example. *'You're just a tragic woman with zero self-respect and even less for the men you sleep with.'*

Ouch! That hurt. I want to defend myself. To say that I'm tragic. That I had lost my self-respect because my husband had stolen it, but now I have refound it. I want to say writing my blog had helped me to be a better person. That I am actually helping people. Saving relationships, encouraging new ones.That I haven't hurt any of my lovers because. . .

newsflash. . .

I haven't slept with anyone.

But the fear of discovery silenced me.

To Eugene, I am some slut who doesn't care. But I do care. That's just it. I care too much. All my life I obsessed so much about what other people thought that I could hardly move through fear of doing the wrong thing. Saying the wrong thing. Being the wrong thing (mental note to self: check to see if there is a disorder, 'afraid of not being liked').

I'd married a man everyone approved of. Dressed the way he wanted me to. Allowed him to make my decisions for me. Shut myself off from the world when he told me he'd prefer a wife that stayed at home. Stopped paining because he thought it was messy and something only poor people, who can't afford to buy real art, do.

Nobody had ever accused me of not caring before. Now a complete stranger had the nerve to tell me I didn't care about anyone except myself.

But for the first time in my life I am both anonymous and infamous.

Sandy Lee is no one's wife.

No one's daughter.

No one's mother.

No one's best friend.

Sandy Lee is a figure of my imagination made real through the power of the Internet and *she can do what she damn well pleased.*

I savor the words. *She can do what she damn well pleased.* I throw back my head, stretch my arms in the air and laugh —completely forgetting about the bowl of quinoa salad in my lap.

The whole dish fell like a pile of sand tossed from a child's bucket. It landed in an indelicate mound on the floor then splattered across the room.

Normally, I would have been up like a flash and cleared the whole thing up. But today I refuse to allow this little domestic intrusion to ruin the incredible sense of liberation I feel

I shake my legs and dislodge some of the salad clinging to my ankles and begin to write. I choose my words carefully.

'Dear Eugene, I'm sorry if we have to break up over this.
Love and sex always,
Sandy.'

I feel ten feet tall. Instead of agonizing for weeks and allowing his criticism to infect every fiber in my cells, I've stood up for myself. Best of all I've used humor to do it.

I glance at my watch. 2 am. Where on earth has the time gone? They say time flies when you are having fun but fun or no fun it is time to go to bed.

Reluctantly I tear myself away from the computer. I may not like cleaning up the mess but I sure as eggs wasn't going to sleep surrounded by salad.

Snoutts, our walking vacuum cleaner, will be back

tomorrow and he'll willingly take care of it, I remind myself as I survey the mess.

I side-step the quinoa disaster and pad down to Millie's room.

It is in its usual meticulous state. Her books are arranged in alphabetical order and categorized into subjects. Her study desk is clear, with all her pencils and papers neatly stored in drawers.

She is like her father in that way. A place for everything and everything in its place. Being tidy came naturally to both of them. I've always been a bit of a fraud in that respect. I do my best to look like I'm organized but I feel as though I spend most of my life picking things up and putting them away somewhere else.

I get undressed, dropping my clothes on a heap on the floor and drape my blouse over the framed picture of Jonathan, Millie and I, beside her bed.

As I slip beneath the clean, crisp cotton sheets and snuggle beneath her blankets I feel an incredible sense of lightness. The sort of lightness that only comes when you are no longer burdened by the thankless task of trying to be all things to all people.

I've survived the meltdown of my marriage and experienced my first Internet break-up. No groveling. No trying to be liked. No anger.

The breakup was final.

Or so I thought.

17

ONE MR. WONDERFUL, TO GO

"Chanel's right," I tell my old school friend Lisa, when we catch up over coffee. "Looking for the right man for me is like looking for the right job. Perhaps if I'd done that in the first place before marrying Jon I would have made a different choice. But I was young. We both were. Things change. People change. Jobs change. Everything changes. Still, he was a match which my hard-to-please parents seemed intent on securing. Marrying him finally give me an escape from home."

"Are you going all spiritual on me? You're sounding awfully philosophical all of a sudden," Lisa says pouring boiling water into a mug. "Earl Grey or herbal?"

"Herbal."

Lisa raises her eyebrow. "You *are* going spiritual."

"I'm on a five-day detox. Time to flush all the crap out of my system and begin my new regime."

"What? Just because you got caught flashing your buttocks in broad daylight?"

"I've seen my rear end in the mirror and believe you me it's not a pretty sight. My butt looks like a ball of Swiss cheese gone off. Why is it," I ask taking the cup of elder-flower tea, "that women get cursed with cellulite and men retain their figures?"

"I don't know about that. You haven't seen Peter naked. But the lovely thing about being married to someone who knows you so well is that they love you just for being you."

I gaze into my teacup.

"Oh, god...I've put my foot in it. I'm sorry," Lisa says giving me a hug. "I keep forgetting. . .put it down to menopause. I'm sorry."

"Forget it. I nearly have," I say.

"Honestly?"

I nod. "Being coached by Chanel is really working wonders. She's got me thinking positively and for the first time in ages, I can honestly say I feel like I am through the worst of it. I'm finally realizing where I went wrong. Somewhere along the way, in the rush to be the perfect daughter, the perfect employee, the perfect wife, I lost sight of me. I was so busy trying to be everything to everyone that I became another one of the thousands of grey people that trudge through their dull, empty, safe lives. I forgot how to take risks. I forgot how to have courage. I forgot how to live out loud. I forgot how to be me."

"Well, I never said it before, but you did lose some of your color when you married Jon. It was like the artist in you died, and in your place, an imposter set up camp. A boringly nice, compliant, predictable clone of a woman. Like a Step-ford wife. "

"Hell, Lisa, why didn't you rescue me?"

"I figured you'd work it out in time."

"Call me a slow learner but eighteen years is an awfully long time. Jon's actually done me a favor. If he hadn't left me

I'd still be living my grey ordinary life. God, horror upon horrors I'd still be wearing beige!"

"So, what have you got planned for the next phase of your life. . . besides a five-day detox and shifting some orange peel?"

"I'm going to live a little and love *a lot.*"

"Go girl. Who's the lucky man?"

"Promise you won't laugh." I reach into my bag and pull out a the collage of my dream man. "I've drawn him!"

"I approve already," Lisa says, studying the images. "Very colorful."

"Tousled hair," I say, pointing, "because he isn't anal about his appearance and believes there's more to life than hair gel and his own reflection. Large chocolate brown eyes because he's like a Labrador—loving, kind and gentle."

"And follows you around like a love-sick puppy," she says.

"Correct!"

"Can you make me one, too?" Lisa said.

"He has a funny quirky dress sense to reflect his sense of humor and love of life."

"It seems like a match made in heavenly heaven. But, and there is a but, the practical me. . . and I don't mean to burst your balloon…because it's great to see you so excited again . . but don't you think you need to be a bit more realistic?"

"Don't worry. I realize he's a dream, but without dreams, life is pretty grey…or beige in my case. I'd rather keep hold of my dream in the hope it might materialize then settle for less. Besides, after years of being at home raising Millie and doing wifely things I've finally got a job with prospects. Once again, I have Jonathan to thank. He may have been gutless enough to dump me via a text message, but he did put a few things in place to cushion my fall. The house for one. And his abandonment motivated me to build a career.

"Give me the goss. I'm dying to know what goes on behind those beauty pageant walls."

"I can assure you that everything about the Miss America pageant is squeaky clean. Well, the bits I get to see anyway. With any luck, I'll get a promotion and move up a rung from Public Relations Advisor to Public Relations Manager."

"You will., Ruby. You've got what it takes. You're one of life's survivors."

I wish I felt as confident as Lisa. But then she doesn't know about the lecherous Matt Loews and his odious blackmail threat.

18

A CHANCE ENCOUNTER?

"What an obnoxious fool," says Chanel.

"Who?" I ask.

"Him, the jerk standing at the bar dressed like a rainbow."

I glance across the crowded bar to where Chanel is looking. "You surprise me. I thought a guy like that would be right up your alley. He even dresses like you," I say. "Confident and flamboyant. A person not afraid to stand apart."

Dangerously handsome, I think as I study him briefly. He was dressed in a broad-striped candy-colored shirt with wide lapels. Swished back hair. Youthful good looks.

I press my hand to her forehead. "Aren't you feeling well? Got a temperature? What's up?" I joke, dropping my hand neatly into the bowl of pretzels on the counter. I try to crunch quietly as Chanel replies.

"Just look at him. Look at the way he has women hanging off his arms. He's supposed to be meeting me here. You'd think I was invisible with all the attention he's giving me," she says sarcastically. She pops a handful of pretzels into her mouth and crunches noisily.

"I thought you liked that in a man? The harder to get the more you seem to fall," I laugh.

Chanel purses her lips." Well. . . perhaps. . . in the past. . . but that was before. . ."

"Before what?"

Chanel stares forlornly into her glass.

"Before the jerk dumped me."

"What do you mean dumped? " I asked. "He's here now, isn't he?" I glance over, my eyes meeting his as he looks in our direction. I quickly look away. "I think he's going to come over," I whisper.

"I don't want to see him."

Chanel is acting very oddly and something just isn't adding up. "Okay, spill what's going on? You're keeping something from me."

"Well if you must know. . . and promise, cross your heart and hope to die, not to tell a single living soul. . ." she says as she looks at me earnestly and waits for me to cross my heart. "I took him home last night. . . well, not home exactly. . . I took him. . . well. . . I tried to take him. . . damn, this is harder than I thought. I mean imagine — me...sex siren of Manhattan, relationship columnist. . ."

"Spit it out. The suspense is killing me."

"*He spat me out*! He didn't even want to kiss me. Shagless for the first time in more years than I care to remember. I failed to score."

"*No way*!"

"Would I lie?"

"No, no way. So what did happen? Why is he here now?"

"All he did was interrogate me like some cop or something. Wanting to know if I had sex with strangers. I said to him, 'What's with the questions, darling? You with the FBI or something?'"

"Maybe he's a pimp and he'd heard about the men you shag." I joke trying to console her. "Perhaps you're stepping on his patch? He looks like a pimp. No offense but get a load of his outfit. Kind of a mix of that rapper Puff Daddy and that English oddball actor Austin Powers."

"Yeah, but I like that in a man. I don't want a rule follower. I like guys who splash a bit of color around," she says wistfully. "He's no pimp. It's something else. I think it's me. I'm losing my pulling power."

"Absolutely not! You're the most irresistible woman I know. Think Samantha, in Sex in the City. Think modern-day sex-changed Casanova. You run rings around them, hands down. You're the mean, lean, sex machine queen."

"Oh, you're so sweet, darling," she says cheering up slightly. "But be honest. Please. I need to hear the truth. Do you think I'm slightly off? I've never had a man turn me down before. It's going to seriously damage my reputation. How on earth can I be a relationship coach if I can't even pull?"

"There's a bit more to a relationship then just mastering the art of getting a guy to bonk you in the broom closet, Chanel. Maybe he's kind of like your life lesson—someone who's here on earth to help you find the road back to you."

Chanel rolls her eyes upward and groans. "You've spent too much time listening to me and Dr. Phil. I don't want to be a loser. I've spent years cultivating this look, this image, this brand. Remember? I changed my name just to get away from my wretched past. I've always wanted to be someone else. Someone like Coco Chanel—someone who overcame their past and went on to inspire thousands of people. She never married. Never needed to. . . but she always made time for her lovers. . .always made time for *l-amore*."

Chanel threw her hands to her face and held them over

her eyes. She shakes her head back and forth and groans. "I've failed my muse. I can't even pull a clown in a candy striped suit!"

I've never seen her this vulnerable. I feel gutted for her. Whatever he had done or said to Chanel must have been cruel. But why was she here? Why was he here?

I put my arm around her. Out of the corner of my eye, I see him glance in our direction. "You must have done something right because he keeps looking over."

"It's too late," she says defiantly. "*I am so over him.*"

"Well, you're going to have to tell him to his too good looking face because he's heading this way."

"Get rid of him," she says.

"Why me?"

"Because I've lost my voice."

"What?"

"I refuse to talk to him. Do you know what the prat said? He told me that I was better off without him because I'd only get too attached. Jerk!" She glances dismissively in his direction before turning her away. "As if I'd been even remotely interested. God, just look at his color sense."

There is no doubt about it. He does have an odd sense of color. Mind you so did Chanel.

There is something wildly hypnotic about his deep brown eyes. Something devilish but totally disarming. I lower my eyes deliberately trying to avoid falling under the spell he had obviously cast on Chanel.

But I couldn't stop thinking about him. As I dropped my gaze to the floor my eyes fell upon his shoes. He wore the weirdest pair of shoes I've ever seen. Bright orange. Obviously expensive Italian leather. Tied with pink laces and set off with lime green socks. Very odd, but kind of endearing.

Especially in a bar full of black-suited men with regulation black socks and polished black shoes.

Black. Black. Black.

Yuk. Yuk. Yuk.

I hate black. It is too close a reminder of the life I have left behind.

"Hello, ladies." his smile lit up his face. He spoke with a heavy Irish accent and carried the sort of confidence that men secure in their looks ooze. He was too good looking. Too confident. Too polished.

I didn't want to like him. He had hurt Chanel's feelings, I reminded myself. And now she has tasked me with getting rid of him. We ignore him and continue with our conversation. I lean close to her so he won't overhear.

"Jeeze, Chanel," I whisper. "I really don't see what you like about these toy boy types. His skin is so smooth you could roll a marble over him and it would keep going and going and going. Besides, I thought you only went for blondes." I do my best to say what I think she will find comforting to hear. I don't say, 'I'd like to try a younger man.'

"'Why don't you try him?"

Has she read my mind?

"After what he did to you? Gee thanks."

"No seriously! Besides, I think we could have ourselves a bit of fun," she says turning to face him.

"Well hello, stranger," she purrs. "I wondered when you'd get that hot bod of yours over here. Turn around let me take a good look at you."

He wiggles his hips and shimmies full circle in front of us.

He's obviously an exhibitionist. I am liking him less and less. Only I like his attitude. What on earth was Chanel up to

I wonder as I watch her lean over and whisper something in his ear.

"Hello ladies," he said, in deep, sonorous voice voice the texture of Baileys Irish Cream. He didn't take his eyes off me as he spoke. A strange look slid over his face as though he was trying to suss me out.

"Do I have food stuck in my teeth?" I finally ask.

"What? Ohh, sorry. I didn't mean to stare. It's just you're different from what I. . . I mean. . . no. . . oh, I forgot my manners. . . I'm Fergus. Fergus O'Farrell."

"He's Irish," Chanel says enthusiastically as she runs her fingers over his shoulders. "Isn't he divine? Don't you just love his accent? It's gorgeous!"

Her miraculous change in mood doesn't surprise me. Chanel has always been the consummate actress. Very rarely does she ever reveal what is really going on in her busy head. Chanel is always playing a part, always working the audience. I admire the way she can pick herself up and reinvent herself again, and again, but I am still totally in the dark as to her real agenda.

I study Chanel's face closely as she talks with Fergus. On the surface, she seems to have it all going for her. But for some odd reason that I totally don't understand she is always having sex with the wrong people. She never seems to care whether she ever sees them again.

I sense that despite what she had said earlier about him Chanel really wasn't into Fergus O'Farrell either. Maybe it was just his rejection that had stung.

For one, her body language gives it away. Her legs are turned away from him and she keeps one arm defensively across her chest.

How did I suddenly become an expert on body language, I hear you ask? I'm not. But work had just put us through a communications skills program as part of our professional development. It's a very handy skill but a little unnerving.

Especially as everything about Fergus's body language yelled that he was interested in. . .

me!

I should be flattered. Excited even. He isn't half bad looking and there was something mysterious about his smoldering dark eyes and totally enchanting smile. His clothing yells 'good time'—in a funky kind of way. Obviously he is sporting the current English-inspired mod fashion look. But Chanel was my childhood friend and despite her claims that she didn't care, he had hurt her terribly.

"Right!" she says as Fergus gets up to buy us both a drink. "Here's my plan. I want you to lead him on."

"I don't even like him," I lie. "He dumped you."

"That will make it easier."

"Easier? I don't follow."

"When you dump him," Chanel says.

"Now I am confused. You want me to lead him on and then break up."

"Exactly. Quick, look alive. Here he comes. Now do your thing. Show me what a good student you've been, darling."

Talk about being put on the spot. I suddenly feel like I am in one of those wretched assessment centers like the one the recruiters had put me through to get my job. As uncomfortable as I feel, I didn't want to fail the task—and worse, I didn't want to fail Chanel.

As Fergus hands me my glass I drape my fingers over his hand. "My what smooth hands you have."

I know it's a crappy line but it is all I could think of.

"All the better for touching you with," he said, grinning. His eyes met mine and I held his gaze.

It was supremely hard to take this seriously. Especially

with Chanel giving me the thumbs up. '*What lovely eyes you have,*' she mouths, prompting my reply.

He grins and leans so close to me I could feel his breath on my face and the lovely citrus sent of his cologne.

"All the better to. . ." he whispers in my ear. He leans back and stares right at me. Through me. "…look into your beautiful eyes."

Heat rises to my face and I shift uncomfortably in my seat. I feel like such an amateur. He is a professional flirt and I feel like a total clutch.

"Get a room," one of the guys Fergus has been drinking with calls out.

"Is it hot in here, or is it just me?" I say, fanning my face and reaching for my drink.

"It's hot. Really hot! Look at the steam coming off your friend over there. Why don't you invite him over, Fergus?" Chanel says.

Fergus eagerly obliges. A little too eagerly. Suddenly we are a foursome. Egged on by Chanel I continue my attempt at seduction while she busied herself with his friend.

"Don't forget your mission," she whispers, as she leaves the bar draped around the stranger.

Right, back to work. I've temporarily forgotten what I was supposed to be doing. You could say I got a little lost in the moment. But now, with my renewed sense of purpose and Chanel's beady, evaluative eyes off me, I feel quite powerful.

Fergus is obviously into me and I really, for once, feel quite distant. Sure he is hot, but I have his card marked. He is a player, and a commitment-phobic, judging from what he'd told Chanel. The old 'don't fall for me you'll only get hurt,' pretty much gave his game away.

Buoyed on by my bevy of unsuccessful dates and the

stupid lines and dull routines men spun designed to get into my pants, I'd had enough and was going to call it a day.

Leading Fergus on will be a nice way to wrap things up I figure. I will pay him back for the way he treated Chanel and making him a scapegoat for the whole of his gender. I am surprised by the amount of passion I feel for my cause. Little, quiet, shy me was getting a whole lot more bolshy.

Perhaps it was rage that made me do it. Perhaps it was a desire to get even. Maybe, and probably more likely, it was stupidity. Or was it as Chanel always said, 'passion is like a horse that runs away with you.' Whatever it was I suddenly find myself thinking the unthinkable.

"Where are we going?" he asks as I lead him through the crowds.

"Somewhere more private. Somewhere we can. . ." I say turning to him and tracing his chest with my fingernail, ". . .talk."

I lead him to a quiet corner of the bar.

He presses himself firmly against me.

I run my fingers over the button of his trousers. Yay, no belt buckle.

He moves his hands over my breasts. Ohh that feels surprisingly good.

He brings his mouth down to mine. I hadn't expected him to kiss me. I don't know why. I just didn't. But it did provide me with the perfect way to distract him. So I kissed him back.

Wow!

I definitely didn't expect to actually enjoy it. I literally melt. Shame Chanel thought he was so rotten, I muse as mini fireworks explode in my body.

Damn, he's a good kisser. Stop! He's a *Casanova*, I remind myself before I fall too deeply. *Keep your mouth on the job!*

As our lips lock together I gently guide his body around, following the beat of the bar music until he is facing the room.

"I love your accent," I say, and lean in for a deeper kiss. Then quicker than a flash of lightning I undo his button, unzip his fly, pull out his erect penis, and cry, "cocktail anyone!"

I didn't wait to see what happened. I ran out the door and into the nearest restaurant where I promptly washed my hands.

I've never touched anyone's penis before!

Not a stranger's anyway and certainly not in a crowded bar. As I wash my hands and look in the mirror I burst out laughing.

The look on Fergus face was priceless.

Thank god I didn't live small-town Alabama. In a city as large as Manhattan I'm pretty confident I will never run into him again.

Or so I thought.

19

I don't feel like writing my blog tonight. I know my fans will be cranky. Withdrawal symptoms are always tough on the soul. Of course with a little embellishment, the scene in the bar would have made a great story.

Sandy Lee, sex nymph, would never have left without finishing the job. She would have had him. Lured him to the toilets. Unzipped his fly, hitched up her skirt and had wild, hot sex propped against the toilet wall.

What would Sandy care if he was the type of guy that probably wouldn't even ask her name? What would she care if he told her not to get too attached? The truth was that she'd be saying exactly the same thing. They'd be totally on the same wavelength.

So I could have written a great scene, possibly the best in my whole blogging career. Especially now that I had actually touched another man's penis.

"Ohhhh", I clench my eyes and let out a long groan. "I can't believe I did that."

Snoutts, who is lying contentedly at my feet, lifts his ear, cocks his head, and gazes at me with a look of total bewilderment.

"I picked up a complete stranger's penis, ran my hand over it and then. . . then I did I truly terrible thing," I tell him.

Snouts still doesn't seem any less in the dark so I continue on. As much for my own clarity as to salvage the owner-dog relationship.

"I know what you're thinking. I must have liked him? Why else would I put my hand down his pants? Secretly deep down in my subconscious, I want him."

I swear Snoutts nods his head. He definitely wags his tail. What am I doing, talking to a dog? I should be talking to a counselor.

"Well, I don't like him one little bit!" I say with finality before padding down to the kitchen and fixing myself a hot chocolate.

Snouts dutifully pads after me. It is nearly ten o'clock and the house is unusually quiet. Normally Millie would be blaring her stereo. I walk over and read the note on the kitchen table.

Doing homework with Jordan. Going to stay over. See you tomorrow. Love you lots, Millie. P. S chocolate donuts in the fridge :)

Oh, I wish she was home more, I think as I read her note. I hate coming home to this empty house. If Snoutts weren't here I think I would die of loneliness.

I reach into the fridge and console myself with a donut.

As I walk back upstairs, hot chocolate and doughnut in hand, I can't get Fergus's face out of my mind.

He looked totally mortified. I hadn't expected that. I thought a guy who fancies himself like he seemed to wouldn't mind flashing his pecker to a crowd of admiring onlookers.

I remembered the whoop of applause that went up and the wolf whistles that reached out onto the street as I made my getaway. Besides let's not forget that he hurt my best friend. Chanel practically told me to make him suffer. He had it coming to him. But if we was so right why did I feel so wrong?

Part of me knew I'd scored a victory for all the women out there who he had treated like heartless vaginas by men who discarded them like products who'd exceeded there 'use by date'.

But there was another part of me, the part that had been with me prior to my *reinvention* (Chanel's term for what she calls my miraculous mid-life make-over—again her words).

This old me, the part that until now I thought had died, felt truly mortified. I, *the old I*, hate making anyone suffer. The old I definitely would have gone out of my way to ensure I never did something to make someone not like me.

"It doesn't matter if he hates me," I assure Snoutts. "I'll never see him again."

I sit down at my computer to check my emails. Blog Boy has written to me. I feel instantly better. We've been email flirting for weeks now. Ever since he came across my *Sex With Strangers* blog.

At least someone besides my dog and my daughter loves me. In a weird kind of way, I felt like Blog Boy really knew me. The true me. The old, but slightly new, me.

His first comment on my blog had been so sweet.

'I've been reading your blog now for eight months. You seem like a red hot wild woman. . . deep down I sense you just want to be loved. Loved in the way that only a man that understands what you need can.'

Of course, I had my blog reputation to uphold. So I emailed back. "Honey, what I need is seriously good shag.'

As the emails continued I decided there was something irresistible about him. Unlike the other emails I received, he had touched my heart. Silly I know. But you should read some of the blog comments I get. Smutty and pornographic put it mildly.

Anyway, our email relationship went from there. To him, I was Sandy Lee. I never admitted I made up my sex conquests and of course I never told him my name. But we did share things that were happening in our lives and the kind of things we were interested in.

Harmless but intimate things. The kind of things that none of my other bloggers ever asked. They just wanted to know what my favorite brand of condoms were, did I get discounts for bulk purchase, had many guys had I had in one night, and what was my favorite position?

But Blog Boy asked me things like what was my favorite color (Irish green, because it reminds me of my Celtic roots). Favorite book (Pride and Prejudice—who doesn't drool over Darcy!) Favorite movie (Roman Holiday —okay so I'm a bit of a romantic!)

So still protected by my anonymity, we went from there.

But now he wanted to meet!

20

A SURPRISE ENCOUNTER

We decided to meet at Bellismo's on 47th. It is a funky wine bar and public enough to be able to make a quick getaway if things turn out badly.

It is Tuesday night and raining heavily. I arrive early so I can watch the door carefully and exit out the back if Blog Boy looks like a total freak.

As I 'd hoped Bellismo's is not too busy, but not too quiet to be awkward. It is the perfect venue—kind of like Goldilocks porridge. Not too hot and not too cold. Only I'm not eating porridge. I'm having what I hoped will be my first, genuine encounter with someone I really fancy.

On email, Blog Boy stacks up perfectly. Funny, intelligent, caring and a little bit. . . I don't know. . . a little bit edgy. If you know what I mean.

Blog Boy had the x-factor. Because we met on the Internet I guess you'd say the e-Factor. He has Internet charisma and loads of promise.

I position myself right at the door so I can catch his eye when he arrives.

'I'll be reading my favorite book, Pride, and Prejudice', I told him when he'd asked how he would recognize me. *'Oh, and just in case someone else if reading it is after all one of the most popular books of all time, I'll carry a yellow rose — my favorite-next-favorite color.'*

I decide against giving him a physical description just yet as I want to maintain my anonymity. That way I can run without hurting his feelings.

Blog Boy told me that he'd bring his favorite book too. *'That way if it turns out to be the date from hell, at least we won't look like complete idiots. We can read our books instead.'*

His joke made me smile. That was exactly was I was thinking. You can always hide in a book. My parents did that all their married lives. Never really saying a word to each other, and quite happy about it.

When Blog Boy told me his favorite book was *The Bridges of Madison Country*,' my heart skipped. Only a true romantic would love that book. Either that or a bridge fanatic.

I prefer the first scenario. The first time I read *The Bridges of Madison Country* I devoured it in one sitting and cried for days. If only the lovers had had a happy ending. I'm determined to get mine.

I'd scanned the bar quickly before sitting down. No books of Bridges and no one who looked as handsome as I was sure Blog Boy would. And there was no one wearing a bright green jacket.

When Blog Boy told me that he'll be wearing a jacket the color of freshly ripened limes I figure it must be because he didn't want me to confuse him with anyone else. He is definitely going to stand out that's for sure. I just hope it isn't in the creepy Santa Claus way.

The bar is full of people wearing the Manhattan black. Sophisticated and professional. Demure and classical. Boring and boring. Just like beige. Once it had been my favorite color but now beige stood for bland. It symbolized everything I chose to leave behind.

Tonight for our first meeting I'd chosen to wear red. Racy red. Sexy red. Take-me-I-want-you-red. on the color wheel. On the color wheel red is the complement of green. I pray we'd *compliment* each other.

As I had got dressed that evening I was also mindful of the fact that I had my reputation to keep up. Sandy Lee is a woman who is confident with her sexuality (I have forgotten what it feels like to be sexual). Sandy is hot for sex (the idea of having sex with a stranger still leaves me cold). Hopefully I'll warm up when I can finally get out of my head and into my body—my very naked, lying next to Blog Boy body.

Sandy loves standing out (I am happiest remaining in the background). To be honest I've never owned a red dress. Once again Chanel came to my aid and took me shopping. When it comes to couture Chanel didn't let her namesake Coco Chanel down.

We found the most gorgeous, seductive knee-length silk dress. It was the color of Valentine's Day roses and silky to the touch. The plunging v-neckline disappeared almost to the waist and fell in soft folds that prevented too much of me from falling out. Not that I had too much.

We picked out a sexy push-up bra with a generous amount of padding from Victoria's Secret to help with the cleavage and the curves. The effect was transformational. I felt like a new woman. The sort of woman who maybe, just maybe, might be up for having sex with a stranger.

At least that was how I was feeling when Chanel helped

me get dressed that evening. Armed with what seemed like a whole bottle of the perfume *Seduction* sprayed all over my body, a generous layer of racy-red lipstick, and long shapely legs courtesy of all the walking I had been doing with Snoutts, and bolstered by diamanté studded black stilettos I really felt the part.

I chose to wear my hair down, slightly tousled to create the just-got-out-of-bed-but-could-happily-go back-there-with-you-look. Chanel's term.

Somewhere between leaving the house and arriving at Belissimo's my confidence wanes. As I sit in the bar alone, surrounded by a room full of strangers I feel awkward and overwhelmingly self-conscious.

What say he doesn't come? I'd look like Nancy-no-friends. Or worse, the rotund man sitting down from me, with the florid face and the watering eyes that bulges from the side of his head like fish eyes, might come over. He is sitting two seats away and gave me the once over as soon as I arrived.

And he isn't the only one.

I blame the dress.It doesn't leave much to the imagination and my push up bra is truly a wonderbra. Even I can't stop admiring my new expanded, protruding, mountainous breasts.

I can hear two guys sitting to my left having bets about who will take me home. One of them isn't too bad looking. Blue eyes, dark hair, dressed in an expensive suit, with dazzling teeth. But the earring in his left ear lets the look down. And the high shrill pitch of his voice really offends my senses.

Not that I am in any way tempted. I am waiting for Blog Boy. The guy who I hope is the man of my dreams.

Feeling a little nervous I order a large velvety glass of Pinot Noir to help boost my confidence. I glance at my watch. Two minutes to seven. He will be here soon. I open my book and flick over the pages. The words pass in a blur. I can't concentrate on a single letter,

"If anyone gives you any trouble just let me know," the barman says as he places the glass in front of me.

"Thanks," I say gratefully. "I'm waiting for a friend."

"Sure," he smiles. "Most of the girls from Danni's pick up their clients here."

"Danni's?"

"The strip club around the corner," he says casually as he walks back toward the bar.

He thinks I'm a stripper! Great! There I am thinking I look sexy and sophisticated and the bartender thinks I look like a hooker.

"You must be new. I haven't seen you before," bartender-guy says.

For a moment I temporarily forget my other personality—Sandy Lee, the sex with strangers queen. It's hard juggling these split personalities but perhaps I've pulled it off, after all. Although, I'm not sure being mistaken for a hooker is a bonus. Externally I might look like a woman up for sex. Inside I still feel like the old, scared-middle-aged me.

I look up nervously as I hear the bar door open. 7:10 pm . He is late. But instead of my Blog Boy two middle-aged women dressed in red slippery fabric that cling to their disproportioned curves saunter in.

Black fishnets wind up their lumpy legs. The teeter precariously on their cork heeled red patent leather shoes and scan the bar. They spy the two men I'd overheard and slither over to them.

After five minutes of foreplay, money changes hands and they all leave arms around each other, the guys squeezing the girls butts. So that's what sex with strangers looks like?

I sip my wine and did my best to look less like a call girl

and high-class—like a movie actress. Cool, calm and hopefully soon to be) collected.

Where was he, I wonder apprehensively, looking at my watch again?

"Another drink?" the bartender asks, noting my empty glass.

I nod.

He brings me another red and I settle into my book. I'm only a few pages in when I am interrupted.

"Cocktail?"

"No thanks," I say not looking up. "I'm fine with wine."

"Surely you'd like to grab a cocktail?" the stranger with the Irish lilt to his words persists. "I seem to recall you can handle your cock. . ." the accent was familiar. Horribly familiar.

I look up slowly.

Fergus!

My face turns a deep shade of merlot as I flash back to the previous night. All I can see was is his penis in my hands. I gasp a great gulp of air. It's not a pretty sight. Me I mean. Not the penis. The penis is great. Really great.

I shoot a panicked look toward the door. What say Blog Boy comes in when I'm talking to Fergus? What if Fergus makes a scene? What if. . . a thousand scenarios race through my mind. I have to get rid of him. And fast.

"I'm expecting someone," I say, trying to sound nonchalant.

"Mind if I take a seat," he says ignoring me. He signals to the bartender. "Whiskey. On the rocks. Irish malt if you have it," he says turning his attention back to me. "All I alone I see."

"Please leave. I'm waiting for someone."

He doesn't take his eyes off me. "Been stood up?"

"No, I haven't," I thrust my arms across my chest." I'm waiting for a gentleman. A really nice man. The sort of man who wouldn't leave a girl like me alone in a bar. I am sure he has a good reason for being late."

"Lucky guy." Fergus's brown eyes glowed with a turquoise blue-green that was striking against his darker features.

"Please go away. He'll think I'm with you."

"Would that be so bad?" he asks looking directly into my eyes. His gaze is arrogant, amused and unwavering.

I am not in the mood to be played by an accomplished seducer. I avoid his far too handsome face and look around for the bartender.

"Is everything alright?" he asks, putting down a coaster and placing Fergus's drink before him.

"This man is bothering me," I say.

The bartender looks at Fergus and then back at me. Fergus beams, a mile-wide smile. The bartender hesitates.

"I'm sorry mate," I hear Fergus whisper as he leans in. "Early onset of Alzheimer's. Sometimes the wife forgets we ever met."

"I'm not his wife," I protest. The waiter glances at my ring finger. Damn, I wish I'd listened to Chanel and got rid of the stupid thing. "I've never met this man before. I swear."

The barman scratches his head.

"She's become obsessed. It's a little embarrassing. . ." Fergus says, gesturing with his eyes in the direction of his crotch. "She's obsessed with exposing men's pecker in public. It's a strange side effect of her medication."

The barman's dark brows furrow. "We can't have any of that in here. We'd lose our license."

"No problem. I"ll keep her on a firm leash. It's why I'm here."

Anger saturated with humiliation wells inside me. "Ohh, you really take the money…"

"Please honey, no outbursts. You heard the man."

My face crimsons.

"It's our anniversary." He leans over and caresses my arm. I pull away.

"I have never met this man in my life…and as for touching peckers…I can explain," I look earnestly up at the barman before scowling briefly at Fergus.

"Look you two. I'm busy. I'm used to people playing out their fantasies. I see it all the time. Couples pretending not to know each other. Picking each other up as if it is the first time. Any other night I would have helped you out. . . but tonight we're one man down. Now if you don't mind I have work to do."

"I don't mind at all," beams Fergus. "I've had the pleasure of being married to this woman for over twenty years. She's given me thirteen wonderful children and a lifetime of memories. This woman is no stranger. I know her like. . ." Fergus gestures to his crotch. the palm of my hand. "If it's not *Pride and Prejudice* I'll take the shirt off my back and give you $100 bucks on top."

My heart stops. *Pride and prejudice*? How does he know? I shut the book and turn it face down on the table. Fergus must be Blog Boy.

My heart plummets thirty floors. Manhattan had suddenly shrunk to the size of a pea. How the hell did he find me?

My Blog Boy is the arrogant man I'd humiliated only nights earlier. Here he is, sitting opposite me, grinning like a Cheshire cat. Any self-respecting man would have seen me, down a u-turn and left. Either that or angrily accosted me.

I guess I should be grateful, but instead of relief, I feel immensely disappointed. I'd built Blog Boy up in my dreams. In my mind, he was a cross between Johnny Depp and Gregory Peck—funny, slightly childish and quirky. But sophisticated, and grown-up at the same time.

Okay, Fergus was all these things, but he was also an annoying, arrogant, rude man. He is so totally self-obsessed and into himself that he refused to get the hint and leave.

"Do you enjoy torturing me?" I mutter under my breath as he pries my fingers off the book and turns it over.

"*Pride and prejudice*," he says loudly turning to me and then at the barman. "What did I tell you?"

"It's just a coincidence," I protest. "This book is a classic. He just got lucky. You said if anyone annoyed me you would get rid of them and now I'm asking you to do just that."

The barman shrugs his shoulders.

"Ohh honey," Fergus says getting up from the table. He reaches across and before I can protest kisses me on the lips.

My face reddens further. But more worrying then my reddening face was the way my heart is responding to his kiss.

"Please stop pretending you don't know me. The game's up. This very astute man has figured out how we like to get it on. Let's go home, make wild passionate love, and do our thing."

My body trembles and my head is spinning. I fan myself as he slides across the bench seat, and slips his arm around me.

"Would you like another drink?" The bartender asks wiping the table and placing down two clean toasters. "Something stronger?"

"No, I'm just leaving." I reach for my coat and place my book in my bag.

Fergus grabs me gently by the arm. "Please let me buy you a drink to make up for the one you lost down my pants."

"I wouldn't have a drink with you if you were the last man in Manhattan."

Fergus winches. "Ouch! Okay, I can take a hint. You're disappointed. I can see that. You were expecting someone else. I thought we got on pretty well actually. All those months of emailing. I was looking forward to meeting you."

Months!

It was true, we'd been hitting it off for a long time.

"At least do me the courtesy Miss Elizabeth Bennett, of telling me, why you are so prejudiced against me. What did I do to deserve that little stunt the other night."

What can I say?

"Still," he says smiling, "I've got to hand it to you it was a real original. Girls are always trying to catch my eye but you blew them right out of the water. You certainly caught my attention."

"You arrogant. . ."

"Ssshhh. . .my darling wife," he says putting a finger over my mouth, "don't say anything you might regret."

I push his finger free. "You think women are like ATM machines. Holes in the wall that you make deposits in and then withdraw without leaving a trace."

"I'd never thought of a woman's body being like an ATM machine. What treasures are you hiding in there, Miss Bennett?"

"Don't play coy with me. You know what I mean. Chanel. You lead her one and then you dumped her."

"I think you have the wrong end of the stick. Don't you have the same laws here as we do in London—innocent until proved guilty or something?" He looks at me earnestly. His Labrador brown eyes pierce my protective armor. Labrador just like the image of my dream man. Cripes! Now I am in trouble.

"Not in this case," I say grabbing my coat and dashing out of the bar. I need to get away before I do something I might regret.

21

I hail a cab and head home. No matter how much I try I can't stop thinking about Fergus. The weird thing is that even though I acted angry I really don't feel that way on the inside.

And while I am disappointed that my Blog Boy isn't the tall, dark, mysterious stranger I've been hoping for, Fergus is annoyingly sexy.

He looks more Italian than Irish with his twinkling coffee-brown eyes and model-like stubble. He reminds me of a cross between those drop-dead gorgeous guys in *Il Divo, the* classical crossover vocal quartet.

He is intriguing. On the one hand, Fergus has the edgy, sexy look thing going on like the modern Italian opera singers. But on the other, instead of going with a stylish black jacket he wore the most unusual assortment of clothes I had ever seen.

No wonder Chanel had been attracted to him. His dress sense, or lack of it, perfectly complemented her own. The lime green jacket with ultra-wide lapels looked like albatross wings, and the white bell-bottom trousers, and iridescent technicolor shirt gave him a rockstar look.

A little laugh bubbles to top of my mouth as I think about him. Perhaps I have judged him too harshly.

The night I'd exposed him I'd acted totally out of character and I felt ashamed. I'd only given him the slimmest of opportunities to explain himself. And if I'm honest, which I am, almost to a fault, what he had told me had softened my hard opinion—just a smidgen.

At least he had tried to be honest with Chanel and spare her a broken heart later. Except he'd misjudged her. Chanel was the last person on earth who wanted to form an attachment.

Much like me. For the first time in ages, I am having fun dating and I didn't need a man to complete me. No, I resolved, I was going to live in the now and be grateful for what I had. I pick up my passion diary and added my list of gratitudes.

Number one on my list, I am grateful for my health. I have two arms and legs, and eyes to see with.

Number two, I am grateful for my gorgeous fun, confident, happy, well-rounded daughter Millie. If it hadn't been for Jonathan I never would have had her so I guess I should put more effort into being grateful that we had what we had.

But that doesn't mean I have to be grateful that he did what he did. The tosser. I take my pen and write in large letters, "I am grateful he is gone." I can't believe I was pathetic enough to want a cheater back.

I add, 'I'm grateful to be divorced because the whole sorry episode has unleashed my creativity.'

Number three, 'I'm grateful for my friends. I may not have oodles and oodles of them but the ones I have are cool.

They lift me up when I'm down and they're great fun to be around.'

Closely related is the fact that I am super, super grateful, ecstatic in fact, that someone wants to publish my book. It's a dream come true! I am still pinching myself! Did I tell you?

In less than three weeks the whole deal will be signed, sealed and courier delivered. I'll be independently wealthy. Fabulously wealthy and finally free of the last tentacles of control Jonathan wields over my life.

It had never occurred to me just how much I truly had to be grateful for. I didn't really want for anything. Okay, so I was a little lonely in the intimacy department, but right now a full-time man would only complicate things.

I certainly didn't need to think that a bit of eye candy like Fergus was anything more than a fling. Cute but dangerous, and distracting, I resolve, trying to oust him from my mind.

He, however, refuses to go. Like one of those blasted pop up ads, he keeps flashing up on the computer of my mind. Just fantasizing about him makes my stomach long-vault.

Fergus has *bad boy heart breaker* written all over him. Thank god my head rules my heart and not the other way around. Logically there was nothing going for him at all. He was arrogant, cheeky, bad-mannered, told fibs. But, damn— there had to be a *but* didn't there?

But I can't stop thinking about him and what he'd said. He told me that Chanel had come onto him. That stacks up. She had told me that she had lured him into the toilets, or more correctly he was in the toilets and she had lured herself there.

So, that stacks up too.

He had tried to free himself from her clutches. I'm not sure about that. What man could refuse an attractive woman who was putting out for him? He'd tried to tell her that she'd only end up getting hurt (what's that about?)

Tonight in the bar all he had done was suggest a truce of some sort. For some reason which completely alluded me, instead of mending picket-fences, I'd behaved like a twat and stormed off.

I can't think what's wrong with me. I'm acting completely irrationally.

I check my calendar. Feb 2nd. My period is not due for another 20 days. It must be something to do with the planets I decide, tucking myself into bed.

Still, Fergus would not budge from my consciousness. I clench my eyes and still, he is there. I try counting sheep but Fergus is there shepherding them with me.

I begin to wonder if life is trying to tell me something. Did Fergus hold the key to some karmic lesson I needed to learn?

I don't have any answers, but what I did know was that whenever he was near little butterflies took flight in my stomach and a tingle surged through my body like hundreds of stars sparkling in unison.

Fergus woke something deep within me. Something that had been dormant for years. Something that scared the heck out of me. But I wanted to feel the fear and have sex with him anyway.

Did I love him?

Impossible.

What a ridiculous thought.

I've only just met him and he irritates the hell out of me, I remind myself.

But I had all the classic symptoms. Erratic thoughts, sleeplessness, inability to stop thinking about him, trembling when he was near and my stomach is in a constant state of upheaval.

Lovesick, definitely.

I reach for the thermometer in my bedside cabinet and pop it into my mouth. 98.6 degrees Fahrenheit. My temperature is normal. How odd. But, I just didn't feel my normal self.

I hadn't exactly been acting normally either. I Ruby Evans, born, bred and married into wealth, manners and etiquette, had gone up to a complete stranger, unzipped his trousers and lifted his penis into my hands.

I shudder and shake my head in disbelief. What the hell is happening to me? Maybe I need to see a shrink, after all.

Is it possible to love someone you hate?

I punch my pillows. Maybe that's where the term love-hate relationship comes from, I wonder as I toss and turn. Finally, I give in to the fact I am not going to nod off to sleep peacefully.

After a restless night, when I wake the next morning I go to the bathroom and splash my face with water. As I look at my reflection in the mirror an image of Fergus appears beside me and kisses the back of my neck.

I shake my head vigorously to dislodge him. A sharp pain pierces my heart. The pain began slowly and then gained momentum. Fergus puts his arms around me.

Salty, bitter tears well in my eyes. Fergus hugged me tighter. As I imagined his arms wrapped around me, tears spill down my face—slowly at first like droplets of rain. Then they gave way to a torrential pour as I sobbed uncontrollably.

At first, I wonder if I am having a breakdown but then I recognize it as grief. Grief trapped inside me that until now I have never allowed myself to express.

Part of me, I later realize was grieving for my lost marriage. But a bigger part, or maybe it was inextricably interwoven part, was an overwhelming feeling of sadness and loneliness.

I yearn to be touched. Cherished. Loved.

But why Fergus? Why now? As far as I can make out he is the sort of guy that went through women like toothpicks. If I was ever going to have sex with a stranger, I'd like to at least have the illusion they cared. Even if it was just a teensy, weensy little bit.

I dab my face dry and head back to my bedroom. The computer is staring at me. I turn my head away. I can feel it calling me.

Log one. Log on.

After fifteen more minutes ignoring it I can't resist any longer. I'm dying to know if Blog Boy has been back online. Just in case he is maybe a little bit interested in me after all.

Why do I care?

Just because for some stupid crazy reason what he thinks matters.

22

———

I DON'T CARE

I haven't heard a word from Fergus for days. After months of enjoying the email banter Blog Boy and I have enjoyed, hearing nothing was like withdrawing from heroin cold turkey. Well, perhaps not that bad, but bad enough.

My mind races with scenarios. He hates me. I've hurt him. He thinks I'm ugly. He's found someone else. My pessimistic thoughts ran away with me until I force myself to get a grip.

You don't even care about him? So why are you worrying?

Four days later I finally receive a blank email from him with a jpeg attachment. For a brief moment, I wonder if he is sending me some terrible Trojan virus.

I didn't take him for a techno hijacker and click open the file. My finger is poised to shut it down if it looks in any way suspicious.

I grin when I see the image. Three rings of white ethereal smoke float on a cloudless sky.

The next day another email arrives. This time with the

words *Truce* and an image of a white flag. Cute. A like his sense of humor.

Thirty minutes later another email invites me out to dinner.

I feel torn and nervous. Fergus is making an effort, and during the last few days, I've found myself thinking about him constantly.

Yet, on the other hand, I had decided to opt out of love in the real world. All my attempts had been a disaster and Fergus had danger written all over his sexy body.

My job was going well and it looked like I was finally going to get the recognition I craved. The last thing I needed right now anything upsetting my hard-won balance.

Certainly not Fergus O'Farrell who is more interested in getting his leg over than in anything remotely meaningful.

I know, I know, I'm supposed to be preparing myself to bonk my way around Europe but the truth is I really couldn't give a toss about all that sex and free love crap Chanel had spun me into believing I needed

My self-esteem is doing just fine now that I've done time single. I have a great job, a wonderful daughter and a lovely home. Life had never looked so good. Why wasn't that enough?

"He probably likes a challenge," Chanel offers when I confide in her about his persistence. "Perhaps I shouldn't have come on so strong when I first met him," she says, her voice disappears into a glass of New Zealand Chardonnay.

"Say I were to go on a date with him. . . how would you feel? Hypothetically speaking," I say.

"Darling," Chanel says, placing her glass down. "I couldn't care a rats. People aren't possessions. He's not a handbag. I don't own him."

I pluck a few of Snoutts hairs off my skirt and avoid her

gaze. "It doesn't matter anyway. I'm not interested. I just wondered that's all," I say.

"You're a typical Libran, to-ing, and fro-ing over the simplest decisions," Chanel says. "Just go out with the guy and get him out of your system, darling."

"I just don't want to get hurt," I admit.

"Protect yourself then. Don't get involved. Just make your mind up but watch your naivety. He's a first-class charmer but something tells me that he's broken goods too. Whatever you do, don't try to fix his tortured soul."

"Broken goods?"

"Good looking, eligible guys like him are single for only one reason," Chanel says. "They're wounded."

"I've got enough wounds of my own. I'm not interested anyway."

"The hell you're not. You haven't stopped thinking about him since you first clapped eyes on him."

I keep forgetting Chanel's an intuitive coach. I wish I had the ability to tap into other people's thoughts. What a godsend that would be—especially if I could tap into mine.

No second thoughts that would be a nightmare. Chanel's right, these days I change my mind more than a whore changes condoms.

Could she really be right about Fergus? Was he really damaged goods?

Empathy stirs in my body. Everyone deserves a chance and right now he was sounding more and more like someone I have a surprising amount in common with.

23

THE DATE

After much indecision and a flurry of emails from Fergus, I finally consent to meet him for dinner. This may sound like a no brainer. *Handsome guy wants to take an average looking single parent to dinner at a swanky Manhattan restaurant.*

You're thinking I'd be mad not to go, right? On paper, it sounds easy but in real life? Now that's a whole different ball game. For one I have nothing to wear and no idea how I am going to fill an evening with scintillating conversation. Whenever Jonathan and I had gone to dinner, which was as rare as a blue moon, we spent most of the time sitting in silence.

I open my wardrobe door where I have blue-tacked my *ideal man criteria*. I ran my eye around the picture I had drawn and read the words out loud: *creative, funny, good-looking, sociable, outgoing, confident.*

I look at the other 'must-haves' and wonder whether Fergus would be a perfect match after all. *Sexy, energetic, fun, generous, sexy voice, not effeminate at all. . . but caring.*

On and on the list went. A tall order, impossibly beyond

the reach of any mere mortal, but quite a delicious idea to hold onto. And Fergus seemed to match many of my must-haves.

Maybe Fergus would end up being the perfect casual fling —a man I could actually fall in love with. A man I could build a future with. A man who could offer Millie and I lasting happiness.

I know I'm getting ahead of myself. I know I am contradicting myself. I know I am confused. What do I want?

Before you say anything, I haven't forgotten Chanel's warning about broken goods. But I'm a Libran ruled by Venus, and I love being in love. For me sex and love are inseparable.

In the interest of obeying my life coach and because it's time to experience other things in life I am happy to try sex without love. Everyone else seems to have flings? Why can't I? Why can't I settle for a one-night passion thing? Why does it have to be more?

I spray perfume behind my ears. I've deliberately chosen *Seductress*. Dark floral notes waft through the air, merging with patchouli, musk, and amber. I spray more behind my ears and inhale. It's dark, provocative, and sexy and promises to transform me into a long-lasting femme fatale. Seductress indeed! I hope it lives up to the marketing hype.

"A seductress," says Chanel as she sprawls on my bed enjoying the late evening sun, "is confident beyond confident. She knows what she wants but she doesn't act desperate. In fact, to her prey, she looks like she is disinterested. Disinterest drives a man wild. You'll be able to reel him in and then pounce. . . elegantly of course. The art is to look like you are not pouncing."

"Let's get this straight," I say. "I have to be confident

beyond confident. I have to know that I want him but not let him know that I know that I want him."

"But you have to dress the part too, darling. Think 1950's. Do you remember those scenes in *Cat on a Hot Tin Roof* with Elizabeth Taylor?" Chanels says. "Remember how she stood, her white chiffon dress gushing around her, her head cocked and one black brow arched, fondling the charm at her collarbone with a lazy wrist, lips plump and faintly parted, her neckline scooped so low that it abandoned the camera frame?"

"I can honestly say I wasn't paying that kind of attention," I reply tugging on my zipper which refuses to glide over my buttocks.

"In that moments," says Chanel getting off the bed and coming to my aid, "Liz coerced an entire generation to adore her. Think Mae West, Greta Garbo, Marilyn Munro —all great seductresses are unique. But they are all classic, chic and sexy."

Chanel tugs the zip firmly. I suck in my stomach to aid the effort. Success!

"Femme fatales leave nothing to the imagination," she says, flopping on the bed again. "Satin dresses hug their figures like cling film and plunging necklines make their boobs practically land in the guy's hands. Only a man can look but he *can't* touch. That's important. Don't let him sample the goods. Make him wait."

"You have anything to worry about there, Chanel! I've been on over thirty dates and I've not so much as a snog. One guy did manage to break through the lip barrier but only because I was trying to hail a cab at the time. As I turned my head he thrust his lips to mine and in instant panic, they sprung shut like prison gates. The guy either got a hell of a fright or he decided I wasn't worth wasting any more time on.

Either way, he did a runner and I was left like a reject on the curb. His parting words *'are you frigid or something?'* hissed between clenched teeth. Do you think I might be frigid, Chanel?"

"Hardly, slow off the bat and fussy. . . maybe. But frigid, definitely not. You just need to relax a little. I think you're suffering from performance anxiety. It might help if you pretend to be someone else. Why don't you try to be Greta Garbo or Elizabeth Taylor for the night? Your problem, darling, is you think having more than one man in your life makes you a whore. Liz dangled men off her arms like the diamonds dripping off her fingers. She wasn't loose and no one called her a whore. Giving a man what he wants ultimately will give you what you want. Which we both know is to get married again. But, here's the secret sauce. Men want to be entranced by a woman. They may not admit it openly, but they want to be lured, mesmerized, bewitched, possessed and seduced by a woman. And they don't mind surrendering to her siren maneuverings and being rendered powerless by her. A man would gladly give anything to the woman who can make him feel good. Even his heart— and his last name—if that's what you really want. Trust me."

"I've never really thought of myself as seductress material. But it does sound like I could have a lot of fun and it does sound a bit more glamorous than slinking off to the pub looking for a shag—as you so elegantly put it!"

"Great. You've already got a few of the basics courtesy of my top flirting tips. But here are a few others. Seduction is simply the act of tempting, persuading, attracting and ultimately getting someone to have sex by using either a romantic or deceptive approach. It's an art in the truest sense of the word. To master this art you have to be able to create an ambiance that exactly meets the deepest desires of your target. Your tools of the trade? Why nothing beyond a good grasp of the workings of the human mind and body. And my darling, that is where I come to your aid."

"This is beginning to sound kind of manipulative," I say laughing nervously.

"Funny you should say that," Chanel says. "The word seduction is derived from the Latin *seducere*, to lead aside. It denotes the illicit, even the criminal—a deviation from the right path. Being led on by a lie."

"Now I am nervous."

"Relax! Would I get you to do anything I wouldn't do, darling?"

I shoot her a doubtful look.

She smiles cheekily. "Even in the prudish 1950s, people pinned Liz Taylor up on their walls. And not because they thought she was creepy, or sinister but because she was attractive, exciting, alluring. . . and just a little bit forbidden. . . a little bit out of their reach."

"Out of reach I could handle," I laugh, putting on my diamond earrings. "So tell me, just so I don't confuse myself and do the wrong thing tonight, how is flirting different from seduction?"

"Think of flirting as the entrée and seduction as the main course. Your aim is to work up to the dessert. . . hot, passionate sex with lots of extras on the side."

I fan my face. "Is it just me, or is it hot in here?"

"It's about to get a whole lot hotter," Chanel reaches into her bag and pulls out a tangled mass of wires. "Here pop this down your front."

"Is that what I think it is?"

Chanel nods and passes me a small electronic bugging device. "I'm going to be your date coach just like on telly.

We're going live in the streets of Manhattan. All you have to do is say exactly what I tell you to say."

Now I am nervous.

24

Fergus stands out immediately from the rest of the suits gathered for after-work drinks on Friday. He wears a pale blue shirt with wide colorful candy stripes of fuchsia pink, lavender purple, and cherry red.

He sat facing the door and gets up immediately when he sees me. His shirt hangs out over his jeans and his hair is gelled into irregular waxen waves. My stomach pings with anticipation.

"Don't look too excited. You'll blow it," Chanel cautions in my ear.

I've managed to conceal the microphone and micro-video camera in a large red silk flower which I've strategically positioned near my heart and changed my diamond earrings for Chanel's costume jewelry. The earrings are big enough to eat off but conceal the single air plug wonderfully.

"You look gorgeous," Fergus says in a thick Irish accent.

I swoon. It isn't just his accent but his drop-dead handsome looks. His eyes dance mischievously and his broad smile fills his face with light. He looks genuinely pleased to see me.

He kisses me on the cheek and leads me to his table.

"Don't walk like an elephant," pipes Chanel, "act like the sex siren you want to be. Wiggle your hips, push out your chest, throw back your shoulders and take your time getting to the table so he can admire you."

It feels odd, but I do as instructed. As I walk past the other diners I can't help but notice a few lingering stares from men and some jealous glances from women.

As Fergus pulls out the chair I glance down and see my old-baby-belly protruding. Thank goodness, his eyes transfixed on my plunging neckline. I reminded myself to suck in my stomach for the rest of the evening.

"You look beautiful," he says earnestly, picking up the long-stemmed red rose lying on the white table cloth and passes it to me.

I blush and take the flower. My heart is beating so rapidly that I'm sure it must be leaping through my dress.

"Every guy thinks they can win a girl over with flowers. Don't fall for it," cautions Chanel. "Now drop your eyes, flutter your lashes and then hold his gaze."

"Thank you," I say, dropping my eyes and smelling the rose briefly. I looked up and smiled demurely, holding my lips in place and lock my gaze with his for a few moments longer than I feel comfortable. Fergus holds my gaze, a bemused look glides over his face.

Despite my nervous awkwardness, it is a fabulous night. The waiter approaches our table and told Fergus the table he'd reserved outside is ready. Fairy lights sparkle through the trees and instrumental music filter gently through hidden speakers.

The tables looked like they had been set for a wedding with white linen, crystal glasses, sterling silver cutlery, and garlands of spring flowers.

The waiter pours us each a glass of champagne and disappears into the restaurant promising to return shortly to take our order.

"Here's to a new beginning," Fergus says raising his champagne flute in the air.

"To new beginnings," I smile, bringing my glass slowly to his.

We sip in silence.

"Get him talking about himself," instructs Chanel. "Men respond well to a woman who makes them feel all important."

"So what brought you to New York?" I ask, taking another sip from my champagne.

"I've always had a yearning to visit. Who wouldn't? This place is such a buzz," he says enthusiastically leaning toward me.

"So far so good. Check out his body language. He's so into you. Yours, on the other hand, needs work," Chanel cautions. "Do a Mae West."

As I listen to him talk, I fondle the charm on my necklace and part my lips provocatively.

Fergus stumbles over his words slightly as his gaze follows the movements of the charm wedged between my breasts. "Er. . . um…yeah enough about me. How about you? How long have you lived here?"

"Go, girl!" Chanel encourages from the sidelines. Now it was my turn to falter. This three-way dialogue was distracting.

"I'm sorry, what did you say?"

"I was asking about you. You know I was kind of surprised by your little stunt the other night. You didn't seem like that kind of woman."

"Don't get suckered into the past. Stay seductive. Arch your eyebrow or something," Chanel says.

Arch my eyebrow? Just one? How?

"Are you okay?" Fergus asks as I attempt the Elizabeth Taylor cocked eyebrow seduction thing. "Do you have something in your eye?"

"Actually, you know what, I think I do. Can you please excuse me for a moment," I say as I get up from the table, "I think I'll just go and fish it out."

"What are you doing?" Chanel asks.

"You said it yourself, things are going well," I say into the microphone as I make my way to the restroom. "He likes me. His body language is good, we're talking, for the first time in ages I'm feeling like maybe I could actually fall for someone again."

"Be careful, darling. Remember what I said."

"Yeah, I know—*damaged goods*. Well, newsflash, so am I. Show me someone in this town who isn't."

"Jonathan for one."

"Thanks, Chanel. Did you have to bring him up?"

"Sorry. Below the belt. You're a big girl. Go have some fun. Just watch yourself. I can't put my finger on it but something about this guy doesn't feel right."

"You mean besides the fact that he's wounded?" I say, impatiently.

"Look, Ruby I'm not trying to rain on your parade but the more I think about it the more think he staged the whole encounter with me just to get to you."

"Now you're ridiculous. Why would he want to get to me? Let's talk about this tomorrow, right now I've got champagne to drink and a man to seduce." I rip out all my wiring and saunter back to join Fergus.

"I was just about to send out a search warrant," Fergus

laughs. He signals to the waiter who reappears moments later with a selection of pasta. "I wasn't sure what you'd like so I took the liberty of ordering a little bit of everything. I hope you don't mind."

"I don't mind at all. I love pasta, I purr, sliding my fingers up and down the stem of the crystal flute, "and you've just saved me having to make a hard decision."

I twist the fork around the pasta and then lift it to my mouth, allowing the tip of my tongue to quiver slightly before closing my mouth slowly over the fork, then pull it gradually from my mouth.

I can see the hunger and longing in his eyes. Everything about his body language tells me he is as attracted to me as I am to him. Chanel is right, being a seductress is fun.

"So you were going to tell me about yourself," Fergus continues. His deep brown eyes study me intensely.

I feel suddenly vulnerable. Caught between the past I want to forget and the life I want to create. Caught between a lie and the truth. Caught between who I was and who I want to be.

I decide not to bring up the whole divorced, single parent, still nursing a broken heart thing. I don't have to be Einstein to know those topics of conversation would be passion killers.

"A lady never reveals her secrets, darling" I laugh, putting on my best Chanel routine. "But I can tell you I'm the real deal—a true blue Manhattan woman. My grandparents immigrated from Ireland when my parents were young but so have half the people born here."

"No way. I'm Irish too!"

"I had kind of picked up the accent," I laugh. "I bet it's a real hit with the ladies."

"Is it a hit with you?" He says staring at me seriously before breaking into another smile.

Heat rises to my face and I nearly choke on my drink. Is he flirting with me? *Hey, I thought I was supposed to be the seductress.*

"It's very sexy, " I say, fondling the charm at my collarbone again, this time with a lazy wrist. I run my tongue over my lips and leave them faintly parted. My Liz Taylor routine seems to be working. He leans forward slightly in his chair and gazes directly into my eyes. I return the gaze with a smoldering look that I've practiced over and over in my bathroom mirror.

"You're a very attractive lady. The minute I saw you I thought wow, that girl's a knockout. Chanel tells me that you're not seeing anyone. I can't believe it."

Chanel has coached me on this one. So I had my reply hot and ready and delivered my line like a pro. Instead of bursting forth with an honest explanation and a string of gushy comments about how I'd tried to meet men for months now and he was the best guy I've seen ever since I started dating, how handsome he was, how I loved his accent, how I want to jump his bones, how I was desperate to break the drought, I sip slowly from my glass.

I look him straight in the eyes, arch my eyebrow and say, "I'm not really the settling down sort of girl. I just want to have fun." I run my foot up and down his leg. "Do you want to have fun, Fergus?"

His smile tells me he did, but his leg jiggles under the table.

"I don't usually ask girls out," says Fergus. He sits up straight and drew a deep breath.

"I'm glad you made an exception," I reply twisting a strand of hair around my forefinger.

"I'm new to New York. It would be nice to know a few more people." He gazes directly into my eyes, "I'd like to see you again. That's if you'd like to, I mean."

"I'd like that," I reply trying to conceal my excitement.

Bingo I'd struck the jackpot. He isn't a commitment-phobe. He is keen.

"I'd love to take one of those hansom cabs around Central Park. Would you be up for that? I know it's kind of touristy but then I am a tourist," he says.

"Would you believe it if I told you I've lived here all my life and never been in one. I'd love to. I really would."

What a catch! Romantic, handsome and undamaged. Not that I could see anyway.

"What say we skip dessert," he says reaching across the table and holding both my hands, "and go catch ourselves a horse."

His touch is electrifying.

He hands the waiter his credit card, before excusing himself to go to the restroom.

I take the opportunity to phone Chanel. "Oh my god, He is drop-dead gorgeous. Absolutely, and everything is going really, really well. I'm holding in my stomach, maintaining eye contact, doing sexy things with my food. In fact, I'm having a ball. . . yes. . . yes. . . totally. And he is the most romantic man ever. He's paid for dinner and now we're going to grab one of those Hanson cabs and go for a night ride through Central Park. Ohh, Chanel, I really do think you're wrong about him. This is the most fun I've had for ages. Gotta go, he's coming back and I have to look all calm and collected."

Fergus is nearly at the table when his cell phone rings. He frowns and looks quickly at me before speaking in a hushed voice to the caller and walking back into the restaurant.

I knock back another drink, completely forgetting about the warning on the new anti-histamine tablets I'm taking, not to drink.

Fergus is taking forever. What's keeping him? Curiosity gets the better of me and I get up from the table and go to look for Fergus. My vision is a little hazy but I put that down to the gray-film wafting from a couple of smokers standing on the corner near the restaurant.

The unsteadiness on my feet I put down to the ludicrously high Manalo Blahnik skyscrapers I'm wearing. But then I start having crazy thoughts, like wondering if there is another woman in Fergus's life. Maybe a wife.

I've been so besotted I'd totally forgotten to ask. But I did check his wedding ring finger and he isn't wearing one.

Fergus is standing by the door with his back to the restaurant. I hear him say something about being on the case, nearly reeling the big fish in, something about money in the bank and all going according to plan.

Relieved it wasn't a woman but obviously a work-related matter I go up to him and throw my arms around his neck. I know, I'm supposed to be treating him mean. I'm supposed to be feigning indifference. I know—pretty quickly, that I've overdone it.

He looks pale for a moment and flips his phone shut.

"Hello gorgeous!" he says, too quickly.

"Hello," I reply cooly, remembering Chanel's advice not to come on too strong.

"These are for you," Fergus says, pointing to the waiter carrying over a small parcel wrapped in glossy gold paper and placing in on our table.

We sit down, and I carefully unpeeled the paper taking great care not to rip it. "Oh my God," I cry, looking down at the exquisite box of chocolates.

"Pierre Marcolini! I love him. He's like the haute couture of chocolate. Wow, you really know how to make an impression."

I guess in hindsight it shouldn't have been that much of a surprise. I'd casually dropped my love of Marcolini chocolate in so many of my blog entries.

Still, I'm flattered and a little knocked off my feet. No man has ever brought me chocolate. Not even Jonathan who was always hiding anything with even the remotest hint of sugar from me.

I gobble up a chocolate there and then and Fergus joins me. As I've posted on my blog I've always believed you can tell a lot about a man by the sort of chocolate he is drawn to. Fergus chooses a truffle with a liquid center and slightly crunchy exterior covered with deliciously crunchy cocoa nibs.

As he carefully bites into it, a sweet and spicy vanilla-like aroma and herbal fragrance permeated the air between us. Funny how you can be so wrong about people, I think. I would have taken him for a tough nut kind of man.

Me? Well, I choose a chocolate-covered marshmallow, with a raspberry center. What does that say about me, I muse as Fergus and I leave the restaurant?

"I'm going to be a tourist in my own home town. What fun," I giggle as the horse-drawn cab pulls up beside us.

The white horse curtsies as the driver, dressed immaculately in a tuxedo and top hat, helps me into the lilac-and-gilt-trimmed cab.

Fergus slips his arm around me and pulls me close. Electricity surges through my body. My heart flips out of my chest.

For a moment I wonder if, for the first time, I am feeling real love flowing through my veins. Fergus didn't try anything more and I guess it is fair to say I was a little bit disappointed. But on the other side, his chivalrous behavior totally surprises me too. I find myself drawn to him.

"OH, that was so much fun! I haven't laughed so much in ages," I giggle as we disembark. Fergus, as though sensing I am about to face-plant the pavement, grips my arm.

"I had a great night too. Fabulous company with a very beautiful, sexy woman."

"The night is early. The fun has only just begun," I slur, tracing my finger along his shirt collar and into the bare skin of his neck. "Mmmmm, I love a man with a hairy chest," I say stroking the hairs on his chest.

"I'd love to party on believe me. But something tells me that when you wake up tomorrow you'll be glad I didn't. Besides I'm behind on a deadline and my boss will have my balls if I don't report in with some progress."

Was he rejecting me? I did my best to conceal my hurt. "You never did tell me what you did? Are you in the CIA or a spy catcher or something?" I slur. I stumble and nearly career into a lamppost.

Fergus reaches out and grabs my hand, and drapes it over his shoulder. I lean against him for support.

"Yip, you could say that," he draws me closer to him, bends down and kisses my forehead. "Did anyone tell you that you look kinda cute when you're drunk?" He smiles briefly and then looks at his watch. "It's 11 pm in New York and tomorrow already in London. I've got an early start. Can I take you home?

"I thought you'd never ask," I say snuggling under his arm and gazing up at him.

"I mean home-home."

I stiffen. "But I thought you said you didn't have a girlfriend."

"I don't."

"You're married?"

"Nope. As I said, I'm free as a bird."

"Aren't I pretty enough? Don't you want to have sex with me."

"You're cute as a button."

"But I want to go home with you."

"Sure you do. *Tonight*. But tomorrow you'll thank me. Believe me. Right now I'd feel better if I just made sure you got home. This is New York after all."

"New York's not such a bad place. Really it's not. . ." I mumbled drowsily. "It's had a bad rap that's all. . .but it's okay now… honest. All the baddies have gone. . ."

"I think you've had too much to drink, young lady. Nowhere's safe for a lady at night, especially one that's had one too many."

"I'm alright, honest. There's practically a cop on every street corner. Ever since Sept 11, I don't think you'd find a safer place on earth. I'll be alright really."

He steps onto the curb and hails a cab, opens the door and then, after I get in, slides in beside me. "I'd feel better if I saw you home." He puts his arm protectively around me and draws me close.

"Where are you two love birds heading?"

I whisper the address into Fergus's ear.

"21 Manhattan Avenue, thanks," he says.

As I snuggle into Fergus's chest he smells divine. A mix of the fresh night air, sandalwood and musk cologne, and strength.

I feel happy and sad, my heart trembling with excitement

and heavy with the knowledge that soon we would be saying goodbye.

It's the first time I've ever got close to wanting a second date and definitely the closest I'd gotten to wanting to have sex with a virtual stranger.

I steal a sideways glance at him. What would he be like under all those clothes, I wonder? His arm feels strong and muscular.

My eyes linger on his lower region far more than is polite. I bet the hard theme continues all over his body. I gaze into his eyes. He meets my stare and holds it and smiles cheekily. I haven't asked how old he is. I know he is younger than me. How much younger I don't want to know. What does it matter if I'm called a baby snatcher? No one cares when men date younger women. Why should I care if I date a younger man?

The cab pulled up outside my place all too soon. Fergus pays the fare and hops out, opens my door, and helps me from the cab as my vision blurs in a drunken haze.

'Wait here for me, mate. I'll just see that she gets in safely."

We walk up the four stone steps to my brownstone and I rummage in my bag for the keys. I pull them out and lift my hand unsteadily to the ruby red door.

"I love the color," he says, taking the keys gently from me and fitting them into the lock. "Let's get you into bed young lady," he says as the door opens.

"Sounds wonderful," I mumble as I feel for the light switch and turn it on. Home looks good, I muse as the edges of the room move in and out.

He stands in the hallway and looks around. "Upstairs or downstairs? "

"Up Fergus. Up. . ." I say, tottering unsteadily on my feet.

"It's a tairway to heaven," he says looking up the steep

wooden staircase that curves its way up the to the next landing. "I should have known. Here, let me help you," he says, coming toward me.

Before I can protest he lifts me up and throws me over his shoulder. "This will be way quicker and safer."

I let my body go limp and dangled my arms and legs playfully like a rag-doll. "Ooooh, how romantic…just like in the movie," I giggle. "I'm not too heavy, am I?"

"Light as a bubble," he says, steadying himself against the wall. Freeing one hand he wipes the small beads of sweat settling on his brow, sucks in a whoosh of air, and continues up the stairs.

As we near the top, my shoe slips off. I watch as it tumbles over the banister and bounces down the stairwell. My Manolo lands with a clank onto the cobbled kitchen tiles two floors below."

"Sssssshhhhh," I giggle, peering over the edge." You'll wake up the mice."

Fergus pushes open the bedroom door with his foot and flicks on the light. He stands robotically still as though photographing the room with his eyes.

"Nice," he says, as he places me on the gauzy canopy bed. "Not exactly as I had imagined, Sandy. I kind of figured you were going for the seductress look. You know red satin sheets, mirrored ceilings, shagpile carpet."

I follow his gaze as he takes in the moody, textually rich gray velvet walls.

"I wasn't expecting you so soon. (hiccup) The decorator is coming tomorrow. . ."

"No, leave it. I like it this way. A woman's room should radiate romantic vibes. It's nice. Soft. Feminine. Dreamy. I like the evocative paintings. Who's the artist?" He asks, studying the minimalist abstracts.

"Me," I mumble.

'Wow. They're good. Hey," he says, turning to face me. "Drop the seductress thing. You have it all going on already. You're a beautiful lady, really."

"You're beautiful too. . . so beautiful. . ." I murmur, closing my eyes.

"Hey, don't go to sleep on me, princess."

As my eyes flicker in and out of consciousness I'm aware of him looking down at me as I lay spread-eagled on the bed. My dress rides up my thigh and my left breast has burst free of my cling-film dress. But I don't care.

Alcohol has taken my tongue, my mind and my body to another place. I want him to join me there. I want him to touch me in places no one has ever touched me. He's such a cutie. Such a hottie. Such a. . .

Disappointment.

To my dismay, he pulls my dress so my thighs are covered, and places the mohair comforter over me.

Even though I'm feeling completely sizzled, I'm coherent enough to stop myself from feeling spurned. I writhe my body and then make my best attempt at looking like a modern-day sleeping beauty.

I know my pale skin is slightly flushed with a rosy-glow. I pout my lips so they looked like cupid's—just begging to be kissed.

It feels like Fergus and I are cocooned from the outside world. The neon light of the cab rises from the street below— a sobering reminder that soon he will leave.

He sits down on the foot of the bed and gazes around the room. I know what he can see. My sanctuary. Soft walls with original art, a bookcase full of romantic novels, candles by my bed, a dresser scattered with colorful beads, make-up heaped in small wicker containers.

My bed is an old antique sleigh bed, on the right are two large double-hung windows with French-style shutters, my writing desk with my Mac book pro.

He grits his teeth and looks at the closed laptop for a long time, then back at me, raking his hands through his hair.

"I really should go." He gets up slowly and walks over to the window and glances down at the street.

"Thank god for cabs," he murmurs as he glances at me once more. I keep my eyes slightly shut and feign sleep.

"Goodnight princess," he says as he tip-toes across the room and partially closes the door behind him.

Regret washes over me like a cold tap. My body is on fire, heated with need. I so, so, so wanted him to kiss me. I thrust my arms around my pillow. I want to scream. Instead, I imagine my pillow is Fergus and I smother it with kisses.

"Who the hell are you?" Millie's angry voice followed by Snoutts' furious barking stops me kisses my pillow.

Still feeling woozy I pad to the door and peer through the gap. She is brandishing a baseball bat with one hand and holding a snarling Snoutts on a leash with the other.

Fergus covers his balls instinctively.

"Who are you? What do you want?" Millie cries lunging at him with the baseball bat.

"I'm Fergus! Who the hell are you?" I can hear the adrenaline spiking his voice.

I should have told him about my daughter. This is not going to end well.

"Millie," she growls."I live here."

Fergus uncovers his balls and looks at her.

"Ohhh," he says as though a lightbulb had just gone on. He looks back through the crack in the door to me. "I see the resemblance. I've just brought your sister home."

"My sister? I don't have a sister."

"I used to deny my family too. But there's no getting away from hereditary. You look the spitting image of her."

"Her? Do you mean my mother? I don't look anything like her. I'm a quarter of a century younger for a start." Millie says, lowering the baseball bat. Snoutts flops onto the floor and begins licking his balls.

"Your mother?"

I'm not sure if it's surprise or mortification that grips his larynx causing his voice to spike like a needle.

I decide to continue feigning sleep in the hope when I wake up this whole terrible scene will be water under the bridge.

Well, I can hope, can't I!

"Where is she? What's she done now?" Millie asks sounding like my mother.

"Your mom is bit under the weather if you know what I mean. I brought her home to sleep it off."

"Has she been drinking?" Millie let out an exasperated sigh. "I told her not to mix her medication with alcohol. I keep telling her to be careful, but she doesn't listen. Sometimes I wonder who is the adult and who is the child in this relationship. Thanks for bringing mom home. I'll take it from here," she says walking toward the stairs. "Ohh and sorry about the bat thing."

"Hey, no problem. I'm glad to see a girl who knows how to look after her mother. You don't hear about that much."

Millie walks Fergus down to the door and unbolts the deadlock. I pad to the landing and carefully looked over the railing.

"We'll be seeing you then, kid," he says, walking down the steps to the waiting cab.

"Sure," she says, looking him over. "That'll be cool."

As he approaches the waiting cab his phone rings. He

reaches into his pocket and checks the caller ID. For a moment he hesitates.

"Worse thing ever invented," I hear the driver curse. "Always at people's beck and call."

Fergus nods in agreement and takes a deep breath. "Boss!" I hear him say. "You've been on my mind a lot. . . yeah. . .yah ..don't worry I'm onto it. . . I've been working the bars. . . going to the places she goes to. Her story seems to stack up. . . you expected something by now? Really? Hang onto…calm down. . . you sound upset. . . yelling won't help. . . your ticker. . . take a chill pill. . . trust me—you taught me everything you know. What do you mean, that's what makes you nervous?"

"Where do ya wanna be dropped, buddy?"

Fergus places his hand over the receiver, "take me to the Big Chill, 9th and 21st."

Fergus holds the phone out away from earshot before getting in the cab. "Stop yelling. Don't worry…I'll get the story . . . Yeah. . .yeah. . .sure thing. Tomorrow."

I watch the cab pull out and tip-toe back to bed. It suddenly strikes me that I never did find out what he did.

25

A SURPRISE VISITOR

The next morning I wake with a hangover. I slowly prop myself up and reach for the glass of water by the side of my bed and gulp it down.

"Ohhh," I groan clutching my head. Sitting up isn't such a great idea. My head throbs. I lie slowly back again, glad of the softness of the feather pillows.

The marketing blurb is true; they are like lying on a bed of soft clouds. I wonder with alarm how I had managed to get naked, but then recalled waking in the night and peeling off my dress.

My head is pounding too horribly to ignore anymore. I get out of bed and reach for my favorite pair of pajamas, slowly put them on and then slink off to the bathroom, placing one foot carefully and slowly in front of the other and holding my head perfectly still as though I was in deportment class balancing books on my head.

Today I feel like I'm balancing 70 stampeding elephants, one roaring train, a ten-ton oil tanker and, dread the thought, one Dr. Seuss character holding a plate of green eggs and ham.

I quicken my pace to the bathroom and only just make it to the toilet bowl as I vomit violently, No diced carrots, but plenty of pasta, I notice as I briefly study the contents of my stomach.

The good news is I no longer feel nauseous. The bad news is I still have the caste of characters perched on my head; only now they've been joined by the Rolling Stones playing *Brown Sugar*.

"Millie! Millie!" I cry, clutching my head. No answer. I crawl out of the bathroom, lean over the wooden banister, "Will you turn down that racket!"

As the music dulls to a quiet whisper I pad back to the bathroom. I take three painkillers and grip the side of the basin as I chase them down with a vitamin tablet in water.

I glance at my reflection in the mirror and instantly regret last night. I look like death microwaved.

My nose is running like a hose and my mascara has pooled into dark panda bear rings around my eyes. Lipstick smears across my face like a bad special effect. Usually, I am fastidious about removing my make-up.

I groan with embarrassment holding my hands over my head as one terrible flash back after another replays in my mind. God, had I really been that seductive? If only someone had talked some sense into me and saved me from making a fool of myself.

"Mom!" Millie calls as she bounded up the stairs.

"Ohhh, I'm never drinking again. Take a long hard look at me. This is what happens to people who drink, Millie. Let your mother be an example to you."

Millie looks at me oddly.

"Why are you staring at me like that?"

Millie shrugs and steps aside and Fergus appears at the top of the landing.

"How's the patient?"

My heart plummets 20 floors. I wish I could follow.

"Cute PJ's," Fergus laughs ignoring my distress. "I'm a big fan of Mickey Mouse myself."

"Oh god!" I shoot Millie a cross look and lock myself in the bathroom. "Give me a minute," I call through the door, pressing myself against the wooden panels and looking with horror at my make-up streaked face.

"I was just practicing for Halloween. I thought I'd get in early."

Fergus chuckles.

"Millie, take Fergus back down stairs and make him a coffee. I'll be down in a minute."

When did I start looking so old? I wonder as I run the hot water and wipe the steam from the mirror.

Not even a thick layer of foundation is going to hide these crows feet, I muse as I run my fingers slowly over my wrinkles.

I massage the extra-firming moisturizer over my neck and lift my chin to stretch some of the extra folds.

That's better, I think. Only I can't go around sticking my neck out like an ostrich. Oh god, what's the point? I may as well face Fergus and get it over with.

I glide some mascara over my lashes, dab on some gloss, sweep my cheeks lightly with blush. That will have to do, I think to myself, feeling too ill to really be bothered with anymore effort. If he doesn't like the stripped-down me, he's just not the right man.

Yeah right. Who am I trying to kid? Jonathon virtually had a fit if I ever appeared without make-up on, I recall, as I leave the safety of the bathroom and slowly navigate the stairs.

"You scrub up well," Fergus says brightly, getting up from the couch and kissing me lightly on the left cheek.

"Thanks. It's amazing what a bit of make-up can do." I look down at my feet momentarily, suddenly feeling incredibly self-conscious. "You look pretty good yourself."

"Aww yuk," Millie grimaces. "I'll get you a coffee. Want another one Fergus?" Millie asks over her shoulder as she disappears down the stairs into the kitchen.

"Sure, that'd be great." Fergus waits until she disappears and then lifts a large gold box from beside his feet.

"Here, something to help you recover."

I meet his gaze and hold it, studying his face. "Two presents within 24 hours!" I smile as I take the box from his hands. "Thanks. You shouldn't have. It's awfully nice of you."

I walk downstairs with him and place the box on the coffee table. We sit down on the couch and I gently lift the lid. "Oh, what a nice surprise. Champagne and strawberries. . .and another box of chocolates."

"It's your anti-hangover cure. We call it the hair of the dog back home. There's nothing like a wee sip of something to put the hair back on your chest… that and some fresh air. I thought we could go for a picnic in Central Park. It's a smashing day and it's another one of those 'seen it in a movie got to do it' things I want to do while I am here."

I laugh. "Well I'm not sure about the hair on my chest scenario but a walk sounds great. Do you know I've lived here all my life and I've never even had one picnic in Central Park? I think your cure is beginning to work already."

"How about Millie, would she like to come?" he says loudly, as he walks over to the door where Millie is eavesdropping.

I hear Millie scuttle back to the bench and clang together

coffee cups as she attempts to pretend she hasn't heard a thing.

"How about it, Millie? " Fergus calls again.

"How about what?" she says, handing Fergus his coffee.

"A picnic in the park," he replies. "Snoutts can come too. I bet you'd like a walk, wouldn't you, Snoutts?" he says smiling at Millie as he walks toward the dog.

Snoutts wags his tail excitedly and leaps around the room.

"Wait, I'll just go up and change," I say.

"Why, you look gorgeous as you are."

Gorgeous? In my old tee shirt and jeans? For the first time in ages, I feel happy. The sort of happy that comes from being with people who take you as you are.

I steal a glance at Fergus who is playing a ball game with Snoutts. He is such a refreshing change from Jonathon, who always demanded I wear dresses and that I was perfectly made up and manicured.

I have to give it to Chanel, I muse as I grab my jacket before heading out the door. She is right—when you seduce a man they usually end up giving you what you need.

But what stumped me was why my getting drunk, looking ghastly and then going on a second date in my old clothes appealed to him. I couldn't fathom it.

Everything seems to be going so well. Too well. And then the roller coaster feelings came back again. I am excited and afraid all at the same time.

Don't get too attached, I warn myself.

He's only here for a few weeks, and then he'll be gone from your life forever.

26

PRACTICING THE ART OF DETACHMENT

"Help!" I cry, throwing my bag onto an empty cafe chair and plonking myself down next to Chanel. "I'm falling for Fergus and I don't know what to do."

"Hmmm, I see the problem. You've met a hunky guy; he's drop-dead gorgeous, kind, romantic, and available. And you haven't found any wounds. I'm not sure I've got the skills to help you with this one, darling."

I shoot Chanel a warning look. "It's not funny, it's serious. He's the first guy I've cared about since Jonathon and I'm scared."

"What's there to be scared of? I'd kill for a piece of that action."

I sit up straight. "You? Queen of one night stands? You would kill to have someone more serious?"

"Don't look so surprised, Ruby. Deep down I yearn for a bit of romance too. The most romantic my men get is dialing me a cab and sending me on my way after we've done the deed." She looks down sadly briefly before tossing her hair back and putting on a bright smile.

"Less about me and more about you. That's my job—to

listen to you and help you achieve your perfect life, not prattle on about mine."

"But Chanel, I'm your friend. I'd like to. . ."

"Enough," she says raising her hands theatrically. "Shoot, what's got you spooked?"

"I'm afraid of how I'm going to feel when he has to go back to London. He's not here for long. He just has to crack some job he's working on and bang he's gone. Just like that, out of my life. I don't think I could bear it."

"I'm not surprised. You haven't even shagged him yet. You must be hurting already."

"What is it with you, Chanel? There's more to a relationship than sex," I say crossly.

"Come on admit it."

"Well, I must admit, it does seem a bit weird that we haven't. It's not as if there's no chemistry. There is. But to be honest it's a bit hard with Millie around."

"I thought she went to her dad's every alternate."

"Not since their baby arrived."

"How about a honeymoon hotel?"

"I want our first night to be wonderful."

"Keep visualizing it—I'm sure if you keep your thoughts centered on what you want and how you want it you'll soon bring your dreams into reality."

"Yes, but it's not just Millie and wanting to protect her."

"Blow me down with a feather. Of course, it's not. I could see through that old excuse, darling."

"I thought your idea of sex with a stranger was a bit yuk at first, but I agreed with you, it seemed like a good way to get over Jonathon and not leap into anything more serious. But I never did it."

"You never did it? But what about all these stories you

told me. What about the lap dancer, the bartender, the guy at the bus stop?"

"I made up every one of them. And that's the other thing. . . promise me you can keep a secret."

"Promise."

"Cross your heart?"

"And hope to die," she says.

"Believe me if this gets out someone will die. Me! Of shame. Oh, Chanel, you're not going to believe what a mess I've got myself into"

"After that last little load that you just revealed nothing would surprise me."

"You're angry with me."

"I'm pulling your leg, darling. You didn't really believe I fell for all those erotic tales of sexual conquest, did you? Like you said before, I'm the queen of one night stands. You, my darling, are just a mere student. And a poor one at that. You haven't so much as snogged another man, let alone got down and dirty."

"But how did you know. Why didn't you let on?"

"I read my fair share of erotic romances, Ruby. Where do you think I get my continual source of tips and techniques from. I can recall practically every scene I've ever read, and most of those you've recounted back to me. Your creative writing is good, I'll give you that. In a less skilled hand, you could be had up for plagiarism, but you've altered things, added your own little twist. You should write a book. With my book idea about the art of seduction and yours on virtual pornography we could both top the best sellers."

"I *have* written a book, Chanel! That's the thing. And it's going to be published."

"Whoooa, back up a little."

"I've been posting my stories of . . . er . . . sexual

conquest. . . pornography, as you put it, on a blog site... It started out as a little bit of self-help. . .you know 'act as if...' and all that."

"Wait. Don't tell me—you've started a movement like that kid in the movie *Pay it Forward.* Only it's a movement for sexual retards."

"Sexually liberated women, like you Chanel," I correct her. "Millions and millions of people started tuning in for my updates. They were insatiable. So to feed the beast and keep them happy I wrote more and more posts."

"You devil! I've just moved your grade up one notch. You're my best student. You've exceeded my expectations."

"The trouble, well it's not exactly trouble yet, but it could be, is that I've been approached by Randomz who want to publish a book, *Sex with Strangers*.

"Who would have thought I'd be best friends with a real live Carrie Bradshaw. I hope you'll still remember your friends when you're rich and famous and swooning around Beverly Hills with Jackie Collins and all those Hollywood stars."

"Be serious, Chanel. Can you imagine, how my family, my boss, god forbid, my daughter, would react if the story ever got out? They'd have kittens."

"Does Fergus know?"

"Fergus? You must be joking. He's the best thing that's ever happened to me. The last thing I want to do is have him thinking I write porn on the Internet. Oh god, this is terrible. What the hell am I going to do?"

"Why not take the money and run. People write under nom de plumes all the time. Sign your contract via email and no one will ever be the wiser. What's do you go under, anyway?"

"Sandy Lee."

Chanel broke into pearls of laughter. "Sandy Lee! Perfect," she cried, breaking into song, "Sandra Lee, lousy with virginity, can't go to bed until I'm legally wed, I'm Sandra Lee."

I glance around the café, "Shhhhh, quit it will you. Do you want to bust my cover? Besides you've got the wrong song. Olivia Newton-John was Sandra Dee in *Grease* not Sandy Lee and my story is about something way different than a high school crush and summer love."

"You can say that again, darling. I take back what I said about being a poor student. That was harsh. You've been great. But to score excellence you'll have to actually do the deed. So where are things with Fergus?"

"Well, that's the other thing. What with the book deal and everything hanging over my head, and the fact that he's going back soon, things have cooled a little. I don't know quite what I should do. Take it to the next level, or pull right back?"

"What would Sandy Lee do, Ruby?" Chanel asks.

"Sandy would have fun. Loads of fun. And she wouldn't get attached. She'd just see it for what it was. A brief fling with a man who's looking for the same thing."

"I think you have your answer, Ruby. . . I mean, Sandy."

"Let's make your first night with Fergus one you both remember for a very, very long time to come."

27

FUCKING IN THE RIGHT IN THE RIGHT PLACE

C hanel says that developing and maintaining my own interests is a very essential part of mastering the act of detachment.

"Men don't like needy women, Ruby. The last thing you want to do is start filling your diary with all the things he wants to do. You'll need to have plenty to get on with when he goes back to London."

I know only too well what happens when a relationship ends and you have nothing to fill the void. The trouble is I'm not sure what I want to do. I know what I don't want. I don't want to join a book club, I don't want to join a knitting circle, and I definitely don't want to go back to Ceroc.

Ceroc was a nightmare.

"If you're going to be a romance writer, it makes sense to master your craft. Why don't you join a local chapter of Romance Writers of America."

Chanel's idea is brilliant.

It doesn't take me long to find one that I liked the sound of, plus it's far enough away from home for me to keep some degree of anonymity. This is becoming increasingly important.

Ever since the book deal was announced I've had more and more hits on my site and people are starting to get a bit too curious about who Sandy Lee really is. So traveling to New Jersey, once a month suits me just fine.

Today is my first romance writers group meeting and I'm amazed. All sorts of people write romance novels. They totally blew my stereotypes about what a romance writer actually looked like.

Of course, I have read zillions of romance novels and nearly all of them have a mug shot of the author on the cover, but those are the authors who have really made it big. They can afford to get dressed up and look like regular citizens.

I figure everyone else, especially the smuttier ones, judging from some of the hot stuff published by the Orange Giselle label, would be wearing fishnets and suspenders. The stuff that the label produces is tripled x-rated and should be sealed. Dominance, submission, female bisexuality, graphic anal sex, spanking, and multiple partners. It's mind-blowing and totally beyond anything I would want to write about. I'm tolerant of other people's vices, but it's not just for me.

Yet, here I am sitting in a nice suburban household in the middle of suburbia on a Saturday afternoon enjoying cups of tea and fairy cakes with pink icing listening to a young housewife talk about her research for her book.

"My husband's always wondering what I'm up to when I'm busy Googling. If only he knew," she giggles, popping several chocolates into her mouth. "My next novel is about a sex-shop worker. It's fun researching. In the interests of authenticity, of course," she smiles.

"Of course," the group choruses back.

"Do tell," a plump, middle-aged woman with a violet rinse through her hair encourages.

"This morning I learned all about vaginal pumps."

The group nods knowledgeably. I don't have any idea what a vaginal pump is, but not wanting to sound naïve, I keep my mouth shut.

As I look around the group I feel totally at home. I should do, the house has the same net curtains as my mother's, the same paisley carpet, the same 50's wallpaper, and the same china dolls carefully placed on the highly polished furniture to protect against marks.

I glance at the family portraits proudly placed on the piano aas Doris, the host, a 70-year-old grandmother, read out her latest sex scene. I couldn't help but wonder if her grand-children knew what kind of stories she wrote.

"'Take me, take me, I gasped as he lay me down on the stack of hay,'" Doris read, panting for added effect.

I look out the window at her husband mowing the lawns and wonder if he helps her conduct her research. Surely not. Not at his age!

"Of course you have to make sure you fuck in the right place," Doris says solemnly.

"I'm sorry, could you repeat that?" I ask. Did she really just say that?

"You have to fuck in the right place."

Color flys to my cheeks. "Yes," I stammer, "That's what I thought you said."

"Too much swearing weakens the storyline," she explains solemnly.

I suddenly feel self-conscious thinking that they must all realize that I had missed her initial point and my smutty mind had wandered down completely the wrong track.

I am saved by Melinda, a willowy, woman, with long thin hair that dangles lifelessly down her back.

"People should get a life," she says quietly, "The problem in this world is there's not enough fucking." She leans forward and dips her celery into a bowl of cream cheese.

I gulp my tea and hide my smile behind my tea-cup. Imagine if I was still married to Jonathon. He'd be mortified if I told him that I want to spend the 4th Saturday of every month right here in this living room talking about sex.

"So what are you writing, Sally?" Melinda asks me. Sally is another of my fictitious names. I don't want to blow my cover before my book comes out. There's obviously no way I can be Sandy Lee here, and I certainly can't jeopardize my career by being myself. So I'm Sally. Sally Spoon. Before you ask, I just liked the way it sounded.

"Oh, nothing really. I'm just in the beginning stages of becoming a romance writer."

"Have you written anything?"

I bite into a fairy cake. I can't tell them about Sandy Lee and my blog site yet because then the cat really will be out of the handbag. I opt for the safer option of the short story competition.

"Well…yes…" I say, swallowing hard. "I entered a competition but I'm afraid I didn't do very well."

"Did you get some feedback?" they ask empathetically.

"Yes, it wasn't terribly encouraging. My heroine was shallow and my hero was crass…oh and they didn't think they should have sex quite so early."

The group roars with laughter.

"See. Melinda is right. Not enough fucking in the world," Doris laughed. "More tea dear?"

As the meeting progresses my sub-personalities and I felt

more and more at home. We sit there quietly taking it all in and by the end of the afternoon I've soaked up heaps of tips to help with my new romance writing career.

Hopefully my date with Fergus tomorrow fuels my inspiration, too.

28

HOW TO HAVE SEX LIKE A MAN

Before I leave for the night Chanel and I meet for a drink and she gives me some final coaching on how to have sex like a man.

"First you need to set the scene. So far you've been on a couple of dates and no sex. Guys like to be champions and true champions are the ones who can turn a casual date into a bonk. You must be sending out the wrong vibes or he would have bonked you by now, darling."

"We've just been having so much fun, enjoying each other's company that it's never come up," I say, despondently.

Chanel arches an eyebrow, "It's never come up? Believe me, with men, it always comes up." She raises her forefinger in the air to add further affect. "You need to take control and break the physical boundaries."

"He kissed my cheek. Does that count?"

Chanel rolls her eyes up to the heavens and back.

"Alright point taken. Maybe he's just not into me."

"He's calling you, isn't he? Showing you attention? Asking you on dates…believe me, he's into you, darling. He just needs a little encouragement."

"I don't want to seem too forward. Shouldn't guys take the lead?"

Chanel's hands flew to her hips. "What have I been telling you all along?"

"Guys need to be given the nod," I reply.

"Exactly! So while you'll out tonight *accidentally* brush his leg with your hand. Smile a lot. Show him you're having a good time."

"That shouldn't be hard. We're going to a comedy club!" I tell her.

"Good. Smile, even if the jokes aren't funny and make sure you make eye contact, all the time. Don't break it. That's fatal. Toward the end of the evening give him your best bedroom eyes. Eyeball him with '*I want your body*' emblazoned in your eyes. This is crucial, but I recognize that it doesn't come naturally to most people. It definitely doesn't come naturally to you, "Chanel says. "Only a small number of people have their bedroom eyes on all the time. These people can be digging in the garden, singing in the choir, cutting their own hair, or filing their income tax, but their bedroom eyes are always on."

"That sounds hazardous to your health."

"Yes, in the best way possible," Chanel laughs.

"They must be getting propositioned all the time! How's this?" I say trying to put on my best bedroom eyes.

"Fine if you're trying to say, '*can you pass me the remote*', but crap otherwise. Geeze, Ruby, you can write the sex stuff but when it comes to getting hot and saucy you look like you've got stage fright. It's more like this."

Chanel tosses back her hair and then lets it fall forward. She lowers her head then looks up slowly with her best '*come hither you sexy beast, take me, take me into your cave and make me your women*' look.

She would win an Oscar for her outstanding performance.

"When you finally get him into the sack," she continues, "and believe me that shouldn't take long once you give him the nudge, I guarantee he'll take over. Oh, that reminds me, whatever you do don't apologize for your body."

"But my breasts sag, I have stretch marks. . .and. . ."

"Stop! What have I told you about that negative self-talk? Five self-esteem press-ups on the spot!"

"I'm loving, I'm loyal, I'm fun to be with, I'm. . . I'm generous. . .I'm. . ."

"You're sexy, Ruby. *Sexy.* Think like a man. Men are attracted to women because they have all the bits and pieces they don't have. They couldn't give a monkey's what state your bits and pieces are in as long as you have the opposite bits to them. Variety is the spice of life— especially for Aquarians like Fergus. Strut your stuff in the bedroom and he'll go wild for you."

"Okay! Okay! Strut my stuff. Maybe I should play some music to get us in the mood."

"Sure why not. Leave it with me. I'll load some up in the iPod — just leave it to me. All you'll have to do is push play. I'll cobble together a few appetizers for you too. Just to help get things in the mood. The way to a man's hot spot is through his stomach."

"Ohh, you mean to serve him food like asparagus and other aphrodisiacs."

"I was thinking more along the lines of edible underwear and chocolate tattoos with erotic words etched in tantalizing places!" Chanel says.

"Gosh, there really is a lot to do, isn't there. When Jon and I had sex we'd just roll into bed, wham bam three minutes it would be over, thank you, mam."

"Bad sex is easy to whip up—like instant noodles that

still leave you unsatisfied. If you want great sex that takes planning. You need to create an atmosphere, you need to create some mystery, some excitement, some sense of longing and lingering—not plunging in like some kid diving in a pool."

"Gotcha. But where am I going to get the edible underwear?"

"Don't worry. I'll handle that. We can go together if you like. There's a great sex shop on Columbus Street."

"I don't know, Chanel."

"Put it down to research for your blog. You may even find a naughty nurse's uniform. Didn't you say that you thought Fergus was coming down with a cold?"

"Look, I'll try the edible underwear, Chanel, but only because I'm curious, but there's no way you're going to get me to dress up as a nurse," I say half-seriously as I gathered up my things. "I have to fly. I've got an important press conference for work."

"One last piece of advice before you go. . . Enjoy yourself! " Chanel passes me a bottle of oil. "This will help the passion flow and anxiety go."

"It's my special seduction blend. Ylang-ylang, rose, jasmine and cedarwood. It will help loosen you up and turn him on. But be warned—a little goes a long way," she says.

I kiss her and head out the door.

"Don't forget to make some noise!" she yells. "Men like to know a woman is having a good time. Grunt, groan do the lot. Tell him how good it feels and enjoy those orgasms."

Well you could have heard a pin prick. The whole bar comes to a stop as people turn and stare at me. I stand as still as a startled deer in headlights, too mortified to move.

"She's having sex for the first time since her divorce. This will be the second man she's ever done it with. I've been helping her master how to have sex with strangers," Chanel crows proudly as she hands out her business cards.

So much for discretion and the confidentiality of the coaching relationship, I thought as the Italian bartender a round of applause cracks through the air.

I throw Chanel my best *I'll get you for this* look and run from the bar.

I ARRIVED at work thirty minutes later to finish a few last minute things, followed by creepy Matt Loews.

"I was at *Deliciao*…I couldn't help but overhear—hell they may as well have used a loud hailer. So, you're going to score? Who's the lucky man. Anyone I know?" he moves closer towards me. "I've always had a thing for you Ruby, I'd be happy to give you some first hand coaching, if you get my drift," he says, pinching me on the bum.

I spring back and slap him. "Thanks but no thanks, Matthew, my husband has taught me very well. Now, if you don't want to end up with a harassment suit, I'd suggest you keep your hands to yourself."

"Word on the street is your ex-husband was the three minute noodle—laziest shag on the block," Matt says dropping his hand casually. "I feel sorry for you."

"You know what they say, longer's not always better, Matt. You of all people should know that."

Matt scowls briefly then snickers. "If I were you I wouldn't make an enemy out of me, Evans." He places a short stubby finger on my chin and slowly traces it down my neck, then dips it under my collar and brushes his hand close to the cup of my lacy bra.

"Before you get any idea, Evans, this never happened," he says pinching my nipple before withdrawing his hand.

"Nobody believes a jilted woman, especially a single mom. We all know you're horny for it. My advice is don't fight it. I know you want me." He steps away and stops in the doorway, smiling lecherously, "and I know you want to do well in your career."

That slime ball is proving to be a real problem. The worst thing is he's already sprung me surfing a porn site I'd been referencing for my blog. At a drop of a needle he could call in computer forensic people and I'd be kicked out of here so fast my feet wouldn't touch the asphalt. I'm not sure what is worse. Being jilted by Jonathon or the lecherous advances of my boss.

My mind wanders to Fergus. Handsome, funny, unpredictable Fergus. I can't wait for the end of the day. He makes me feel like a princess and I can't wait to sample more of what life with him tastes like.

Actually, if I'm honest I couldn't wait to taste him.

I rush home and scoot up the stairs. Only one hour before Fergus picks me up. Finally, he is going to tell me what he does for a job. I can't wait.

"I'll get it, Millie. It'll be Fergus," I skip down the stairs to answer the knock on the door.

I get the surprise of my life. Instead of my date, a shiny, leaf-green frog stood before me. I try to shut the door.

"It's me. Fergus!" the frog cries.

"Fergus?" I say uncertainly.

"Who else?"

You look. . ."

"I know. I look great, don't I?"

He hops around in a 360 degree circle so I can admire all his angles. When I say hop, I mean that literally. He is clad head to toe in a shiny green skin-tight suit. Actually, it is more of a stocking than a suit. I don't think they make suits in Lycra.

He sports large webbed feet and hands, and the most ridiculous mask I have ever seen.

I lean out of the door and look up and down the street. "Come in! Before someone sees you!"

Attracting attention to myself had never been my forte, let

alone being the subject of gossip. I can hear the dear old biddies that live in the neighboring houses now.

'There are *old goings-on in the house over there. I always said there was something not quite right about divorced women. Do you know her husband left her? If you ask me she dabbles in the occult. Anyone in their right mind knows you can't turn a frog into a prince. But not her. No. She's forever trying."*

"A quarter for your thoughts," interrupts Fergus.

"I didn't know you were coming in fancy dress. Couldn't you have worn something a little more normal when you came and picked me up?"

"I'm a comedian."

"That's what you do?"

"It's a passion-project. This is part of my routine. Catching the subway and watching everyone's reaction gets me in the mood. It's a crack up. You wait and see. You look nice by the way. Really nice."

'We're catching the subway?"

"It's more fun." He leans over and plants a kiss on my cheek. Instead of pulling away he lingers, his cheek pressed against mine. "Mmmmm, you smell really nice." His nostrils flare as he inhales. "*Really nice.*"

"Just a wee potion I whipped up," I laugh. If only he knew the lengths Chanel and I have stretched to create this special passion blend.

Chanel said it would be effective, but never in my wildest dreams did I think he would love it so much. But then I didn't know I was going on a date with a frog, either. Thank goodness I've only put on a wee dab behind my ears. Having hot passionate sex with a green man isn't exactly what I had in mind for tonight.

"Do I detect a glimmer of mischief in those pretty green

eyes?" he asks, stepping back and staring at me. A grin stretches across his face. He looks me up and down and nods in appreciation. "You look stunning."

"If I kiss you will you turn into a prince?"

"Try me."

I wrap my arms around him and kiss him.

Chanel and I had tonight all planned down the last detail. Tonight is going to be the night. I've chosen a very sexy violet chiffon dress which had diamanté's scattered across the plunging neckline, and strappy red sandals, with diamanté clasps.

Of course, neither of us have anticipated Fergus would be wearing a frog suit. But hey, I'm becoming better at improvising.

I had to.

Spending these few days with him has really opened a whole new world up to me. Nothing he does is predictable. I love his spontaneity and the way he makes me laugh, and the way he manages to pull me way out of my comfort zone, and somehow make it seem like the most natural thing in the world.

"I hope you have a change of clothes for later," I say, as we head out the door. As we walk through the streets toward the subway nobody give him a second glance. *This is New York.*

"The secret is to look confident," Fergus says.

"I don't know how you look so nonplussed wearing skin-tight fluorescent lycra," I say shaking my head. "You're acting is as though you're going to work in your business suit. Your acting so completely normal that it's abnormal."

"But it is my suit," he laughs, "and I am going to work."

As we stride onto the train nobody bats an eyebrow.

"I'd heard New York commuters are used to seeing

eccentric, colorful, characters on the subway but I had to be sure. If this was Ireland people would come and have a yarn with you. In London, they'd have you institutionalized. But here, it's cool. I like indifference."

"It's probably more about fear," I warn him. "Whatever you do, if you want to avoid trouble, don't look anyone in the eye."

His eyes lock with mine, and we hold each other's gaze. We must look a right pair. Me, dressed up to the nines, and him, dressed as a frog.

"I take it then, Miss Lee, that you're rather partial to some trouble."

"After tonight," I finger my necklace provocatively as I smile, "We'll both be in a bit of trouble."

We get off the train at 42nd and take a cab across town to 9th. I'd heard about Harry's Comedy shop from some of the guys at work but never had the courage to go in.

Secretly I fear that I might be hauled up on the stage or in some other way made a fool of. The club is sultry and dark. Small, round tables covered in black satin dot the room. Candles on each of the twenty or so tables give the room a soft glow.

Fergus sits with me for a while before disappearing into the dark recesses of the room. Suddenly the thick sooty curtain drew back, and there he is, my very own frog prince. His face is hidden by a Kermit mask and a spotlight illuminates the ridges of his muscular torso.

I'll let you figure out what else swelled under the spotlight when I blew him a kiss!

He quickly has the crowd belly-laughing as he jigs across the stage in a hilarious Irish stepdance. The projectile sex toys from hecklers don't face him as his story-based jokes meander off on a tangent, before arriving back at their intended punchline.

A gag about a BB King concert almost immediately veers off into an extended tale that covers religion, circumcision and the sounds made when a man's genitals get caught in his zipper.

As his 70-minute routine ends, Fergus tells everyone how nice it is to make them smile. I'm thinking how glad I am to be wearing waterproof mascara. That was a really brilliant idea of Chanel's.

Her other idea is even more brilliant. Read on!

30

GIMME SOME HOT STUFF

After Fergus had finished his routine, he changed and came and sat down at the table we had reserved and we watched the rest of the acts.

I felt proud when people came up and tell him he is the funniest act of the night. I feel even prouder knowing that soon we will be having our own performance under the sheets.

We sit opposite each other which is great for the bedroom eyes and smiling but not so flash for the accidental brushing of the leg with my hand. So I do a David Beckham move instead, and gently glide my foot up and down his calves, and smile seductively at him and give him my bedroom, *'take me, take me back to your cave'* look.

It's just as well I'm good at multi-tasking. I'm happy to say Fergus is good at multi-tasking too. He caresses my leg back, smiles, reaches out and caresses my hand.

"Let's say we go somewhere more comfortable," he says. His voice has dropped a notch, and his gaze lingers over every part of my body as he undresses me with his eyes. My sexual organs stir in a way that is entirely inappropriate in a public place.

"I know just the spot," I say reaching for my purse. Of course, I do!

I don't let on that I've already arranged everything in advance. Instead, it just *happens* that when he suggests that he'd like to do wild, naughty, passionate things with me, by a fluke of luck Chanel's apartment is nearby, I have the key, and she happens to be babysitting Millie for the night.

Chanel had told me it was imperative that I make everything look like it was all very spur of the moment and not terribly orchestrated.

"He seems like the sort of guy who's big on spontaneity. We on the other hand love to plan," she'd said. "And we don't want the planning to get in the way of passion do we?"

"No, we don't," I concurred.

Fergus comes around behind me and pushing the chair back, helps me to my feet. Two brownie points for you, I muse, as he takes my hand and leads me through the crowd. I love a man with manners, I think as he hails a cab.

"Where to?" the cabbie asks.

Fergus looks at me, "Anywhere the lady wants." He goes to get in the cab then stops. "Damn, my coat…wait for me will you?" he says running back into the club. He returns minutes later with a long summer-weight trench coat.

"Not another routine?" I laugh, it from him as he slips beside me.

The driver glances at us through his rearview mirror. "7th and 44th," I say happily, cuddling into Fergus's chest, "I have an all-night pass. Chanel is babysitting Millie and has given us exclusive use of her apartment for the night."

He leans over and kisses me. His tongue explores every crevice of my mouth. The kiss deepens. A long lingering throaty kiss that rocks my world. I arch my back and slide further into the rear seat.

"Hey you two love birds," the cab driver calls, "Get a nest." He throws his head back and roars with laughter, "My heart can't handle the excitement."

"Sure, if you do us all a favor and step on the gas, or you won't be able to hold me accountable for what's going to happen," Fergus calls back.

The driver tips his cap, smiles and accelerates. "Anything for love," he chuckles.

Ten minutes later as he pulls to a stop outside Chanel's apartment he turns to us. "For what it's worth. You look good together. I pick up a lot of people but I've got a good feelin' about you two. You're goin' make it."

Fergus hands him his fare and tips him generously. The cabbie hands back the tip.

"Keep your money. I mean what I said." Then he drove off into the night, the screech of his tires and the friendly toot of his horn blending with the shrill of sirens punctuating the night air.

A tremor floods my body as I stand at Chanel's door and turn the key. Fergus stands directly behind me his breath warm against my ear. The smell of his cologne, the warmth of his touch, the sexy sound of his voice as he speaks, make me giddy with excitement. But I am still nervous as hell.

"I loved the smell of an aroused woman," he says, kissing the back of my neck.

Trembling I push open the door. I flick the switch, adjusting the dimmers as Chanel has instructed. The subdued lights cast a mellow glow over her apartment.

She's been busy. Along with the usual collection of crystals, beads, and other offerings to the spirit world that enthralls Chanel, a trail of rose petals peppers the hallway.

Ambient music plays in the background and the smell of Ylang-Ylang, Jasmine, orange blossom, and cedarwood gently warming in aroma burners adds to the carefully curated sensual atmosphere.

Fergus acts as though being lured into a mystical sex haven is the most natural thing in the world. He stands back and takes it all in. Mind if I take some photos?" he asks, as he plucks a bottle of champagne from the ice bucket on the side-board near the entrance, and begins to pour two glasses.

"Sure, why not," I reply. I didn't say that I thought it is a bit of an odd thing to ask. He takes out his iPhone and begins clicking away. Now that I think about it, he's been snatching photos of me ever since we first meet.

Most of the time he assumes I'm not looking. Only I am, of course, carefully maneuvering myself so he always captured my best side. To be honest, I am kind of flattered that he wants to take photos of me. But that could be the warm glow of alcohol whispering.

"Mmm interesting array of food you have here," he says, taking some shots. "Spring onions, asparagus, sardines, garlic, oysters, lettuce, radishes, and broad beans."

He puts away his iPhone and smiles at me as he holds the asparagus erect in the air, "Open wide," he says as he places the asparagus in his mouth. He walks slowly toward me and guides the tip into my mouth. Our mouths touch lightly as we nibble at each end.

"Lucky for you I like shellfish" he laughs, as he walks back to the entrees and holds an oyster suggestively in his mouth, then suckles on an oyster.

"Mmmm," he groans, licking his lips suggestively, "very nice but not as good as the real thing," he curls his finger and beckons me toward him.

"Can I offer you a radish, perhaps a bit of lettuce, a carrot, or perhaps some garlic?" I suggest nervously. Now that it comes down to getting down and dirty I have lost my nerve.

His confidence burns a hole within me, a cavernous void into which I feel as though I might disappear forever.

"Not going all coy on me are we, Miss Lee?" He growls playfully coming toward me. He draws me toward him and encircles his hands tightly around my waist and then lifts me up into his arms.

"While I love all that sex food you needn't have bothered, my libido's great, and when it comes to being with you, I'm all yours. You're a sexy, desirable, woman, and I want you. All of you. Every way possible."

Heat rises to my face. "Did you bring any condoms?" I stammer. God only knows why I asked that then but at the time it seemed like the most logical thing to ask. I'd never used the things in my life but I knew, if I am going to do the wild thing with a virtual stranger, protection is a must.

"As it happens I did," he replies putting me carefully down on the floor.

Of course he does.

He grabs his lapels and throws his arms open. "I've got a trench coat full of them! How creepy is that!"

"A swift-moving tide of mortification engulfs me. Perhaps this isn't a good idea, after all, I thought, looking for the best path to escape. "Very creepy," I whisper. "You obviously have sex with lots and lots of strangers"

"No, it's not what you think. I'm picking up some extra cash as a condom tester for Durex. I thought tonight would be the perfect night to try out the full range."

He throws his coat to the floor, lifts his head to my face and lightly nibbles on my neck. "so, you're not a man whore," I murmur, surrendering to his advances.

Encouraged he peppers my chest with kisses and then

peels my dress back. He flicks his tongue playfully around my hardened nipple. I moan. Not because Chanel has told me to make lots of noise, but because it feels so damned good.

"The bedroom's down the there," I pant, writhing with desire. I dig my nails lightly into his back and nibble on his ear lobes as he carries me down the hall.

He taps the door open and he walks in and lays me down on the gold satin sheets. Rose petals lay strewn over the bed and on the side table is a little box, marked *'edible me'* written on the front.

I reach out for the remote control as Fergus lifts my dress around my thighs and peels off my stockings with his teeth. I lay back enjoying Fergus's tender touch as I wait for Chanel's specially chosen playlist to begin.

Looking for some hot stuff baby this evenin'
I need some hot stuff baby tonight
I want some hot stuff baby this evenin'
Gotta have some hot stuff...

I quickly click fast forward. Donna Summer's *Hot Stuff* isn't exactly the music I had in mind. Maybe in a few weeks when I have some more experience, but right now the words only make me feel inept. The next song is even worse.

Sex bomb, sex bomb, sex bomb, you're my sex bomb. And you can give it to me when I need to come along give it to me. Sex bomb, sex bomb, you're my sex bomb. And baby you can turn me on baby you can turn me on. You know what you're doing to me, don't you? Ha, ha. I know you do.

"Good song," Fergus beams reaching for the remote and taking it from my hand. He turns up the volume and straddles my body.

"You're my sex bomb, baby," he sing, looking deep into my eyes and peeling back my shoestring straps.

"You can turn me on baby, you can turn me on," he

continues to sing at the top of his Celtic lungs as he lowers my dress.

I glance down as my lacy pink bra pops into view. He draws his hands into my bra and cups my breasts, gently squeezing them. So far so good. He hasn't noticed they sag. Thank goodness for Victoria's Secret.

Burying his head in my breasts he lowers his lips to my nipples and brings them into his mouth, then slowly runs the tip of his tongue down my body, my belly, and lower—much lower—until I cry out. "Stop!"

Be playful, I remind my self. You're a sexy, desirable, gorgeous woman. "Wait. I haven't got my edible knickers on," I blurt.

His eyebrows arch and a wicked smile spreads across his lips as I wrestle with the box Chanel has left by the side of the bed.

"I won't be a tick," I say, feigning confidence as I slip out from under him and make my way to the bathroom.

I splash my face with water. *Get a grip, girl this is it. This is your chance. Don't blow it,* I say to the flushed face in the mirror. I slip off my knickers. I look to stow them out of sight in the cupboard under the basin, and spy anti-cellulite cream.

"Better late than never," I say, as I generously smother my thighs and buttocks in the thick white cream.

I take the edible knickers carefully out of their wrapping. They are as thin as a sheet of filo pastry. I can't resist knowing how they taste and have a wee lick. Obviously not Pierre Marcolini chocolate I decide as the taste of synthetic chocolate sticks to the roof of my mouth.

Carefully stepping into them to avoid tearing, I wrap a towel around me, take a deep breath and slip back to the bedroom. I flick the light off.

"Leave it on," Fergus murmurs. "I want to see you. All of you."

Thankfully something miraculous happens between leaving the room and returning from the bathroom. Maybe it is the excess alcohol I'd drunk for Irish courage, or maybe the aphrodisiac platter is catapulting me into a brave new world, but I suddenly feel emboldened.

Relieved of all my sexual hang-ups and nervous angst I drop my towel and thrust my chest up and forward as I perform my best Mae West pose.

"Let me take your photo. You look divine."

Before I can reply Fergus grabs the iPhone he seems permanently attached to. As he lay on the bed he clicks a series of photos.

"Promise me you'll delete them," I say, between poses.

"Of course," he looks at me so earnestly it doesn't occur to me to doubt him.

"Come here. I want to ravage you," he says, finally putting the camera down.

I lie back on the bed. He spreads my legs and goes down on me. I writhe in ecstasy as Tom Jones belts out *Sex Bomb* again.

"Mmm, you taste like Ben and Jerry's chocolate and pretzel flavored ice-cream," he says in between licks. "But there something else too, I can't put my finger on it," he murmurs licking my thighs.

I decide now is not the time to tell him about the cellulite cream. I turn over and reveal the "tasteful tattoo" Chanel has stenciled in chocolate on my butt.

"Don't mind if I do," Fergus says enthusiastically reading the words '*eat me*' emblazoned across my cheeks.

I giggle hysterically as every tickle-sensitive cell in my body comes alive.

"Can you stencil me?" he asks. I lean across to the bedside cabinet and open the drawer and bring out the jar of chocolate frosting, the paintbrush and the stencils we had used earlier.

"Where do you want it?"

"Here, where else?" he smirks, pointing to his private bits and bobs.

We are both impressed that I could write the words '*delicious*' up the whole length of his shaft.

"Want to know what delicious really feels like?" he teases, sliding me on top of him.

He slowly removes my bra and what is left of my edible knickers. I pull his shirt over his head and throw it to the floor. I wrestle with his belt buckle before allowing him to take care of his lower clothing.

My heart leaps as he takes off his socks. All my married life I'd had to endure Jonathan's socked feet while we made love. Finally, we are standing before each other clad in nothing but our birthday suits.

I'm probably making this sound like the most natural thing in the world, but believe me, underneath I am trembling like a leaf.

I am going to go all the way. It isn't a game. This is for real. With a man I am falling in love with.

Gone is the bullshit bravo, gone is the 'I don't care, this is only a fling,' and all the rest of the performance anxiety that comes with doing it for the first time with someone you feel intimately about. Someone you hope feels the same about you. And hello to 'I care about you, I want you to care about me',

For the last ten years of my marriage, even my husband hadn't got this up front and personal. Most of the time I wore a full-length Mickey Mouse tee-shirt to bed, and he'd slip under it with this hows-your father, do the deed and them slip out again. All over in three minutes.

How the hell had I convinced myself that was good sex? The 30 minutes of foreplay that I'd just had with Fergus is far beyond all the cumulated three minutes of the real thing for the length of our marriage.

So to be standing here, with the lights on, in my birthday suit with nowhere to tuck in my post-baby roll of skin, and no way to angle the light away from the tell-tale pockmarks of cellulite, is a real revelation.

The way Fergus looks at me tells me everything that I need to know. He likes the way I looked, he loves my generous curves, and my pock-marked skin, and as he grabs a handful of breast, I knew he does't give a damn that they droop and aren't firm like watermelons stuffed with silicon. I am a natural woman and for the first time in my life, I'm proud of it.

Fergus and I go at it like rabbits in season. He blows my mind. Chanel needn't have worried about me staying silent, I whoop and yell and scream like a girl going mad in a game park.

Sex with Fergus is fabulous and fun. None of this 'lie back' and keep you mouth shut stuff that Jonathon preferred.

We laugh, eat, have sex, talk, eat, laugh and on and on. We go through the whole new summer range of Durex condoms. Ribbed, thick, thin, sheathed, unsheathed, we try them all.

I prefer ribbed, by the way.

We make love until every single cell in my body sparks like firecrackers about to explode. I discover parts of my body that I never knew existed and try out hundreds of sexual positions that even the most experienced yoga teacher wouldn't be able to contort her body to do.

.   .   .

WHEN MORNING COMES we do it all over again. Thank god Chanel had thought to leave some condoms just in case.

"You were amazing last night. Just amazing. I love a woman who is so sexually adventurous and in touch with her body. It's a real turn on," Fergus gushes peppering my body with kisses.

I shed a tear, both of happiness and also of grief as I finally allow myself to let go once and for all of any misguided notion that Jonathan and I would ever reunite.

I hadn't realized how much it had hurt to admit that I had failed—as a mother to save my marriage and give Millie the kind of life she deserved.

And now here I am in bed with a man I barely knew having just had marathon sex.

"What's wrong?" Fergus asks detecting my sober mood.

"Nothing's wrong," I say as brightly as I can. "It's just a turning point."

I just had sex with a stranger and nothing will ever be the same again.

31

WHEN LIFE TURNS TO CUSTARD

After I leave the apartment I decide to walk to work. Suddenly there is a lightness in my step almost as though little fairies are cushioning every stride. Everything seems more colorful, more alive, and more intense somehow.

Is this love?

I have never felt this way ever before. When I married Jonathon it had been all arranged. Our parents had been long-time friends who moved in all the right circles.

It was a good match, so my mother told me.

Jonathon was ambitious, successful, well connected and on his way to being a serious contender for district court attorney. He was destined for The White House.

We lived in the best suburb, the best house, we ate at all the best restaurants, mingled with all the best people, and I wanted for nothing. Until now.

I'd had a life of unparalleled privilege. I had dozens of staff to wait on my every need. A personal cook to prepare my favorite dishes, a personal doctor to attend to my health, maids, and servants to pamper me.

I mixed with rarefied company: royalty, stars of stage and

screen, heads of state—sheikhs. My clothes were tailor-made by the world's most famous fashion houses. I lived in the most opulent residences - of which I had many. I traveled the world in first-class luxury and saw sights that most people will only ever see in books. I had it all.

But now, I realize that the price of that life was my freedom. Freedom to do as I pleased, dress as I liked, eat what I wanted, hang out with whom I desired. And more, much more than that, to be totally reckless, carefree and unworried about trying to always be, say and do totally the right thing.

Spending a lifetime trying to be the perfect daughter, sister and wife had zapped the "me" from me.

But now ever since meeting Fergus, I can see so much more clearly how everything that I thought was real is a sham. My life is a façade, empty and soulless.

I am empty and soulless.

Jonathon would never have lowered himself to catch the subway, let alone be caught dead in a skin light-lime lycra frog suit in central Manhattan.

I giggle. In fact, ever since I had met Fergus, I can't stop smiling. I have a grin that stretches from ear to ear.

I walk up to a street vendor and purchase a bunch of daffodils. I inhale their scent, before giving them to a little old lady walking down the street. I felt happy and want to share this with the world.

Why then, had I left the apartment in that way? Cool as a cucumber instead of the hot chili pepper I felt inside. It's a four-letter word. . . begins with F. . . ends with R.

Yes, fear.

I'm also afraid.

In the heat of the moment last night Fergus had told me he loved me. Really loved me. That he wanted to share his life with me. To marry me.

Marry me!

I have to pinch myself. It is more than I dared imagine. But ever since I had met him it is all I have thought about. The first time I met Fergus, spoke to Fergus, brushed past Fergus's body, the sparks soared. Even when I was trying to be angry with him because of the way I had thought he had treated Chanel, deep down I still wanted him.

As I spent more and more time with him I really felt 'it'. He made me love him. His unpredictability, the way he didn't care a hoot about what other people thought of him, his generosity. The way he cared for me so tenderly that night when I was so out of control and drunk.

Was it the drink again or the crazy hormones circling through our bodies that made him ask me to marry him and for me to say, 'yes?'

Yes! Yes! Yes! A thousand and three times yes. Were we both crazy? We barely knew each other. We'd spent two weeks together at the most. When I woke in his arms and looked across at him I scarcely dared allow myself to believe that it could possibly be true.

Fergus loved me!

Perhaps that's why I ran. To protect myself from the horrible feeling that he might change his mind when he opened his eyes. Even if he hadn't changed it, I felt sure sooner or later he would. Maybe, Chanel was right all those months ago when she said that I feared abandonment.

Perhaps that explains why I automatically reacted in such a way. To distance myself. Or was I acting on Chanel's *keep your man* tips? She'd told me so often that 'the way to a man's heart was to treat him mean, keep him keen' — and, most importantly not to be needy.

So I did my brisk, *Good Morning Man in My Bed routine,*

"That was fun, but now I have to go to work. . . let yourself out, will you?"

I can still see his face, he looked stunned. Ashen. Confused. Oh god, why had I blown it?

I did take the precautionary measure, so as not to be too ice-queenish, and kissed him before I flew from his bed. Or Chanel's bed, to be correct.

I can still feel the love butterflies. Everything and I mean, everything, stirred in my body when he uttered those words. It's stirring now just thinking about it. . .

him. . .

love.

Nothing stirred like that with Jonathon. But with Fergus, my whole body was wired to explode on a kiss. He looked happier after that, but I sensed a flicker of vulnerability and I hated myself as I pulled away, got dressed and walked out the door.

Why then did I still feel so high? Because he had asked me to marry him that's why. Ruby Evans isn't going to be a left-over-girl for the rest of her life. Ruby Evans wasn't going to have to go on endless inane dates with lecherous, appalling men.

Ruby Evans wouldn't have to bonk her way around Europe on a Contiki bus full of drunk teenagers and several desperate middle-aged women.

Ruby Evans was going to get married.

I beamed with happiness. I stopped to get a latte and pick up the paper.

The gasp-worthy headlines stop me in my tracks.

Sex Blogger—Eight-Figure Book Deal About to Get Hotter.

My mind races as I read the article. They are on the hunt

for the author's true identity. What to do? I haven't told Fergus who I really am. What will I say? What will he say?

'Oh, by the way, Fergus before we get married I need to tell you something. There's no easy way to tell you this so I'll just come out and say it.

I'm not really Sandy Lee. I'm Ruby Evans.

(Dramatic pause)

I write a sordid sex column about all my hot escapades between the sheets. Only it's not really me. I just make it up.'

How could Fergus possibly reply?

'Sure no problem, I understand completely. . . you write erotic romance. . . it's just something you do on the side. It's all in your head, you don't practice, or do field-research, or anything steamy and sordid. It's just mindless made-up sex.'

Yeah right, as if.

And what about my book deal? I've always dreamed of being a published author. What will happen if they find out nothing I write is true. That the whole thing is fake news.

My sizable advance will evaporate. My sordid sex life won't be nearly as interesting made up as it was true. Then there is work. God, life really was going to turn to custard.

True or not true, no one likes a scandal. One of the girls from my writing group was politely 'encouraged" to resign from her job when they found out she'd been writing erotica. I doubt there'd be much politeness at all.

Matt Loews would make sure of that. He's been either wanting my tail or on my tail for years. There's nothing like a spurned suitor to dish the dirt on you.

And what about the effect this will have on Millie? How will she ever live it down? The shame and stigma of having a mother who is a porn star. The fact that I could deny it all will only add fuel to the fire. People will revel in the gossip, the dirt and the speculation. I'll be lucky if Millie ever forgives me. She's at such a sensitive age.

Why didn't I think first, write later?

My head throbs with the worry of it all. Just when I should be the happiest girl in the world everything is caving in on me.

How the hell am I going to get out of this mess? Coming clean is lose-lose. Preserve the status quo? That's too risky. The press is getting uncomfortably close.

Someone has been visiting all the places I write about, asking questions, trying to find out who I am. This makes me nervous. Some of the details they have discovered are so intimate I've even begun suspecting my friends. How bad is that? Who close to me would ever stoop so low? I'm becoming paranoid.

The very thing I turned to as a bit of harmless self-help suddenly looks anything but helpful.

32

NOT MY REAL NAME

Well, the shit has proverbially hit the fan. Big time. I should have known it would happen. But who is doing the digging? Some ferret of a journalist? A jilted lover?

Only there are no jilted lovers. I've made every one of them up. Except Blog Boy. I shouldn't have written about my sex between the sheets with Fergus, but I wanted to share with my fans what true intimacy felt like. But I never shared his true name. And I'd never talked to journalist. Perhaps I should have covered my tracks better. Perhaps I shouldn't have been so real with the settings and rendezvous of my sexual escapades.

But I had to make something real. I was having trouble enough inventing my sex scenes let alone trying to create believable Manhattan bars.

When I first started writing *Sex With Strangers* it never occurred to me to create it in a different country. Why would I? I never expected anyone to read my blog. It was for me. Something to help get me through a blind spot.

I search through my blog and scan back to when it all began and re-read the comments that the nosey rat had left.

'Come out. Come out. Where ever you are.'

I ignored the message at first, thinking it is some crank.

He is persistent (I assume it is a he. Of course the person trying to expose me could have been a she).

'Contact me or else.'

Is he threatening me? With what? Why?

'I take it your blog name Sandy Lee was inspired by the movie, Grease. Only you're not Sandra Dee, lousy with virginity. You're her complete opposite aren't you? Or are you? Contact me and I promise you a great deal for the true warts and all story.'

His email started a horrible avalanche of similar queries. Suddenly everyone is hungry to know who I really am. My whole identity as Sandra Lee is called into doubt.

I start to feel sick. Very sick. What am I going to do? Ignoring them isn't going to work. I'd have thousands emails.

The worst thing is that I had no one to confide in. No one I can trust. I am on my own and this intrusion looks like it is going to be the biggest test of my whole life.

I am only early into my career in PR and I have no idea how to keep this media frenzy at bay. My career, my life, my friendships, my character, my future will all be called in question.

My thoughts tumble into a spiral of despair. To say I am catastrophizing about will might happen if my true identity is revealed is an understatement.

There isn't a word in the whole English dictionary that can accurately capture what I am feeling. *Gloom. Doom. Despair. Hopelessness.* None of them quite do it.

I check my thesaurus in the hope that, like a person without an unnamed disease who feels better once they have a name for their ailment, I will feel instantly reassured.

Desperation? Despondency? Bleakness? Depression? Not

quite depression but I do feel increasingly dark about what might lie ahead.

Why can't people let things be? I'm not hurting anyone. Perhaps someone has caught green-eyed envy when they heard about the book deal I've scored.

Whatever the motivation, it doen't matter now. What matters is averting a potential disaster.

For a moment I wonder if it is perhaps a bluff. Some silly attempt to unsettle me. But in my heart, I knew this wasn't true.

What I have learned in PR so far is that journalists often creep up on you unawares, almost while you are sleeping. They begin quietly and then, bang, pounce on you for the final kill. Most of them hire undercover detectives to scoop up the dirt. They check your trash—nothing is left unturned.

Gossip journalists are life's vermin and stop at nothing until they rip their victim's life and soul from them.

I rake my hands through my hair in disbelief.

In their quest to uncover my true identity what will they do? I'm still fictionalizing my daily rompings with the rest of the world on my blog. But now Sandy Lee's true identity has been brought into question.

I should be pleased. The fact that I write too well has triggered doubts. But now they are close to snaring me. I can feel their breath on my neck. I can see the feverish fire in their eyes. I can taste the celebratory whiskey on their breath as they drink to their victorious success in derobing me.

I can feel the noose around my neck as my life is stripped from me. Money is on my head. Winner takes all. Careers, fame and fortunes rest on my capture. The bounty?

Last time I'd heard a fee of $900,000 was offered for the exclusive story. As I continue to elude them the fee climbs daily. Jesus had been betrayed for far less.

I decide to ignore the daily email invitations to tell my side of the story.

Two days later, my publisher, Julian Wordsmith emails. We have never met. I'd pretended I was based in London. Don't ask me why. I just thought it sounded more professional somehow and I'd always admired the English. My email address is also based in the UK. I never imagined journalists would track me down to living in New York.

In hindsight thank God that I had been clever enough to create some distance, I think to myself as I opened up Julian's latest email. I read his email and brace myself for the worst.

'What's going on? Do you have a twin? People are sending me weird emails trying to track you down. None of them are using your real name. So far I have Penny Adams. Mery-kate horn, Jenny Lust, Ruby Evans, Clare Golightly, Rain Phoenix. . .'

My heart skips three beats. I re-read the email. I suck in deep gasps of air. My heart kick-starts into fast forward, pounding at lightning speed. I clutch my stomach as the contents of my breakfast threaten to spew forth. I swear, the whites of my eyes nearly catapult through the screen.

Buried in cold, dark type is my name.

My real name.

33

DIFFICULT CONVERSATIONS

New York, July, 2006

"All this media interest is great for sales Sandy, well done!' Julian Wordsmith continues in his email. 'We've got enough pre-orders of your book to reach number one on the bestsellers list globally. I'm chuffed."

At least someone is happy. I shut down my laptop. But how will my publisher feel when the whole fake tale is revealed. Everyone knows sex sells. Only this time there is no sex. Not even a hint of it. At least, not the way I've written it.

Fergus is different. Fergus is private. Fergus is love-sex.

As for the rest of it, the lies and the stories and my sordid imagination, I'd be a laughing stock. Frigid Fanny who couldn't even get laid and had to get a coach. The phantom sex nymph who kicks it off by re-writing scenes from the romance novels that line her bookshelves. I'd never live it down.

I doubt the story of Ruby Evans—divorced, getting alimony, and child support. . .and still shagless will cause anyone to shed a solitary tear. And I can forget about the 8-figure book deal.

Being left for a much, much, much younger woman and sitting home alone lathered in anti-aging face cream and creating fictitious sex-scenes isn't exactly a page-turner and certainly not worth over a million dollars.

I still can't believe I've managed to score one of the biggest publishing deals of the millennium. It is unheard of for an unpublished author, topping J.K. Rowling and her phenomenal advance. But only magic, or the most skilled teams of sorcerers conjuring their way into my life, can save me now.

But I'm not giving up yet. I'll just have to stay anonymous for longer. Somehow.

I am still pinching myself. Once this book is released I will be a millionaire! It's crazy money. Crazy and much-needed money. I'll never secure a life for Millie on the salary of a PR person. With millions of dollars I will finally be free of Jonathan and his guilt-induced alimony payments.

I'll be free of groveling for his handouts like a pet waiting for his master to fill his bowl. It's demeaning. I don't care what anyone says. I don't want to be owned or controlled. Earning my own way in life will free me finally. It will be the one thing that will enable me to move forward in my life.

Nausea rises in my throat.

I have to be careful, very careful or I'll be exposed. My whole life will tumble around me like the condemned buildings around the World Trade Center. Teetering on the brink of collapse the smallest crack could send me, and anyone near me, into ruin.

You probably think I'm over exaggerating. Perhaps I am, but you try putting yourself in my shoes for a minute. It's not very comfortable is it! Better safe than sorry I say. That's always been my motto and it's especially relevant now.

Keep my head down and my ears to the ground, just like always. Besides, it's too late to go back, the horse, as they say, had already bolted. I can't simply press delete, even if I want to.

Just imagine if I did come clean? My mother would have a field day. She never thought I'd amount to much. Nor did my father for that matter. After having seven daughters you don't have to be a rocket scientist to figure that perhaps they were hoping for something else. Someone less like me.

'I'm sure you were switched at birth,' they used to say, shaking their heads in despair as I did my best to act like the son they'd always hoped for. Sadly ball skills and I just didn't go together. Me and a hammer didn't work out too well either.

After numerous broken windows and oddly constructed woodworking ventures I gave up and did my best to blend into the background. It didn't help that my birth name is Rubian.

My parents had named me in hopeful anticipation of a baby with a slightly different apparatus. Not on a whim either I might add. The nurse had assured them that I was very well endowed indeed. She'd smothered my mother's protruding belly with a generous lather of jelly and oohed and ahhed.

My parents had wept with joy. But joy soon turned to tears. They stopped trying for a boy after that, the grief was more than they could bear. Especially at their age. My mother was 48-years-old when she had me. So not only do we have gender issues to deal with but we have generational ones too.

I seriously doubt she even knows what a blog is. It would probably conjure up images of smog, or blobs of ink on the carpet or something equally annoying. I can hear the conversation now.

Me: "It's not a blob it's a blog. . . an on-line diary. . .you know. . .where you post your thoughts and people read them and stuff."

"You post them? Through the mail? And people read them? Haven't they got anything better to do? Isn't a breach of privacy illegal?"

"No mom, not through the mail. . .through the Internet. . . and yes, of course, it's legal. . . and no, they don't have anything better to do. . . about the legal part. . . sit down mom."

"I'm fine standing. Don't treat me like I'm an invalid. If you were a boy you wouldn't treat me like that. You'd be bringing me flowers and helping mow my lawns."

"Please mom not now, I have something important to tell you."

"Have you been kicking balls through the neighbor's windows?"

"Mom, last time I did that I was nine. You and dad yelled so much I never touched a ball again."

"When are you going to do something with your life?"

"Mom, I'm trying to tell you something."

"Like the time you told me your marriage was over. That kind of something. I knew it would come to that. I just knew. You've never been good at looking after other people. Always thinking you're special. Trying to be someone you're not."

You're probably wondering where this is all going and how I know beyond any reasonable doubt how the conversation will to pan out. I should know — I've heard the same thing, different words, but the same theme for years now.

Ever since Jonathan left me, their disappointment has

become more pronounced and like a well-loved fur coat she drags it out every chance she gets. Summer, Autumn, Winter, and Spring.

Trying to be someone I'm not? Little did she know that this would come to be true. It shouldn't really come as such a surprise. Especially given my history and the fact that all my life my father has called me Rubian.

I could just imagine the uproar when I share my latest attempt at living with a new identity.

"Mom, Dad. I know I haven't spoken with you much about the divorce (no wonder — they made my life a misery, rubbing salt into my gaping wounds, and blaming me for making him look elsewhere). I know that you think I failed you—the first divorce in the family and everything. I know that you aren't thrilled with the way the press played everything out in the media but I have some good news. The good news is that. . . well. . . that media frenzy was nothing compared to what we may be facing now. . . I really do think you'd better sit down."

My mother will roll her eyes and give my father *the look.* The one that says, 'I told you she was swapped at birth. The good lord would never have burdened us with a child like this.'

She will let out a huge dispirited sigh as she plops herself on the sofa and my father will stand stiffly like a soldier on guard beside her.

"So Rubian," he will say tightly, "what shame have you brought upon us now."

I honestly can't think what Id ever done to make them dislike me so much. If anything, I'd bent over backwards, jumped through hoops and waited expectantly for even the smallest morsels of love and affection. Boozo the dog got more than me. He still sleeps in their bed.

I imagine myself standing up to them for once.

"Is it any wonder I'm such a disaster to you. All my life I've tried to be the boy you wanted. Then when you decide it's time for me to act like a girl, I marry the man you choose, then when he walks out, you blame me for not being a better more feminine wife. Now, I can't even look at another man. . .all I can do is write about my fictitious sex life and how I get it on with complete strangers. . .and because of my screwed up stupid ramblings everyone thinks I'm the greatest thing since gluten-free bread and they want my story. . .only. . .and this is ironic. . .I can't give it to them because. . .I'm not the person I say I am and it's not my real name. . .so I'm screwed. . .only I'm not. . . and I never will be because after this gets out nobody will want to touch me with a ten foot pole. . ."

So you can see why I'm never going to tell them. Nope, telling my parents is the absolute worse thing to do.

34

BREAKFAST – BUT NOT AT TIFFANY'S

My mind wanders back to Fergus. Warm, funny, yet edgy slightly aloof. He's begun to reveal a softer unselfish side I've begun to fall deeper in love.

And for the first time, I admitted that I'm not really into one-night stands and told him that I had really strong feelings for him and was falling in love with him. It was totally unplanned and unscripted.

Chanel will be cross about that. But happy to know that being true to my feelings is the best tip for getting over a break up fast. Love like you've never been hurt. Dance like. . . I couldn't remember the rest of the words but only knew that they spoke of being true to yourself and not worrying about failing.

Only now that he had asked me to marry him, I am afraid of failing. I am afraid of failing again at marriage.

I am afraid of telling him my name's not Sandy Lee. It's not a biggie, right. I mean, it's just a name. He know the real me—the me beyond the name. If it wasn't for my blog we would't have met. It's odd, he hasn't asked me about all the headlines in the newspaper but I just figure he doesn't read.

From deep in my heart I recalled that magical moment when he asked me to marry him. We'd fallen into bed and spend a night of passionate, sensuous lovemaking. It is totally the best sex I've ever had. And then the bliss of finding out Fergus loves with me. Me! Not my name, but me—the woman with the cellulite. Oh, the euphoria. . . and oh the fear in the morning that it had all been a dream.

My phone rang. Fergus. Was he reading my thoughts? I pressed the phone to my ear, swooning as I devour his accent. "Breakfast? Sure great. See you in fifteen minutes."

He arrives looking immaculate as ever. My skin trembles at the sight of him. He looks hot. smoking hot. I visualize him in his tuxedo, standing at the altar like something out of television series *The Bachelor*. In my vision, Fergus is holding a rose and I am the girl he chooses.

He walks up to me and kisses me quickly on the lips. I can't put my finger on it but something feels different, a sort of coolness.

"Is everything alright?" I ask tentatively.

"Sure, just a little tired, that's all." He snaps his fingers and looked impatiently around the room for the waitress. "Expresso," he says curtly as she catches his eye. "What can I get you, Sandy?" he asks, not looking at me.

"Just a bagel. . . oh and an expresso. . . make mine an extra strength." I say brightly trying to look unconcerned. Has he changed his mind? Or has he totally forgotten his proposal? I fiddle with the paper napkin folding and unfolding it, then tearing little bits off the corners as I wait for him to bring up our engagement.

"Busy day?" he asks coolly. He takes the napkin from my hands and places it on the table.

"We've got a PR cleanup job today. You might have read about it in the papers..." I pause, wondering if he'll say anything about newspaper headlines, but he says nothing. "Miss America went mad in some of Manhattan's trendiest bars, drinking too much and smoking pot," I continue. "Anyway, I have to give a press conference today. I'm a little nervous. It's the first one I've done on my own."

I listen as the words flowed from my mouth. Boring, dull, tedious words about work. Not words full of the feelings and dreams I long to share. I want to ask, 'About last night? About us? Did you mean what you said?'

But I keep my mouth shut. In case he feels pressured or I come across as too needy. He'll run a mile then. I've read that in *Cleo* and numerous other magazines. The articles made it quite, quite clear that coming on too strong or too needy is dating suicide. They didn't say if it made a difference if you were engaged. Nearly engaged, that is.

"You're really something in the sack, baby," Fergus says suddenly.

My heart sinks. These aren't the words I long to hear. Anything but. Was that all last night is to him? A romp in the sack? Two days ago I might have been flattered.

Fergus is the first man I'd had sex with outside of my marriage. He is the second man I've had sex with in my life. And he thinks I'm hot. That should be helium gas for my sagging balloon of confidence. That is, if I hadn't gone and fallen in love.

But now all I want is to go back to is the careless, attachment-free, expectation-free intimacy we had shared. The romantic, intimate aspects of our lovemaking. The way Fergus stroked my hair, kissed the chocolate from my belly, laughed, and tickled me. The way he looked when he told me he loved me. Not, 'you were hot in the sack baby.'

Marriage, or talk of marriage changes things. Look at

Brad Pitt and Angelina Jolie. Don't look at them. Bad example.

"Was it true what you said about not turning it up for other boys?"

I flinch. Why is he being so cruel? "Of course it was true. I don't lie." I leave out that I just hadn't told him the truth. I mean, people change their names all the time. Why couldn't I? If I hadn't been Sandy Lee I never would have met Fergus.

He looks at me briefly and then looks away. For a brief moment, I think I see a flicker of sadness.

"Of course you don't. Why should you? You're the nicest girl I ever met."

His words are laced wit sarcasm. Perhaps I'm just being sensitive. After all, I was lying. I did have sex with strangers —just not in the way that he'd hinted.

"Nice girls never lie, do they?" he says looking directly at me.

I want to tell him the truth then and there, but I can't. Things already seem tense and I feel gutted enough already.

Not once over breakfast did he mention his proposal. Not once. I hadn't imagined it. I knew that in my heart. If I was going to salvage what we had, telling him about the sex blog right at this moment wasn't going to be the way to do it.

"Are you sure everything is okay? You seem different. Are . . . are. . . we okay?" I asked.

He lets out a huge exaggerated sigh. "Sure baby. You and I are great. We're just getting started. You're the best thing that happened to me since I've been here. With you beside me, I get a distinct feeling that my luck is about to change."

35

THE VULTURES GATHER

The press room begins to fill. People sit pencils and pads ready while others practice their screenshots for television feeds. As I scan the room my legs shake like trees in a Los Angeles earthquake. My breathing is shallow and short.

I clench and unclench my hands as I take my place next to Matt Loews.

Amongst the thong of faces there are a a few I recognize from sitting on past news conferences. I shouldn't be nervous, I'd watched a million times before, but this is different. This time I'd be getting up there for the first time ever on my own.

In the spotlight. Having to think on my feet. Julianne my boss had been detained by the air traffic controllers strike. She is a seasoned pro. An old hand. Her mind is as sharp as a tack and her tongue even sharper.

Confidence oozed out her. Journalists both admired and feared her. Only the truly brave would ask a question for fear of being made to look small or totally simple-minded.

Me? I only hoped I didn't waffle. I reached into my pocket and ran my fingers over the lucky stone Millie had given me. "It's a magic stone, guaranteed to bring good flow," she promised.

I rub it harder. If a magic genie popped up and granted me three wishes I'd be thrilled. What would I wish for...the ground to swallow me up?

No...don't waste a wish...I wish I could blow everyone away with a truly magnanimous performance.

I wish I don't waffle on or lose my train of thought, get asked a curly one or go totally go blank.

"Public speaking has never been my stronghold. I'm a great speechwriter. Much better suited to staying behind the camera. Get Matt to do it. He's much better at this sort of thing than me." I said to Julianne. But my passionately delivered attempt to persuade her to choose anyone but me had failed miserably.

"You're the best person for the job. Clean image, no prior publicity, a nice squeaky clean face to represent the company. The last thing we need now is another curveball, Imagine them in their birthday suits if that helps."

It didn't help at all. Not one little bit. I don't think Julianne realized how highly visual I have become. Just the suggestion of nakedness and my brain had already stripped everyone of their clothes.

What a disaster. Boris Flanders, New York-based journalist for *The Guardian*, ruddy-faced and potbellied isn't a pretty sight at all.

And just to prove that you can't judge a man by their name Don Sexpot, is anything but sexy. In clothes, he scrubbed up really well, but naked... well, that's another story altogether.

My imagination ran riot. Pimples on his bum, a gut that only his high waisted gut restraining underwear managed to conceal, and hair even King Kong would envy.

Harry Drinkwater looked like he needed to…drink water that is. He'd obviously been out on the turps all night and looked seriously emancipated and dehydrated.

Dan Ramsbottom…well what can I say! One after another, after another…a heaving ocean full of journalists appeared in their birthday suits.

After my initial shock, I start to see the humor in my new gift. X-ray vision isn't such a bad thing at all. Especially if it means I didn't have to endure pairs and pairs of the most depressing scuffled, uncared for and ungroomed shoes.

Did I tell you—I have a thing for shoes? You can tell a hunk by their footwear. And if there's one thing I know about it's shoes. In my next life, I'd love to come back as a shoe designer and travel the world designing elegant shoes.

As I cast my eyes downward a latecomers feet caught my attention. When I tuned down the x-ray vision and spy the most gorgeous Roberto Cavalli pointed-toe python shoes my spirit soars. Elegant, classy and classic, they virtually scream successful and fashionable. Only a strong confident man who knows he looks good and doesn't mind flaunting it would wear elegant black lace-up loafers like these!

I've seen shoes like these before just recently. Now, where was that? I allow myself the luxury of lingering over the fine specimens in front of me a little longer as I try to kick-start my memory.

Nope no good. I can't recall.

I lift my gaze up the long muscular legs, clad in a wide pinstripe, Italian wool. I wanted to savor every moment. There's nothing sexier than a well-dressed man.

My mind flashes to Fergus. Fergus knew the way to woo a woman is by dressing to impress. Heat flooded to my face just thinking about him.

I return to the well-dressed vision in front of me. . .beautiful shirt, juicy vibrant tie. Then I looked at his face.

It is Fergus.

What is he doing here? How did he get past security? This is strictly media only. Everyone has been strictly vetted.

As he walks toward me I see the press pass dangling around his neck. His face is flat, unsmiling.

I force a smile and tried to maintain my composure. He walks closer.

I feel sick.

Closer.

Sicker.

"Not speechless I hope? In your job that would be career suicide." His voice is a harsh whisper, but his eyes tell a different story. He looks hurt and I knew why.

My heart rate soars through the roof. No way. Not Fergus? I hope desperately that I'm mistaken.

". . .I don't understand. How did you get this?" I say picking up his press pass and turning it over.

"It's a press pass. What do you think it is. . . oh yes, that's right you haven't shagged a journalist before, have you?"

"I can explain. Just not here. Not now. Someone will hear you." Thankfully with so many people in the room, the background noise is like a pre-match baseball game.

"I don't give a monkey's if someone hears me or not," he says raising his voice. "That's the least of my worries. Right now there's a blow-by-blow account of my butt on your blog site. The whole world's reading about my penis and what I'm like in bed."

For a moment the world stands still. I suck in great gusts of air and hold them in my lungs. I rattle my brain for a plausible excuse. But I am guilty as accused.

"I hadn't meant my blog post to be a brag-feast. I'd meant

it to be my final entry ever," I say. Now would be a good time to tell him the truth, but I figure he's worked it out already.

"How could you do that to me?" he continues, his angry frown is replaced momentarily with a wounded expression as he searches my face.

I met his gaze. "Please, Fergus. . . don't make a scene. I can explain. It's not what you think. Honestly." I grab him gently by the elbow and attempt to move him away from Glenn Charlett, a reporter for *The New York Times,* and one of the biggest gossips I've ever had the misfortune to meet.

As my hand meets his elbow he stiffens and he pulls angrily away.

His voice trembles as he speaks. "What you and I did was private," fire wells in his eyes. "For us only. . .for a moment I thought it had been special even. . ." I detect a sadness beneath his angry words

"It was. It..it is special . . ." I say softly.

"Spare me your spin," he says angrily. "That's what you do, isn't it? You're a spin doctor who sells yarns for a living."

And you Fergus, what exactly is it you do?" I reply angrily. I reach toward him and lift the press pass hanging around his neck. "I thought you were a stand-up comic?"

"I am. I create skits about people and their sordid lives. . .I paint the truth and lacquer it with humor."

"The truth?"

"Yeah, that's what journalists do too," he says. holding my gaze.

"That's stretching things a bit."

"I guess you could say we're in the same line of work then."

Then it dawns on me. "You've been investigating me, haven't you? You're the one that's been diving deep?" I rake my fingers through my hair. We've both been playing a part.

"Look, this is getting us nowhere. We both need answers. We both deserve to know the truth. Meet me over at the Moon Café in thirty minutes so we can talk."

"I have a job to do, Ruby. Ruby Evans. That's your real name, isn't it? An hour ago I was about to call my boss and tell him to shove his stupid job, but then I read what you wrote and I realized you never cared about me at all."

"You're wrong Fergus, I do care about you. Do you care about me?"

"Yeah, you care about me as much as you care for all those other men you shagged. And to think I nearly fell for it, Ruby or should I say, *Sandy*. You're hot property all over the world. I assume you do know there's a bounty on your head for the person that finds out who you really are. I guess I just got lucky."

Adrenaline surges through my chest. Surely he wouldn't blow my cover. I know Fergus is hurt, but he had the wrong end of the pole.

"Look, I know it looks bad but I can explain. It isn't what you think."

"What do you know about what I think? You don't know a thing about me. I thought I knew about you but I was wrong. Really wrong. You're not the girl I thought you were. You're not the girl that I told I loved."

His voice began to shake and get louder. "Sex with strangers. . . and then there's me."

Heads began to turn toward us. Matt Loews was looking at this watch and shifting uncomfortably on his feet.

"Please," I say lowering my voice and leaning toward him, "not here. Not now. Let's. . ."

"Let's what? Kiss and make up? Or is it kiss, have hot passionate sex and tell?" he says angrily "I don't think so. . .I'm not really up to having my balls spread all over the Internet. You better get rid of what's there already or I'll have you for defamation of character."

"What are you talking about? I never even mentioned your name?"

"How many men do you know that catch the subway in a frog suit?"

"Come on, Fergus. I never meant to harm anyone. You of all people should be able to see the funny side. What's this really all about? "

"What's this all about? It's about you shagging every stranger you meet. It's about you lying to me. . . it's about you being a…"

Matt stepped off the podium and came over. "Is everything alright?" he glanced between the two of us. What a pair we must have looked. Fergus, stood defiantly, lips pursed, eyes cold as the arctic, body tense as steel.

"Lovers tiff?" Matt asks. We both stand silently. "Whatever it is, get over it," he says crossly. "We have more important things to worry about here today than you two quarreling over who left the toilet seat up or didn't put the cap back on the toothpaste."

I tense even more and my face flushes with a mix of embarrassment and anger. Fergus glares at him. I could see he was struggling to regain his composure. Any more provocation and he will blow. One more smart comment from Matt and I could rely on it. I suck in plenty of calming air and resume my most professional composure, inhaling my pride as I did so.

"Yes, Matt, you're right. There are more important things to worry about."

I look at Fergus. He lifts his head, and for a moment our eyes meet. 'I'm sorry,' I try to say with my eyes.

If our eyes are the windows to our soul I hope he can see

my soul aches for him. But he looks right through my retinas and tosses me a stony glare.

"Please Fergus, don't make a scene. Let me explain. Meet me at Moon's."

"What and miss your big performance? I don't think so. In fact, I want to make sure I'm front row. Who knows what sort of questions I'll feel like asking."

My heart sinks. I can imagine exactly what questions he will ask. 'How does The Miss American Pageant feel about sex with strangers? Is it a good idea for a staff member to be having intimate liaisons with men she barely knows? Does this set a good example to young girls? What are your views on the role of those in positions of influence to uphold the values and morals of this country?'

Just my luck to fall for a journalist with a London tabloid. Just my luck to be holding my first press conference and to have it all blow up in my face.

"Fergus. . ." I implore, "I am sorry, really sorry"

"Yeah, darling, of cause you are," he says turning and walking toward the front of the press gallery. I glance around the room. Thankfully all the other journalists are too busy in a relationship with their iPhones or preening and primping themselves and haven't overhead Fergus's outburst.

It's a lose-lose situation, and there is no precedent. I hoped like hell I can just get through the conference without a drama. But more than that I hope Fergus will forgive me.

The worst-case scenario is he'll blow my cover, make a scene and then everything, everything will tumble around me.

I'll lose the contract for the book, my career will be in tatters, I'll be the laughing stock of Manhattan. Mille will want to go and live with her father. And I'd lose the only man I loved.

I knew he was angry. He was no longer my laughing,

funny Fergus. I'd hurt him. Hurt him immeasurably. It was unforgivable.

At that moment as I looked across at him his arms crossed defensively across his chest, his lips pursed, his eyes glazed in a protective layer masking the hurt, I knew that a life without Fergus would be no life at all.

There is only one thing to do.

36

NOT MY REAL NAME

This is terrible. Terrible. Tension wells in my body as I find my personal need to tell him everything, conflicting in a tangled heap with my public and professional duties.

I feel like I am being pulled in two different directions—impossible to pursue simultaneously. In less than five minutes whatever unfolds will emphasize the polarity in my life.

I feel a strong urge to follow my heart, yet at the same time to heed my rational mind which urges me to stay and fulfill my professional duties.

I scan the room for Fergus, but can't see him. 30 minutes and it will be over and I can explain everything. But something tells me I don't have 30 minutes.

Matt Loews looks at me with shock as the unscripted words began to flow from my mouth. Once I'd begun I was powerless to stop them. Everything was breaking down. I'd made the biggest mistake of my life and now only I could fix it.

Rationally I knew what I was going to say was career

suicide. Emotionally I've never felt freer. For the first time in a long time, a feel excited and energized about the future.

I search for Fergus. But I still can't see him. Has he left? Where? Why would he go? I continue with my speech hoping that somewhere in this sea of people he'll hear the words that were meant for his ears only.

Even though I have no idea what I was going to say once I open my mouth the words flow easily.

"Ever since my divorce and especially since meeting the man of my dreams, a man I might add who took me on a date dressed as a frog, I have realized the importance of being true to myself."

A deathly hush fills the room and you could have heard a pen drop. I ignore the horrified look on Matt Loews pallid face.

"As many of you are aware," I continue, "my divorce was very painful for me—you all shared it, many of you wrote about it. Your papers dined out on it for months. So here's something else for you all to dine out on. For the first time in my life, I don't care what you think. What anyone thinks. The only thing that matter is the good opinion of the man who only hours ago asked me to be his wife."

A sea of camera flashes momentarily blinds me. I looked down and steadied myself.

"I feel as if I have emerged from the darkness and into the light." I laugh at the pun and a murmur of laughter ran through the room. I feel emboldened that the joke had not been missed.

"For this reason and to further free myself of the burden of worrying about securing the good impression of all of you, but mostly to free myself from the weight of the lies, I wish to confess. I created. . ." I pause.

There is no point dragging it out. In fact, I feel quite

excited about the shock factor. I allow myself the luxury of imagining how Matt Loews will mop up the mess. I savor the thought a little longer, then let the bomb drop.

". . .the woman you have all been looking for, the infamous sex blogger, the one with the big book deal is. . . Me!"

The deathly silence is fast replaced with frenzied activity as microphones and digital recorder are thrust in my direction and reporters jostle to get the best photo.

"One at a time," I cry commanding the stage as they talk over each other. "You'll all get your turn but first. . ."

I look around for Fergus. My heart sinks. Where was he? Hadn't he heard what I said? Or had he heard it and not cared anyway. I stand in the spotlight as a stadium of cameras and iPhones snaps my picture and microphones are thrust toward my face, looking and feeling like the left-over-girl I'd always feared I'd become.

"What started as a harmless bit of fun," I continue, "has exploded beyond my wildest intentions. I have never spoken publicly about my painful divorce to Jonathan but in the interests of clearing up this whole sorry affair I will say this, I was deeply traumatized by those events one year ago, and found myself quite unable to even begin…"

I reach for a glass of water as I gather my thoughts. This is going to be embarrassing but I want to go on in the hope that Fergus will be watching and listening somewhere.

". . . thinking about having sex with another man felt like climbing Everest with my feet bound. While working with a life coach I learned the principle of acting *as if*. So that's what I did. . . I acted as though I was the most confident, secure, sexy, uninhibited woman in the world. A woman who was unafraid of her sexuality, of loving men, who wasn't hung up about conforming to societal expectations, who did no harm but only created pleasure for herself and for others. I made everything up. Absolutely everything. Except . . ."

I pause again, and then look directly into the camera. ". . . except for the night I spent with the most fantastic man I have ever, ever met in my life. Fergus if you are out there, please forgive me for not telling you the truth. *I love you.* I truly, madly, deeply do. And if the offer still stands I'd like nothing more in the world than to be your wife. . . if you'll still have a girl like me."

Then just like Moses commanding the Red Sea, the crowd parts and Fergus, who all this time has been standing at the back of the room, somersaults his way toward the stage.

"The truth wins," he says. "In the end, it always wins."

"Once a performer always a performer," I laugh, as he bends on one knee at my feet.

"Does this princess take this frog for her husband so that they can mutually adore each other for the rest of their lives," he asks.

"She does," I gush, not caring about the tears spilling down my face. "Happily and blissfully for ever after."

* * * THE END * * *

My book deal didn't crash. They fictionalized my made-up tale after all. *Sex With Strangers* became a multi-bestseller in multiple categories, including, self-empowerment for women and contemporary fiction and best of all, romantic comedy.

My readers feel as I do. They're tired of toxic, demoralizing, negative news. They want to read something uplifting, fun, light, and a little bit naughty.

We all need to love and laugh more, don't we?

It doesn't matter to them that Ruby Evans had told porkies. They loved Sandy Lee, like the world loves all their favorite fictional characters. In a world of fake-news, fiction has become the new go-to. At least when you're being lied to you know it's just make-believe.

Fergus did have wounds. Big ones. He confided in me about his childhood trauma and years of neglect, and how comedy had given him an escape and saved his life. That, and the newspaper editor who helped him forge a career when no one else would. When he first started investigating Sandy

Lee, sex blogger, he'd never dreamed he'd fall for her. Her being me—Ruby Evans. Or who I used to be.

Did I tell you? I have a new name now. One I plan on keeping happily-for-ever-after. Ruby O'Farrell. It sounds good on me, don't you agree?

Oh, in case you're wondering, I don't have sex with strangers anymore. I have sex, lot's of it, with my husband. Fergus has thrown away his press pass, grabbed the mic and channelled his inner comic, taking the healing power of laughter out to the world.

We can all do with more laughter and less tears, right? Laughter liberates us—and sometimes, for the love of laughter, once in a pink moon, we have to play dirty.

AFTERWORD

This story began many moons ago at a romance writer's retreat, facilitated by Mills and Boon authors Robyn Donald and Daphne Clair. The feedback from these wonderful passionate and experienced writers, and others on the writer's retreat, was so encouraging

"I love it!"

"We thoroughly enjoyed it"

"You've got the beginnings of a really good, hip, fun book"

"The chapter heads are just lovely"

"It was a riot. I thoroughly enjoyed it. Great fun!"

"I can see the movie now."

"When are you going to finish it?"

I decided it was time for it to air!

Many of the events are inspired by true stories—both my and others' experiences. I've encountered so many people over the years who are looking for love again, and just don't know how or where to start.

I hope you giggle and laugh from deep in your belly as you read this story. Like I did, remembering and rewriting some of these scenes (and flashing back to events that were true.)

And my hero Fergus O'Farrell? A few people told me that you can't have an Irish hero that wears green pants and is called Fergus. The Fergus I met once, told me a different story.

He was so hunky, he could wear anything—or nothing at all! Think Jamie Dornan (better known as Christian Grey), Colin Farrell, and Pierce Bronsan (the only ever Irish James Bond), the alpha Irish sexy men who rock our world.

Talented, hot-looking and super sexy.

ACKNOWLEDGMENTS

My sincere thanks to Mills and Boon authors Robyn Donald and Daphne Clair who were enthusiastic cheerleaders from the start.

I shall always be indebted to you and so thankful I had the opportunity to attend Kara, your writers retreat.

Bronwyn Sell and Bronwen Evans thank you, too. I'm so happy to have met you at Kara and to see your writing careers flourish.

To my partner, Lorenzo, thank you for supporting my dreams and allowing me to sit down in peace and write.

To the boyfriends and bosses who let me down, you paved a way forward that was entirely self-motivated and without further regret. Every closed door was a window on this path. Thank you for inspiring so many books!

To my fabulous beta and arc readers, I am lucky to know all of you. Not only could I not have continued without you, but I would not be the person I have since become. Tears, fears, doubts, Mallowpuffs and green tea later, I am truly indebted. Thank you for everything, especially for patient and kind guinea pigs with my earliest manuscripts.

Steven Novak, a graphic designer, spent hours perfecting the cover and bringing my vision to life. I love your work!

ABOUT THE AUTHOR

MOLLIE MATHEWS writes fun, sophisticated, passion-filled contemporary romance. She is known for her "sensual, beautiful, empowered stories enveloped in true romance" (5-star review). Her books have resonated with a global audience. She has been featured in magazines, television, and radio.

A former child and family therapist Mollie passionately believes in the power of romance to transform people's lives. She loves Mother Theresa's words, *"We are all pens in the hands of a writing God sending love letters to the world."*

Her stories are unashamedly positive, optimistic, full of fun and passion.

She is graduate of Victoria University, in Wellington, New Zealand and has given keynote speeches at romance writers conventions and international seminars.

Mollie follows the sun, dividing her time between New Zealand and exotic locations—wherever she intends setting her next romance novel. She lives with her very own romantic hero, Lorenzo—tall, dark, terribly handsome and fluent in Spanish!

Follow her on BookBub https://www.bookbub.com/authors/mollie-mathews and on her blog https://molliemathews.wordpress.com

and sign up for Mollie's newsletter at www.Molliemathews.com and receive her FREE gift.

THANK YOU

Thank you for reading *Sex With Strangers*… I hope you loved it. If you did…

1. Help other people find this book by writing a review
2. Signup for my new releases email to find out about the next book as soon as I release it, sign up here http://eepurl.com/ghM501
3. Email me at mollie@molliemathews.com with a copy of your honest review and let me know if you'd love to join my dream team and of advance readers
4. Follow me on BookBub, https://www.bookbub. com/authors/mollie-mathews
5. Stay in touch on Facebook, https://www. facebook.com/molliemathewsnz
6. Follow me on Twitter - https:// twitter.com/Molliemathewsnz
7. Be inspired on Pinterest - https://nz.pinterest.com/

molliemathews and Instagram - https://www.instagram.com/molliemathewsauthor
8. Follow my blog - https://molliemathews.wordpress.com
9. Watch me on Youtube: Molliemathews YouTube

First Published 2020

First New Zealand eBook and Paperback Edition 2020

Cover Design: © Steven Novak

ISBN eBook: 978-0-9951335-0-1

ISBN Paperback: 978-0-9951335-1-8

ISBN Large Print: 978-0-9951335-6-3

ISBN Hardcover: 978-0-9951335-5-6

Also available in audiobook.

book with another person, please purchase an additional copy for each recipient.

Published by

Blue Orchid Publishing

New Zealand

Visit www.molliemathews.com to read more about all our books and to buy them. You will also find features, author interviews and news of author events, and you can sign up for e-newsletters so that you're always first to hear about our new releases.

 Created with Vellum